CU00900657

Wendy was born in Barnsley, a small mining town in South Yorkshire, in 1944. She attended Ardsley Oaks Secondary Modern School and left at the age of fifteen. She married Kevin Gill in 1964 and they had two children, a son, Spencer Gill, and a daughter, Deborah Hotchkiss.

NIPPLES AND CRISPS

WENDY GILL

NIPPLES AND CRISPS

Vanguard Press

A CIP catalogue record for this title is
available from the British Library.

ISBN 978-1-80016-599-1

*Vanguard Press is an imprint of
Pegasus Elliot Mackenzie Publishers Ltd.*
www.pegasuspublishers.com

First Published in 2023

**Vanguard Press
Sheraton House Castle Park
Cambridge England**

Printed & Bound in Great Britain

Dedicated to my husband, Kevin Gill. The naming of this book lands totally upon his shoulders.

To my sisters, Valerie Owen and Carol Wood and for their continued support and encouragement. Also, to Julie Ivory for her friendship and hospitality

Chapter One

It was pitch black, I could see nothing. Something had broken my sleep. My heart started pounding in my chest. Then I heard my staircase creak, someone was creeping up the stairs.

I knew they had trodden on the sixth step from the bottom because it creaks every time I go up or down the stairs myself, it was very annoying, but this time, I was grateful for the warning.

I was sure I'd locked my doors and checked my windows before I had gone to bed. Glancing at the digital clock on the bedside cabinet, I saw it was one-thirty in the morning.

The sound of footsteps was getting closer, I knew it was only seconds before the intruder would open my bedroom door. I panicked, not knowing what to do or what to expect. Should I get out of bed, find something to use as a weapon, hit the intruder over the head and flee for my life?

Too late, I heard the bedroom door opening, I decided to stay where I was, pretend to be asleep and hope whoever it was, took whatever he or she had come for and leave me alone.

They had left my bedroom door wide open, a small window at the top of the stairs was directly opposite the bedroom and the moon was giving off a pale light. The shape of a human body was slowly making its way silently across my uncarpeted bedroom floor.

They turned slightly to their right as if trying to see what my bedroom held, and for a split second I saw clearly, the silhouette of a handgun before the form resumed their advance towards the bed, and the handgun was gone.

I lay motionless until the intruder was within striking distance, then, I threw the bedcover off and my action made Bennie spring into life. He made a dive at the dark shape hovering above me.

The unexpected impact of my dog landing on them, sent the intruder staggering backward. They overbalanced and went crashing to the floor. The sound of metal sliding across the wooden floor broke the silence in the bedroom.

Bennie, landing on top of the body, felt strong hands pushing him off, and he hit the floor, landing on his back. I saw the figure jump up and run out of my bedroom. Giving no thought for my safety, I scrambled out of the bed and gave chase. Bennie was not far behind me, I was just in time to see the figure vanish through the front door which was wide open.

When I reached the door, I slammed it shut, turned the key and pulled the bolt into place. I looked at the lock and doorframe, they were both intact. My door had not been forced open. How had the intruder entered my house? They certainly knew where to find the exit door, because I saw them disappearing out of it. I looked down at Bennie and said, "Good boy Bennie, good boy."

Bennie who had the opposite reaction to me at the unexpected visitor gave me two enthusiastic barks and wagged his tail in delight, he at least had enjoyed himself.

I turned and ran back upstairs, along the landing and into my bedroom with Bennie at my heels. Switching the light on I bent down and looked under my dressing table, and sure enough, there it was, flush up against the skirting board, the black shape of a handgun.

I rang the police and informed them of the home invasion and they said to lock my door and not to let anybody in before the police arrive. They told me there had been a spate of break-ins just recently and the person that was doing the break-ins was becoming violent. I told them the door was already locked and bolted and that I had no intention of letting anybody into my house unless it was the police.

I got dressed quickly and was about to bend down and retrieve the handgun when the doorbell rang. I went down the stairs and looked through the spyhole, Bennie was not barking at the unexpected early morning visitor, so therefore he must have known them.

It was not the police, it was Marley Burton, a neighbour from across the street, he lived in the house exactly opposite mine. While we were not all that well acquainted, and there were weeks when we never saw each other, we would pass the time of day if we were in our respective front gardens.

Ignoring the advice of the police and my determination not to let anybody in, I pulled the bolt across and unlocked the door. Marley stepped inside, he looked harassed and his hair tousled.

"Hello, Jasmin. I was in bed and nodding off when I thought I heard a noise. I glanced at my bedside clock; it was one o'clock in the morning. I thought someone was trying to break into my house. I switched the light on and came downstairs to investigate. If someone was trying to break in, they must have seen the light go on and fled.

"Then I couldn't get back to sleep so I got up and made myself a cup of tea and took it up to bed. I decided to have a final peek out of the window, just in case there was someone still lurking about. I saw your light on and because of the hour, I have come to see if you are all right, make sure nobody has tried to break into your house."

"I'm glad you did because someone has broken into my house. If it hadn't been for Bennie, the outcome might have been worse. The intruder had a handgun and Bennie pounced on them, making them drop the gun, it slid under my dressing table.

"I have rung the police and they are on their way, it shouldn't be long before they arrive. I appreciate you coming over, I must admit it's frightened me. I'm glad I've got Bennie." She bent down and gave the faithful Bennie a rub behind the ear, then she continued. "I bet it was the same person Marley, who tried to get into your house but failed, so they had a go at mine. Have you rung the police?" Jasmin asked.

"No, I couldn't be sure it was somebody breaking in. It could have been a car backfiring, or somebody banging down a dustbin lid, or even a courting couple in my back garden. I'd have felt a right idiot if I had rung the police and when they came, they found a courting couple under my hedge," Marley told her.

This brought a smile to Jasmin's face and she said, "A courting couple under your hedge, it could have been. Nothing surprises me these days, it's a sign of the times."

"I'll just have a quick look around upstairs to make sure there wasn't a second person involved."

"Please don't put yourself in so much trouble, the police will be here any minute now."

"It's no trouble and it's better safe than sorry."

"I can assure you there is nobody else in my house, Marley. If there were, Bennie would have let me know. I'd rather leave it for the police to sort out," Jasmin told him.

Before Marley could reply to this the sound of a car coming to a halt outside her house took Jasmin in the direction of the door, but Marley was there before her and looking through the spyhole, "It's a police car, two policemen walking up the drive. I guess it's all right to let them in."

Once the two policemen were sitting opposite Jasmin and Marley, the elder of the two policemen said, "My name is PC Coltley, and this is PC Harrison, can you tell me what happened, Miss Ward?"

"Not much to tell really. Someone broke into my house. My dog Bennie sleeps at the bottom of my bed and when the intruder came into the bedroom, Bennie jumped on them and knocked them to the ground. The intruder was armed and they dropped the gun.

"It slid under my dressing table. I would appreciate it if you could remove it, I don't like the thought of there being a gun in my bedroom," Jasmin informed the policemen. "If it hadn't been for Bennie, I don't know what I would have done," Jasmin concluded.

"It's a good job Bennie did scare the intruder off. In the last home invasion that I attended, the owner of that house was shot and sadly died. If the gun under your dressing table is a match to the gun that shot the lady, it might help us catch her killer.

"I am going to have to get the crime scene investigators in I am afraid. They will take care of the gun, don't worry about that. We might find some DNA that could help us catch him or her. I think you have had a very lucky escape, Miss Ward. Is there anything in your house that is of any great value that would merit a break-in?"

"No, nothing. I don't have very much and what I do have is of little value," Jasmin replied.

"Do you have any relations that you could stay with for a couple of nights until the CSI people have done what they need to do?"

"No, there's nobody, my mother who was a widow, died some two years ago and I am an only child. It looks like I will have to check into a hotel for a couple of nights but it will be hard to find one that takes dogs and I am not leaving Bennie. He'd hate it in kennels," Jasmin told the policemen.

"You must come and stay with me, Jasmin. Bennie can come with you, of course, we get on all right, don't we Bennie old boy?"

On hearing his name mentioned, Bennie got up from his position of laying across the full-length of the hearth rug and wandered over to Marley and laid his head on his knee, and it achieved the desired reaction. Marley's hand began to stroke the dark brown head.

"That's very kind of you Mr Burton. As Miss Ward stated, there aren't many hotels or bed and breakfast accommodations that will take in a Rottweiler," PC Coltley said.

"I am afraid PC Harrison will have to escort you back up to your bedroom so you can pack a few things that you will need, for a couple of days, might not even be that long. Just to make sure you don't accidentally destroy any evidence that might be of interest to us.

While we are waiting for the CSI to arrive can we have a quick look round? How did the intruder get in?" The officer wanted to know.

"I don't know, I am sure I locked the front door and pulled the bolt across before I went to bed, but when I chased the intruder out of the house, the front door was wide open. No sign of damage and the bolt had been pulled back," Jasmin explained.

"Did you see the intruder's face or any other identifying marks?" PC Coltley asked.

"No, it was too dark, but when they entered my bedroom, from the outline, it looked like a man. The moonlight was behind him, and it looked like he had a balaclava on, no hair, you see. But then again, I could have been mistaken," Jasmin admitted.

"So, you think it was a he?" PC Coltley asked.

"I don't really know, it was the size and shape of them I guess, that made me think so. But there are women that are tall and on the chunky side, I'll grant you that. I am afraid I didn't see if the intruder was loaded up top or down below, so it could have been either male or female," Jasmin stated with a twinkle in her eye.

PC Coltley did not comment but whilst he made a note in his notebook, he had a smile on his face.

"Did you leave the key in the door when you locked up?" PC Harrison wanted to know.

"Yes, I did," admitted Jasmin.

"Then if we find a window broken, the intruder will have entered your house by the broken window, gone over to the front door and unlocked it, and left it wide open before they came upstairs. Just in case they had to make a quick escape. Did they leave your bedroom door wide open when they entered your bedroom? That is their trademark. He or she has used that method of entry and escape in two other break-ins so, I guess if they did, we might be looking for the same person," PC Harrison told her.

"Yes, they did," confirmed Jasmin.

The broken window was found in the kitchen, not broken as in smashed, but it looked like a rubber sucker had been attached to the window and a ring cut out of the glass, big enough for someone's hand to enter and take off the latch on the inside and open the window.

"Well, that answers the question of how they got in," nodded PC Harrison.

"What about you Mr Burton, if you live across the street, how do you come to be over here?"

"My story is exactly like Jasmin's, I was woken by a noise, and came downstairs. Nothing out of place so I went back upstairs to bed. I looked out of my window and saw Jasmin's light on. That was unusual, so I nipped across to see if she was all right. I'm glad I did," explained Marley.

"So am I," agreed Jasmin.

There was a knock on the door and PC Harrison went to answer it. It was the CSI team, so Jasmin,

Marley and Bennie made their way across the street and into Marley's house. Armed with a small suitcase she had thrown a few clothes into before they left her house, Jasmin and Bennie followed Marley upstairs where Jasmin was shown into a bedroom.

Saturday was the longest day Jasmin had ever known and she spent most of the day out on the canal with Bennie and she was pleased when she could excuse herself and retire for the night.

Sunday morning found PC Coltley knocking on Marley's door. When Marley opened the door, he was surprised to see the officer dressed in jeans and a t-shirt.

"May I come in?" PC Coltley asked Marley.

"Of course," Marley stepped aside and the policeman stepped over the threshold.

Marley led him across the hall and into the sitting room, "Please take a seat."

"Thank you, Mr Burton. Is Miss Ward in? I have come to tell her she can go back home now. The CSI have finished over there so there is nothing to stop her from returning home," said PC Coltley as he sat down.

Bennie came ambling in from the kitchen followed by Jasmin and greeted PC Coltley in his usual manner by placing his huge head on the officer's knee, and his head was stroked.

"Oh, there you are Miss Ward. I have come to let you know you may go home now. Here is your house key back." He passed her the key.

"Thank you, that is great news. I'll go up and get my things. I'm sure Marley will be glad to see the back of us," Jasmin smiled. "Come on Bennie, let's get packed and go home."

"Are you working, or is this a social call?" Marley asked when Jasmin had gone.

"You mean my dress I suppose? We've been informed that there is to be a large party on a riverboat moored about five kilometres downriver from Glaston, this afternoon. I'm pretending to be a taxi driver, parked in the taxi rank. I'm hoping to pick up a guest or two who want taking to the riverboat. You never know I might find something out. The odd slip or word. It's worth a try. It might be linked to these break-ins that have been taking place.

"The owner of the riverboat is called George InGuesty. It is a name we know to be connected with drug trafficking, but we have never been able to find anything that connects him to this illegal operation or anything else out about him," Marley was informed.

"What makes you think that George InGuesty is connected to the break-ins?"

"I'm sorry Mr Burton, but I cannot tell you anything else connected to the case. I shouldn't have told you about the drug trafficking really. But I can tell you that the gun found under Miss Ward's dressing table is not the gun used to shoot the lady I was telling Miss Ward and you about. Wrong calibre."

"I see," said Marley. "What does George InGuesty look like?"

"Now that is a very good question. He holds these parties but never makes an appearance. I must be off now Mr Burton, I have stayed much too long, and no doubt said too much." PC Coltley stood up, shook hands with Marley and went back to his car.

"Oh, yes PC Coltley, you have said far too much. But thanks for the information," Marley said to the police officer's retreating back.

Closing the door, he turned and saw his wife standing on the landing at the top of the stairs, "Did you hear that, Valerie?"

"I did. I don't think we should attend the party this afternoon and I think we had better make ourselves scarce. We have failed to get the evidence we were looking for, but I don't think anybody else is aware of the hiding place or even the existence of the DVD or the camera. Do you?

"After all it was under extreme pressure that Clive Huggard told you the hiding place before you silenced him. And I have nearly been caught here twice. Once when you stupidly brought that girl from across the road here, and just now when that policeman called. It would have blown our cover. Thank goodness that woman has gone back home and taken that blasted dog with her. He came sniffing at our bedroom door on more than one occasion and your friend Jasmin had to drag it away."

"I think you're right; we need to disappear. But when I brought Jasmin over, I knew you were aware that I had gone over to see her, I knew you had the sense to keep out of the way until I returned, standard procedure for us. Letting the policeman in put us in no danger either. I knew you were upstairs before I let him in.

"The police have got the gun that I shot Clive Huggard with. Thank God it can't be traced back to me. Better get packing though," Marley told her. "I'll nip across the road and give an excuse as to why I'm leaving, then it doesn't look suspicious."

Chapter Two

Jasmin packed her bag and took Bennie home. Although she had been grateful for the Friday night and Saturday night she had spent across the road at Marley's, it had been an uncomfortable couple of nights. She had the feeling that he was watching her every move. She was glad to be home. *Work in the morning,* she thought. *That weekend has been a write-off.*

She unpacked her bag. Going over to the little dressing table, she put a couple of t-shirts that she hadn't worn back in the bottom drawer. She ran her hand over the highly polished wood that had a black ebony inlay running around the edge of the dressing table top. She had only had the dressing table since Friday night.

Jasmin had gone straight to the supermarket after leaving work on Friday so she would have the weekend free to spend as much time as possible with Bennie.

She had been walking along High Street, her arms full of shopping when she had collided with the dressing table that was standing on the pavement outside a second-hand shop that she had to pass on her way home. Peering around her armful of shopping Jasmin saw a price ticket of thirty pounds.

It was just what she needed for her bedroom, more drawer space. On impulse, she entered the shop and handed over her thirty pounds. The proprietor of the shop whose name is Mr Sackblock told her it would be delivered that evening as he had other purchases to deliver as well.

Whilst Jasmin was waiting for her receipt, a young woman with a pram entered the shop and asked Mr Sackblock if he would accept twenty-five pounds for the dressing table standing outside.

He told the young lady, that unfortunately, the dressing table had been bought by this young lady, and he indicated Jasmin. But he had another small dressing table further inside the shop if she would like to take a look at that one.

The young lady glanced at the other small dressing table and saw it only had a single mirror. Not what she was after. The offer was declined and the young lady looked at Jasmin with interest, which made Jasmin feel uncomfortable and guilty at the same time, then the woman turned and left the shop.

Jasmin watched the retreating figure. She turned, left and headed in the opposite direction that Jasmin was to take. But just for a split second, as the lady turned left, Jasmin glanced into the pram. The pram was empty. No baby.

Jasmin walked home happily planning where the best place would be for her dressing table to stand. She turned up her driveway and disappeared into the house.

Had she been less engrossed with her dressing table and glanced behind her, she would have seen a young woman, on the opposite side of the road, pushing a pram and following her at a discreet distance.

When the young woman with the pram came to the bottom of Marley's drive, she stopped and pretended to look into the pram to see to the baby. But covertly she looked up and down the street. It was empty. She turned the pram quickly and walked up Marley's driveway keeping herself and the pram hidden as much as possible, by walking between the parked car and the side garden fence.

The back door was open when she reached it and the young lady walked into Marley's kitchen and was enfolded in a pair of strong arms and a warm passionate pair of lips.

"Now that's what I call a welcome," said the young lady.

"How did you get on my darling?" Marley asked.

"You are not going to believe this, but the young woman who lives straight across the road from here has bought the dressing table. I missed it by seconds. I went into the second-hand shop to buy it and the young woman opposite had just pipped me to it. I overheard the proprietor tell the young woman it is going to be delivered sometime this evening."

"Well, in that case, I had better find my balaclava out," Marley told her. "This dressing table has been as hard to find as Clive Huggard was. I never thought Huggy would turn on us like that."

"He's out of your hair now Marley. You made sure of that. Good riddance, get rid of the rubbish I say, you did the right thing, it was a case of him or us. Move on Marley, move on," Valerie replied.

"Yes, it was lucky for us that one of the police officers that was sent to Huggy's house after his body had been found floating in the river, works for us. And he found that partly written letter Huggy had started to write to his daughter, but had screwed it up and thrown it in the waste bin at the side of his desk. It was quick thinking on his part to slip the letter telling his daughter about the DVD, into his pocket before any of the other officers saw it," agreed Marley.

"The police were in Huggy's house and before we knew it, the daughter had asked Mr Sackblock to do the house clearance. She didn't waste much time in selling off Huggy's things," replied Valerie.

"I don't think it's a good idea for me to try breaking into Jasmin's house again, not with the police snooping about. I'll get someone else on the job and we'll make ourselves disappear again.

A small white van drove up Jasmin's driveway that Friday evening and two young men carried the dressing table up to her bedroom for her. When they had gone, she spent an enjoyable two hours cleaning out the drawers and then rearranging her lingerie and t-shirts.

Little did she know that this was the start of the adventure that was to follow.

Jasmin had bought the semi-detached house four months ago. It was of moderate size and boasted three bedrooms. Her mother had died leaving the terrace house they had lived in to Jasmin, in her will. She had left everything to Jasmin who was her only child. Her father died when she was twelve years old, leaving her mother to bring Jasmin up on her own.

Her mother had worked in the local supermarket and although they didn't have a lot of money, they had a comfortable lifestyle. When Jasmin left school at the age of sixteen, she found herself a job working at the reception desk in a local solicitor's office.

Jasmin found it difficult to stay in the family home on her own. Too many memories, she needed to move on with her life. So, she sold up and moved into the semi-detached house in Glaston. She had only seen her next-door neighbour once. He was a middle-aged gentleman who told her he worked away from home on the oil rigs out at sea.

She was still working her way through the house, decorating one room at a time and this little dressing table was ideal, not too large, it would fit perfectly into any of the three bedrooms quite easily.

Bennie stirred himself into a sitting position on the bed, all of a sudden, he was alert. Jasmin's heart missed a beat and she strained her ears to see if she could hear what had roused Bennie. The experience of two nights ago, had left her feeling vulnerable.

The sound of the chiming of the front doorbell had made Jasmin jump, *For goodness' sake, this is stupid,* she rebuked herself, and then stood up and went downstairs to answer the door.

Upon opening the door, she found Marley standing there, "Marley, come in. I was just about to put the kettle on."

"Thanks, but no, I have come to tell you that my wife has turned up and we are going to try and make a go of our marriage. We have been separated for twelve months but have decided to try again. I am going back to our family home in Scoresbrook so I don't suppose I will be seeing you again. Make sure all your doors and windows are locked, and good luck for the future."

"I didn't know you were married."

"No, it wasn't something I spread around. The house across the road is rented, so I can leave and go back home if I want to."

While Marley was talking, a movement behind him made Jasmin glance over to his house. Coming out of Marley's house and placing a pram into the boot of his car, was the young woman that had been in the second-hand shop wanting to buy the dressing table. Jasmin found her breathing becoming laboured so she hurriedly said, "Well, all the best to you and your wife, I hope everything works out for you both."

"I'll be off then; we are all packed and setting off now. We hope to be back in Scoresbrook before it gets dark." He turned and walked back across the road.

As soon as his back was turned, Jasmin closed the door and turned the key. She ran upstairs to watch out of her bedroom window and was just in time to see Marley get into the driving seat, lean over to the passenger seat and give the woman, he claimed to be his wife, a quick peck on the lips.

He drove slowly down the drive and stopped for a few seconds to make sure the road was clear before he turned into it. He was indicating right, and Jasmin could see clearly, there was no baby on board as he continued into the road and disappeared from view.

Surely it couldn't be a coincidence, she buys a second-hand dressing table on impulse, and the young woman with the pram, with no baby in it, turns up at the house opposite. Now Marley has come knocking on her door and he claims she's, his wife. He had never mentioned having a wife before.

Thinking about it, Marley had offered to go up and check out her bedroom the day she had the break-in. Why would he do that when he was aware that the police were on the way? She had already told him that the intruder had fled.

And why was he so ready to offer a place for her and Bennie to stay for a couple of nights, after all, they weren't good friends.

A thought went through Jasmin's head as she sat on her bed looking at the dressing table. Was there something about the dressing table that she had missed? If Marley and the young woman did live in Scoresbrook, which was about seventy kilometres away from Glaston, surely, she could have bought a dressing table nearer to home.

Although it was a nice-looking piece of furniture Jasmin didn't think it was anything special, or of any value. There had been nothing in any of the drawers because she had checked them all and cleaned them out before putting any of her clothes in.

Jasmin turned and looked at her dog, she had found him one day sitting on her doorstep under the canopy, sheltering from the rain. He was shivering and wet and his ribs were showing alarmingly through his fur so she had taken him in, dried him off and fed him.

She had reported him to the police in case anybody was looking for him, but nobody had come forward to claim him. That was four months ago when she had just moved into the house. Bennie had not moved out; he had adopted her. But she wouldn't be without him now.

Bennie was supposed to be a guard dog, but he was as soft as a kitten. He loved everybody, but because of his size, people tended to shy away from him. He was Jasmin's best friend.

"What do you think Bennie, is it something to do with the dressing table? Why all of a sudden was Marley being so attentive? He has never come knocking on my door before. Now he is shooting off to God knows where, and with a woman who was trying to buy the same dressing table I had just bought." She looked at Bennie with great expectation in her eyes. "After all," she added, "I was burgled the same evening that the dressing table was delivered?"

Unfortunately, Bennie was oblivious to her questions, but nevertheless, he loved hearing her talk to him.

Jasmin sat looking at the dressing table, the mirror was split into three, and a large mirror sat in the centre with a smaller mirror on either side. It was one of the reasons Jasmin had bought it, you could fold the side mirrors in and it enabled you to see the back of your head. This would help her when she was getting ready to go out. Not that she went out very often, all her friends were back in Tanbrook where she had grown up.

Tanbrook was a very large coastal town and she'd many good nights out with her friends, but over the past four months her friends had slowly diminished, none were willing to put themselves out to travel the twenty kilometres from Tanbrook to Glaston. She understood that because she found travelling the distance back and forth to Tanbrook too much. So far, she had not met anybody in Glaston that she could call her best friend, apart from Bennie of course.

Jasmin reached out to pull the two side mirrors inwards but the right-hand side one wouldn't move. She stood up and pulled the dressing table away from the wall so she could see behind it. On the bottom hinge Jasmin saw a little brown button, she pushed it in, and a long thin compartment shot out from the right-hand side of the dressing table base.

The compartment wasn't very deep, but laying at the bottom was a flat bright yellow box. Taking the box out Jasmin placed it on the bed beside her and asked Bennie, "Blimey Bennie, what do you think we have in here?"

After investigating with his nose, Bennie was not impressed. Jasmin gently lifted off the lid to find what looked like precious gemstones of different colours. Rubies, emeralds, sapphires and diamonds? She could only guess.

What to do now, she wondered. She could put them back into the compartment and pretend she knew nothing about them. But then, were these stones the reason for the break-in? Did the person that broke in know they were there? Will they try to break into her house again to get to them? *Yes,* she thought. *They will.*

Jasmin took the box downstairs. She looked around to find a good hiding place, but there wasn't one. She went into the kitchen to make something to eat and saw Bennie's bed with a big fat cushion in it. Not that he ever went to bed in it, he slept at the bottom of Jasmin's bed. She decided to place the yellow box under Bennie's big fat cushion.

Glancing at the wall clock Jasmin saw it was seven o'clock. No wonder she was hungry, it was way past her tea time. *Work tomorrow,* she thought, what was she going to do with the yellow box? She couldn't leave it in the house, no doubt it could be a good opportunity for the burglar to return while she was out at work.

Nor did she fancy taking it to work with her. So, she changed her mind and decided to leave it in Bennie's bed. Surely nobody would think about looking under a dog's cushion for a box of precious stones.

Her property had a nice, enclosed back garden with a medium-sized wooden shed at the bottom. Because she had to go out to work and it was unfair to keep Bennie locked up in the house all day, she had employed a carpenter to saw the door in half and put two-way hinges on so Bennie could push the door with his nose from either side. Similar to a cat flap but bigger. Allowing Bennie to come and go as he pleased, thus providing him with protection when needed against wind and rain.

He had a second bed with a big fat cushion for him to lie on. Also, there was a workbench beneath a window and Jasmin had placed a wooden box, filled with stones to stop it from sliding, at the side of the window so Bennie could jump up onto the box and then onto the workbench so he could sit and look out of the window. All the comforts of home.

"What am I going to do Bennie? I can't leave this box of stones here indefinitely, I am going to have to take it to the police," Jasmin told Bennie.

Then she had another thought, *What if there is more than one secret compartment.*

Standing, she turned on her heels and went back upstairs, taking them two at a time. Sitting on the bed looking at the little dressing table, Bennie joined her, "What say you Bennie, is there room for a second secret compartment?"

Bennie gave an enthusiastic bark and Jasmin laughed.

"No harm in trying," she told herself. Pulling the dressing table away from the wall again she found another little brown button. The button was pushed in and out shot a second concealed compartment. This time, it housed a DVD.

Taking the DVD out, Jasmin quickly closed the secret compartment, pushed the dressing table back into place and took her DVD into one of the spare bedrooms that she had converted into a computer room. She switched on the computer, waited for it to boot up then clicked on the icon that opened the DVD reader. Not so lucky this time, the screen flashed 'Private and Confidential, Encrypted Information'.

Things were becoming out of hand now, so taking the DVD out of the computer, Jasmin took it downstairs and put it with the yellow box under Bennie's cushion in his bed. It was the only place she could think of to hide them. In the dog basket.

She decided, that when it was her lunch hour tomorrow, she would have a walk and call in at the second-hand shop and see if she could find out where the dressing table had come from, and whom it had belonged to.

At the solicitors where Jasmin had worked in Tanbrook, they had on their books, a company called, IT Intelligence, based in Glaston. When she moved house, Jasmin applied to IT Intelligence for a job. She was given a position in the typing pool, working in a little pod of her own in a room with about twenty other employees.

Sitting in her little pod, Jasmin watched the clock hands go round, it was a long four hours for they seemed to drag, but one o'clock eventually arrived and she shut her computer down and left her pod.

Not that she had a fixed lunch hour. She was allowed to take it when it suited her so long as the work was done.

Walking at a fast pace, Jasmin arrived at the second-hand shop but found Mr Sackblock busy with a customer. Impatiently Jasmin looked around the shop while she waited for her turn with the shop owner.

Mr Sackblock saw Jasmin keep looking at her watch and wondered why she was back. Did she have a complaint about the dressing table? If she did, it was hard lines. He had sold it in good faith.

When he escaped the customer, he had been serving, the proprietor approached Jasmin, "Is there something I can help you with?"

"I bought a small dressing table from you last Friday, I was wondering if you could tell me who it belonged to."

"Was it that dressing table with the three mirrors on, a large one in the middle and two smaller side mirrors?"

"It was indeed. You remember it then?"

"Not likely to forget it. I've had a PC Coltley on my back for the past couple of days wanting to know where, and from whom I got it. The funny thing was though, he never asked me who bought it, just wanted to know how I came by it. It's all right, I didn't tell him about you."

"Thank you, that was very kind of you. How did you come by it?"

"Got a phone call from a young lady, said her father had died and would I be interested in doing a house clearance. Well, running a second-hand shop, I'd have been an idiot to say no. So, I went and cleared out the contents of the house, which included the dressing table.

"It turns out, the old guy that owned the dressing table was murdered. Gave me a right grilling did PC Coltley, but I couldn't tell him any more than I have told you. Never met the poor old guy, but his daughter was a bit of a loser if you ask me."

"Why do you say that?"

"Looks like she eats chip butties for every meal, bit prone to the heavy side. Not much up here." He tapped his temple.

"Do you know where she lives?"

"No, she told me she would meet me at her father's house. I paid her what I thought the contents were worth and we parted company."

"Thank you for your time," Jasmin told him and she went back to work.

PC Coltley had told her that someone had been shot during another burglary. Could he have meant that it was the previous owner of the dressing table, that had been shot? She decided to call the police station and make enquires and explain what she had found in the secret compartments in the little dressing table.

So, on returning home from work that evening Jasmin put Bennie on his leash and they had a leisurely walk to the police station.

The officer at the front desk smiled in welcome as Jasmin entered the police station. She had tied Bennie up outside, because she had found out early on, that all shops and public places, discouraged taking a dog inside the premises unless it was a dog for the blind.

"Good afternoon Miss, can I help you?"

"I was wondering if it was possible to speak to PC Coltley, please?"

"He's off sick at the moment, but his partner, PC Harrison is available if you wish to have a word with him."

"Thank you, I would appreciate that."

"Take a seat and I will let him know you are here."

Jasmin went and sat down and waited until the police officer made an appearance.

"Hello Miss Ward, how can I help you?"

"I've been to see the proprietor of the second-hand shop I bought the dressing table from to see if he could tell me where he got it from. I have found a pen inside one of the drawers and I was going to return it. It's not an expensive pen, but sometimes things have sentimental value to people. So just in case, a loved one had bought the previous owner the pen, I thought he or she might like it back.

"But Mr Sackblock tells me the owner of the dressing table has been murdered. PC Coltley told me that there had been someone shot in the spate of burglaries that have been taking place prior to someone breaking into my house. I have come to see if the incidents are connected."

"Your dog is getting a bit restless, shall we go outside and let him know you haven't deserted him?" The door was held open for her.

Once outside, PC Harrison said, "I've brought you outside to tell you this because it's privileged information. If I am asked if I divulged this information to you, I will of course deny it. But as you are involved, I feel I must warn you to take care from now on. Is that understood?"

Jasmin nodded.

The policeman continued, "We are not sure if the two incidents are connected, but to be truthful there have been some funny things happening just lately and we think they all might be related. Unfortunately, PC

Coltley has come under suspicion, and he has been suspended from duty. Nothing proven, you understand, but evidence has been going missing from the evidence room.

"In particular some DVDs are missing and PC Coltley was the last name in the record book to say he had been in to look for some evidence. I'm sure it's all a misunderstanding, things get filed wrong all the time. Give it a couple of days and call back into the station if you still want to speak to PC Coltley, I'm sure he'll be back by then. You told us about the gun that slid under your dressing table, was there anything else that you might have found inside the dressing table drawers?" he asked.

"Such as what?" Jasmin wanted to know.

"Any DVDs, things of that nature, or even a camera?"

"No, nothing, like that. The only thing I did find was a pen in one of the drawers, it's of no value though," lied Jasmin.

"Well, in that case, you take care and call back in a couple of days if you feel the need, or anytime come to that, we are open twenty-four hours a day. If you find anything or remember anything that you feel might be relevant to the case, please ask for me at the desk and let me know."

"Thank you I will. I don't suppose you know where the daughter of the shot man lives, do you? I would like to go and see her to see if the pen belongs to her and offer my condolences."

"Do you know where the petrol station is on Chubb Lane?"

"Yes, I do."

"Well, she lives three doors down from the petrol station."

"Thanks for the information," Jasmin said and she proceeded to untie Bennie and they walked away from the police station and headed for home.

What was she thinking? She'd lied to the police. When PC Harrison had said DVDs had been going missing from the evidence room, then he pointedly asked her if she had found any DVDs or a camera, she had decided to keep the information she had to herself.

All the information that PC Harrison had revealed to her should not, under any circumstances, have been divulged. Police do not give this sort of information out to the public. Even the receptionist had told her that PC Coltley was off sick. Jasmin felt very uncomfortable about it. She had worked on reception in a solicitor's office and one of the first things that she had drilled into her was customer confidentiality.

By the time Jasmin reached her home, it was well past tea time. She let herself in and turned to let Bennie off his leash. Bennie bounded upstairs and started barking at her bedroom door. Looking in, Jasmin saw she'd had unwelcome guests again. Things were pulled out of drawers and thrown asunder. Her bed had been ransacked and every drawer of the dressing table had been pulled out and thrown to one side.

Jasmin turned and bolted to the kitchen, she pulled Bennie's cushion off and to her relief, her little yellow box and DVD were still there waiting to be discovered.

Chapter Three

Jasmin spent the rest of the evening clearing up the mess in her bedroom. She didn't report the break-in, there was no point. Nothing had been taken as far as she could tell. But then again there was not much to steal. Except for a box full of precious stones that is, and they were safe in Bennie's bed.

The feeling that she was being watched had returned. Had the intruder waited until she was home from work and taken Bennie out for a walk? Yes, she decided whoever it was that broke into her house, didn't know that Bennie would not be inside the house while she was at work.

A thought struck her, how had they got in, her front door was still locked when she arrived home. Jasmin went to see if the kitchen window had been cut again but it had not, the new pane of glass was still intact. The only explanation was, someone had a key to her front door or back door. She looked at the lock in her back door. The lock still housed her key. She tried to open it but the door was locked, the intruder had not used the back door.

She had left the front door key with the police whilst she was staying at Marley's. Could PC Coltley have made a copy? She could hardly accuse him, or anyone else at the police station who would have had access to the key, of doing such a thing. Someone at the police station must have made a copy of her house key, there was no other explanation. She would have to have her lock changed. When she bought that dressing table, she thought she had bought a bargain. It turns out it is costing her a fortune.

The next morning Jasmin took the yellow box and DVD out of Bennie's basket and put them in her bag. It seemed unlikely that PC Coltley was involved in these break-ins because he knew that when she was at work, Bennie was out in the back garden, or in his shed. She had told him this whilst PC Harrison was upstairs showing the CSI team which bedroom needed to be processed.

So that was one theory gone to the wall. There must be someone else involved. She would keep the box and DVD with her until she can think of what she needed to do about them.

The day passed with a lack of excitement and Jasmin, on leaving work, decided to go via Chubb Lane and see if she could find out where the daughter of the murdered man lived. Bennie would have to wait for his walk.

Chubb Lane was a ten-minute walk from IT Intelligence. She walked on past the petrol station and counted the doors of the terraced houses and was soon knocking on the door of the third house down. No movement came from within the house so Jasmin tried again.

This time, Jasmin saw the curtain twitch to the left of her and she smiled at the face of a young woman peeking out to see who was knocking on her door. Then the curtain was dropped and the young woman's face disappeared only to reappear as the door opened, just as far as the metal security chain would allow.

"Who are you and what do you want?" the young woman asked Jasmin.

"My name is Jasmin Ward and I purchased a dressing table from the second-hand shop in Glaston and I found a pen in one of the drawers. I have been told that you are the young lady that asked Mr Sackblock to do a house clearance of your father's house. I have come to return the pen."

"I don't want it, you can keep it," the young woman said.

"I know it's not worth much but I thought it might be of sentimental value to you," Jasmin told her.

"Well, you thought wrong, it isn't. I have had nothing but trouble since that fateful day the solicitor came to my door and told me my father had made me the beneficiary of his will. Go away and take the pen with you."

"You might say the same for me. I have had nothing but trouble either since I bought that dressing table from Mr Sackblock. I have had my house burgled twice and have had to live at a neighbour's house until the crime scene people had done what they had to do. That is the reason I have come to see you; I was wondering if you know what is going on. I didn't find a pen in the dressing table it was just an excuse to come and see you," Jasmin told her.

After a few seconds of silence, the door was closed and Jasmin heard the safety chain being taken off and the door opened and the young woman said, "Hurry up and come inside."

Jasmin did as she was bid and the door was closed behind her, locked and the safety chain was put back in place.

"Come on through, I'll put the kettle on. Sorry about the attitude at the door, but I think my house is being watched. There have been two men standing inside that bus shelter for the past week. I can see the shelter from the kiosk at work and when I'm at work, these two men vanish. When I go back home, they are back. They are there now. Take a peek out of the window."

Jasmin did as she was told and sure enough, there were two men standing under the bus shelter.

Jasmin followed the young women into the kitchen and she pointed to two hardbacked chairs placed at a little wooden kitchen table.

Jasmin was surprised at the size of the young woman. She had only seen her face at the window. Being able to get a better look at her, as Mr Sackblock had said, she was rather a large young woman for her age.

"I know, before you say anything to me, I'm too fat," the young woman said.

"I wasn't going to say any such thing," Jasmin said.

"Well, maybe you are too polite to say anything but I know you will be thinking it. I eat too much and most of it is the wrong type of food. But my mother brought me up and she never chastised me for eating the wrong things. She was an alcoholic you see, and all she thought about was where her next bottle of plonk was coming from."

"What about your father, didn't he try to stop her from drinking?"

"My father? That's a laugh. I never knew my father. It came out of the blue one day. I work at the petrol station just up the road. I had been on the day shift and when I left work at two o'clock, I arrived home to find a solicitor waiting to see me. He told me my father had named me as the beneficiary of his will. I told the solicitor he must have the wrong person, but no, I had to have a DNA test and it was proven that I was indeed, Clive Huggard's daughter.

"Rhoda Huggard is my name. I lived in the same town as my father all these years and I never knew it. Not only in the same town but only a few streets away. My mother always said he was a waste of time and he wasn't worth bothering about. She said that he worked away somewhere, she never did say where and I didn't bother asking. No point was there?

"He never bothered about me, so as I got older, I never thought about him. I did when I was little though. When my mother passed out with the booze, I would have given anything to have my father walk in through the door and take me away with him.

"Then about two months ago this happens. I found myself lumbered with a rented terrace house with tatty contents and not much else. I had to pay a month's rent on the house because it was full of his stuff and I had to get rid of it. I had to wait four weeks before the police said I could move the stuff out, murder scene and all that.

"That's why I asked Mr Sackblock to do the house clearance so quickly. I can't afford to keep paying rent on a house that didn't belong to me. At least my mother had managed to pay this mortgage off before her demise. Probably from the money she made from prostitution. She went on the game to get money for the booze, catch twenty-two, as the saying goes. That's why I eat a lot, of comfort food.

"My father had been murdered, shot once in the head and thrown in the river. When he was dragged out of the river the police found a gun in his pocket. They asked me if I knew anything about the gun. I ask you; do I look like someone that knows about guns? I told them I didn't know my father, let alone any guns he had.

"Not that I give a fig about that, I might have shot him in the head myself if I had ever come face to face with him. But the nightmare didn't end there. Two weeks ago, my house was burgled and I had the police in but nothing ever came of it.

"The officer who came to my house said my father had been an associate of someone called George InGuesty, a smuggler. The officer wanted to know if I had any of my father's things here or any photos. I said I had not. If he had seen the state of the things that were in that house, it would have been a question better not to have been asked."

"Rhoda, just out of curiosity, what was the name of the officer that called to see you?"

"PC Coltley, I think."

"How interesting. That is the name of one of the officers who came to my house when I had the break-in."

"You think he's involved in all this?"

"I think he could be, but some of the things that have been happening don't add up."

"But what do they want, there was nothing of any value amongst my father's things, I checked."

"Look Rhoda, this is becoming a bit complicated. I really must go home. I have a dog, and he has to be taken for a walk. I came straight here from work to see you so Bennie has been locked in the back garden all day. Do you fancy coming back with me to my house and we can carry on trying to sort this out while we take Bennie for his walk?"

"Sorry, what did you say your name was?" Rhoda asked.

"My name is, Jasmin Ward."

"I have nothing else to do Jasmin, so why not,"

A quarter of an hour later, Bennie was being introduced to Rhoda and it was a match made in heaven. Rhoda took to him straightaway, and Bennie, if someone makes a fuss of him, they are his friend for life.

"Come on old fella, let's get you along the canal path so you can get rid of all that energy you've built up during the day," Jasmin said as she attached the leash.

On reaching the canal path, Bennie was given his freedom and he had no objection to taking it, he bounded off along the towpath, stopping at every other blade of grass to have a smell, but keeping his eye on the two ladies, to make sure they were in sight.

"I've lived on Chubb Lane all my life and I've never been along here before, it's beautiful," Rhoda said.

"What do you do to pass the time of day when you're not working?" asked Jasmin.

"Not much, watch the telly mostly. I don't have any friends as such. I did have a friend called Jean, but she stopped asking me out on a night. When I asked her why, she said I put the men off, so I just sit and watch the telly. This is nice though; I like the canal."

"We have a problem, Rhoda. I think I know what the burglars are looking for."

"Really, what is it."

Jasmin looked behind her to see if there was anybody following them, but the path was clear of any other person. It was safe to take the yellow box out. She opened her bag and pulled out the box, then proceeded to lift off the lid. After Rhoda had seen the contents, Jasmin closed the lid and put the box back in her bag.

"Are they real?"

"I have no idea. I found them in a secret compartment on that dressing table I bought. I came across it quite by accident." Jasmin went on to tell Rhoda how she made the discovery.

"You can imagine my shock at seeing these stones."

"Why didn't you take them to the police?"

"I did, but when I got there, PC Harrison took me outside and told me PC Coltley had been suspended for tampering with evidence in the evidence room. He said he wanted to warn me to be careful."

"That was good of him."

"I disagree. He should not have divulged that information to me. That is why he took me outside so nobody else could hear what he was saying. I also, like you, have the feeling I am being watched. I wonder if PC Harrison is involved and that is the reason, he told me where you lived.

"So, whoever was watching us could keep an eye on both of us and see what we get up to. This is a problem, for I don't think I can put my trust in the police now. It has put me back to square one. I could be making a mountain out of a molehill, and it is my imagination that is running wild. I have no evidence that PC Harrison is involved, he might genuinely have been trying to warn me to be careful. What am I going to do with these stones?"

"If we can't trust the police, who can we trust?" Rhoda asked.

"These, shall we say gems for the moment, are yours by rights. Your father left you all his worldly goods and these were included unless, of course, your father knew nothing about them. After all, they were hidden away in a secret compartment What do you want me to do with them?"

"Do with them? I want you to keep them, they are safer with you and Bennie than they are with me. What would I do with a box of gemstones? Buy more food and end up exploding. Anyway, like you say they might not have anything to do with my father."

Jasmin was delighted with her reply and she couldn't help laughing. "I work for an IT company, it's quite a big concern and rumour has it, that the guy who owns the company has a secret room somewhere with a computer in it that can do anything, but the police can't find it. He can access any computer anywhere in the world and hack into it, and it cannot be traced."

"What has that got to do with that box of glass you have in your bag?"

"Because, not only did I find the yellow box in the dressing table, but on the other side there was a second secret compartment and that held a DVD. I tried reading it on my computer but it is encrypted, my computer couldn't open it without a password, and I didn't have it.

"That is why I thought I might try to see the owner of the IT company and ask if he could do whatever has to be done to be able to see what is on the DVD."

"Can he be trusted not to go to the police?"

"I don't know. But I do know he has a reputation from his past. He had a few run-ins with the police when this company first started up, not producing legal stuff, I think. I'm not sure what that means but there's a fifty-fifty chance that he would not go to the police. It's the only thing I can think of to do.

"I work in the typing pool and to be honest, the stuff I have to type up is way over my head. I have no idea what I'm typing, it's all double Dutch to me, but it pays the bills. I also know that Jacob Firth, is a very hard man to see. Jacob being the owner of the IT company. He's a recluse by the sounds of it. He has an office on the top floor and a battle-axe for a secretary who won't allow anyone near him.

"I also know that this secretary leaves her office from twelve o'clock until one o'clock and goes back home to check on her elderly mother, to make sure she is all right. So, I had thought, when I see the secretary leave for her lunch hour tomorrow, I would try to sneak up to the top floor and go and see Jacob Firth. What do you think of that plan?"

"Why do you need to know what is on the DVD?"

"Why were the DVD and box of gems hidden in the secret compartments? I think these two items might be the reason why you and I are being targeted by a burglar or burglars. You are assuming that the burglar was after the box of gems. What if it has nothing to do with the gems? What if it is about the DVD? We have to know. I buy the dressing table and you inherit Clive Huggard's estate and we have both been burgled," Jasmin told her.

Rhoda was silent for a minute then she said, "What you've just said about the dressing table, the description matches a set of drawers I have at home. They were both at my father's house when I went to clear it out. I asked one of the lads at work who has a car if he would be so kind as to collect the drawers and drop them off at my house for me. I took the drawers and left the dressing table there.

"My house isn't big enough to take both of them and the set of drawers fit nicely in my spare bedroom. I had forgotten all about it until you mentioned your dressing table. I did look inside the dressing table before I let Mr Sackblock take it, but there wasn't so much as a pair of underpants in it."

"I think we'd better go and take a look at your drawers, don't you?" Jasmin asked.

"Yes, I think we better had."

Bennie was called back and they turned around and made their way back along the towpath. Bennie was put back on his leash whilst they walked along the causeway to Rhoda's house.

Bennie was in his element, all these new smells and different rooms to investigate and investigate he did.

Up in Rhoda's bedroom, Jasmin looked behind the set of drawers and found an identical little brown button so she proceeded to push it in. Out shot a concealed compartment but alas, it was empty. She moved to the other side of the drawers and pushed the little brown button and a second compartment was revealed. This time it held a long thin envelope and written on the front was:

To my daughter, Rhoda Huggard.

Jasmin passed the envelope to Rhoda and she took the letter out and read:

My darling daughter

If by any miracle you are reading this letter, I will be six feet under. Do not grieve, I have had an exciting life, if not an honest one. Unfortunately, I may have placed you in danger, it was not intended. I have crossed someone I should not have crossed and his name is, George InGuesty, he is a bad man.

The police have never been able to find out who InGuesty is. I have taken a few photos of him and put them on a DVD. You should by now have received the letter telling you where to find the DVD.

On the opposite side to where the DVD is hidden, you will find a yellow box. In this box, there are some precious stones. These stones were bought legally from a jeweller called Billy Greystone. Billy had a gambling problem and when he found himself in difficulty and the gull catches were after him, he came to me. He would bring a precious stone and I would give him money for it and over the years I amassed quite a number of these stones. I put them safely away for my retirement, but that will not happen now. InGuesty is after my blood, and he will eventually get it.

I had a visit from a PC Coltley, and he asked me if I would help him to get some proof of who InGuesty is by taking a photo of him and handing it to the police. I asked PC Coltley how he knew I worked for InGuesty and he said he had been once or twice to a party on board a riverboat and he had seen me roaming about. He assumed I worked there.

He had also overheard a conversation that I'd had with another guest at one of the parties and he'd heard me say I wanted out. I decided that if I did what he asked, I might be able to change my way of life and try to lead a normal life. After all, I don't need money. I have more than enough to see me put to rest and there will still be plenty left for you to inherit.

I paid your mother's mortgage off years ago to keep a roof over your head. I was aware of your mother's drinking habits. I would try and become friends with you. I know you will find it hard to believe but I have followed your progress and I am really proud of the way you have turned out. I know what a difficult childhood you had with your mother, but it was a better life than I could give you.

Unfortunately, InGuesty saw me taking a photo of him and I had to flee. It is only a matter of time before I am caught, I know that you don't cross InGuesty and get away with it.

I hope you have received the letter I wrote to you telling you where to look for all this information. If by chance you find this letter before the letter that I left with the solicitor along with a key to a security box at the Chapel Bank, you will have to work backwards. But be very, very careful how you approach the situation. I don't know who to advise you to get in touch with, for I am not sure that PC Coltley is a safe bet.

Keep safe

Your loving father, Clive.

"My God, it was my father that paid my mother's mortgage off, not my mother. All these years and my mother never said a word to me. But I haven't received any letter with a key in it from the solicitor," Rhoda said handing the letter over for Jasmin to read.

Jasmin read the letter and handed it back to Rhoda, "So the box of stones are precious gems, and they are not stolen. You have suddenly become a very rich young woman. The burglars know nothing about the stones, it's the DVD they are after. Your father mentions taking a photo, I bet that is what is on the DVD. And that is why you and I are being targeted. But I suppose that is something we will never know. PC Harrison mentioned the camera. I wonder how he knew about it?"

"Please, will you keep the stones and the letter? Just until we know what's going on. I wouldn't know what to do with them, and anyway, I am now scared stiff after reading that letter. I won't be able to sleep ever again. I was bad enough after the break-in, I'm sure as hell terrified now."

"Why don't you come and stay with me for a while? I have a spare room and we will have each other for company and support, and then there's Bennie, he'll look after us. If we work together, we might be able to sort it out, or at least find out what it's all about."

"Would you mind terribly? I can't stop here on my own now."

"I would be grateful for your company Rhoda. I am in the same position as you, it's not a pleasant situation we find ourselves in. I can't come and live at your house; I have Bennie to think about."

"Let me pack a few things then, and I'll come back to your place for a while."

Rhoda got her shopping trolley and filled it with what she thought she might need for the next few days and it was not long before Jasmin was unlocking her front door.

Once Rhoda was installed in the spare room, Jasmin made hot chocolate and some sandwiches for them both and they sat on the sofa and enjoyed their feast.

Jasmin broke the silence by saying, "I think the suggestion I made earlier about trying to get to see Jacob Firth, is the best solution to our problem, don't you?"

"If you say so, it's more than I have got. Do you mind if I go off to bed now? I'm on the day shift this week so I'm up and out for six-thirty, start work at seven," Rhoda told Jasmin.

Jasmin went over to a wall cabinet and took out a spare set of keys handing them to Rhoda. "Front door, back door. Bennie will be out in the back garden when you get back from work. I usually leave a key in the back door when I go to work, just to make it more difficult for anybody who tries to break-in. Much good that did. Bennie has all he needs in the shed: food, water and a nice big bed. You can let him back in when you come home if you want, he'll like that."

"Thank you, I'll do that. He's great company."

"Yes, he is," confirmed Jasmin.

The next morning Jasmin awoke to the smell of toast and coffee. She quickly donned her jeans and jumper and followed the enticing smell into the kitchen.

"Jasmin, I hope I haven't woken you and you don't mind me making myself a bit of breakfast," Rhoda said.

"No, you haven't woken me, I am usually up around this time to take Bennie for a walk before I get changed to go to work. Is there any coffee ready?"

"No, sorry. I only made some for myself I didn't think you would be up. I have to go now."

"That's OK. I will take Bennie out for his walk and get something when I get back. See you tonight." Jasmin left Rhoda to her own devices.

Chapter Four

Jasmin found it hard to concentrate on her work that morning. She kept glancing at the big clock that was located above the office supervisor's pod and she thought the hands would never reach twelve o'clock.

She saw Jacob Firth's secretary making her way down the glass-sided staircase to the left of the building. *Time to go,* she thought, so she signed out of her computer and when the secretary was out of sight, Jasmin made for the lift. She hoped it was empty and kept everything crossed that no one in the office would notice that the lift was going up instead of down.

There were two problems with using the staircase. One was the glass side that anybody in the office could see who was going up and down. The second problem was, the double doors opening onto the staircase, were locked. You needed a code to be able to open them and Jasmin was not privileged enough to have the code.

When the lift doors opened on the top floor, Jasmin stepped out. She opened her bag to check that she had brought all that she was going to need when she tried to explain her situation to Jacob Firth. Doubt kicked in, she felt utterly stupid, this was a very bad idea. Why would Jacob Firth want to help her, he didn't know her, and why should he give a damn about Clive Huggard's murder.

The overhead computer screen pinged into life and Jacob glanced upwards. It was a long time since the screen had sprung to life and Jacob saw the corridor to his office appear on the screen. This was one of the security systems that were scattered around the building. If anyone used the lift up to the top floor without permission, the video system kidded in. The usual procedure was if someone wanted to see Jacob, they had to ring his secretary first and she would log the visit onto the computer.

This visitor however had not been authorised and Jacob watched the lift doors open and was surprised to see a young woman step out into the corridor. He watched her hesitate, then open her handbag and look inside. She looked behind her as the lift doors closed and put out her hand to recall the lift, but it was too late, the lift was on its way back down.

The vision on Jacob's screen looked around her, nothing but closed doors. She was here now, so she might as well go through with what she had come to do. Making her way down the corridor, Jasmin read the nameplates on each door but they meant nothing to her until she reached the very end of the corridor and there, firmly standing in the middle, stood two solid-looking oak doors with brass nameplates. One read Jacob Firth and the other, Luther.

Deciding to take the bull by the horns she opened the impressive oak door boasting the brass nameplate of Jacob Firth. She glided in silently keeping her back towards the inner office, closing the door gently before she looked around. There, she was in. So far so good.

Taking a deep breath, Jasmin turned to face the office. What she saw, was not what she had expected. She had expected to enter an outer office where Jacob's secretary worked. She expected this office to be empty because the secretary had gone for her lunch, that was why she hadn't knocked before she entered. But no, she was standing in the main office. Facing her was a wall of glass looking out over Glaston and sitting with his back to the glass wall, was a handsome young man in his early to mid-twenties watching her.

Silence reigned in the office as they both took stock of each other. Jacob liked what he saw. A young woman in her early twenties, with short neatly trimmed brown hair, large sky-blue eyes and wearing a white short-sleeved blouse tucked into the waist of a black pencil style skirt. She wore flat open sandals on her feet and her tiny toenails were painted bright red.

Jasmin's shock at seeing such a handsome young man with wavy black hair and enquiring brown eyes watching her back began to panic.

"I beg your pardon; I was looking for Jacob Firth," apologised Jasmin.

"You have found him."

"You are Jacob Firth?"

"I am."

"Well, I'm not well pleased about that. You can't be Jacob Firth."

"I can't say I'm well pleased by this intrusion either, but I assure you, I am Jacob Firth."

"You are not what I expected."

The office door opened and in walked a gentleman dressed smartly in a dark-grey double-breasted suit with a bright pink shirt beneath and a scarlet tie at his throat. The gentleman stopped in his tracks when he saw Jasmin. He looked over at Jacob and said, "You've kept this quiet. You are a sly old dog, Jacob." He went to sit on the corner of Jacob's desk, folded his arms, and he openly took Jasmin in.

Silence reigned once more and Jasmin's curiosity took in the face of the new addition to the office. The right-hand side of his face was very handsome, but to the left, the vision wasn't so perfect. The absence of an eye gave it a lopsided look, but in a comical way and Jasmin was pushed into saying, "What happened to your eye?"

"Which one?"

"Your left one of course."

"I had a vicious cat, I was laid in bed one day and I opened my eyes, I think the cat thought it was a game, he attacked it with his claws."

Jasmin burst out laughing, "I don't believe a word of it, but a neighbour of ours had a ginger cat and I must admit if you got too close to it, you were left in no doubt you had better keep your distance."

"That's my story, what's yours? What are you doing in Jacob's office? He hasn't mentioned you before."

"That's because I haven't been in Jacob's office before. If I had, I would not be here now. He is not what I expected."

The one-eyed man was beginning to warm to this young woman and he asked, "What did you expect?"

"His father."

Silence continued.

Then the one-eyed man suddenly blurted out, "I say, are you Jacob's sister?"

"His sister. How can I be his sister?"

"You're after his father, the thought occurred to me that you might be an illegitimate child and you have tracked Jacob's father down as being your father. That would make you step-brother and sister, wouldn't it?"

"Well, you are far off the mark there, Sir."

"Yes, I guess so. Jacob's father died when he was ten years old. That's the effect Jacob has on you, makes you old before your time. Look what he's done to me, I'm only eighteen really."

Jasmin couldn't help laughing and she added, "I like you."

"Thanks very much. You like me better than him?"

"I expected to find someone much older, tending to be on the plump side and balding."

The one-eyed man turned to look at his friend and said, "I think this one's a keeper. She likes me better than you. That's never happened before."

Jacob chose to ignore him and addressed Jasmin, "Why do you want to see my father?"

"He has a reputation of being a recluse and a brilliant IT man, and he has a computer that the police can't find. I need to use his computer. I thought if I could see him and explain the situation, because of his years and his reputation of once being on the wrong side of the law, he might help me."

"It's not his father that has the reputation, it's him." The one-eyed man nodded towards Jacob.

"But surely he is too young to hold such a reputation?"

"He started early," declared the visitor.

Delight shone in Jasmin's eyes as she looked over at the patient Jacob listening to the banter between the two.

Then Jasmin asked, "Oh my god, what time is it? I'm on my dinner hour and if I'm back late the supervisor wouldn't be too pleased and she'll deduct the money off my wage."

"I'm pleased to hear it. Why should I pay an employee for dallying about on my time? How did you get past my secretary?" Jacob wanted to know.

"I waited until I saw her leave on her lunch hour. I don't want anybody to know about this. I don't know what I've gotten myself into," explained Jasmin. "How do you know I work for you?"

"You had access to the lift. An outsider would never have gotten into this office."

Jasmin could think of nothing to reply to this so she glanced at her watch. It was all right, she had another half an hour left but she was getting nowhere fast so she decided to call it a day. She would have to think of some other way to retrieve the information from the DVD.

"Please accept my apologies for the intrusion into your office. It has been nice meeting you, Sir." She held out her hand to the one-eyed man.

Jasmin felt her right hand tightly clasped in the gentleman's right hand, then his left hand covered the top of her hand so that her hand was completely encased. It felt good and comforting and also very, very safe. Tears suddenly welled up in her eyes and she pulled her hand free and walked towards the door.

Jacob felt under his desk and pressed a button, the door was locked, and Jasmin was going nowhere.

She tried turning the handle but to no avail and after making three further attempts to escape she gave up and stood with her back towards the two gentlemen and refused to turn around.

"You are an employee of mine and you came to me with a problem. Please come and sit down and tell us all about it. You can trust Luther you know, despite his looks and his name," Jasmin heard Jacob say.

Jasmin turned and looked at Luther and replied, "Yes, I know I can. He is not the problem. I am disappointed in you, I was expecting a much older man, you are nothing like I imagined you to be. Is that your office next door to this?" Jasmin turned and looked at Luther.

"It is. Do you want to come into my office instead?" replied Luther.

Jasmin laughed, "No, of course not. I noticed your name on the brass nameplate on the door. Unusual name, it stuck in my mind," Jasmin told him.

"That makes a change, it's usually my eye that makes the first impression," Luther informed her.

Ignoring the conversation between the two Jacob said, "If you have made an error of judgement you are going to have to live with it, but you never know until you try whether something is going to work out or not. Come and sit down and let us hear what you have to say."

Jasmin went and sat down on the chair opposite Jacob. She glanced up at Luther who looked back at her and winked his one eye. The decision was made, and she would tell her story.

"To cut a long story short, I bought a second-hand dressing table. I discovered a secret compartment, and in this compartment, I found this." Jasmin opened her bag and produced the yellow box and placed it on the desk in front of Jacob.

Jacob reached out and opened the box. Luther whistled.

Jacob looked at Jasmin and she continued until she came to the bit where she discovered the second secret compartment and she opened her bag and laid the DVD on the desk in front of Jacob.

"I'm guessing you've tried to play the DVD and the computer won't allow you to read it?"

"That is correct. So, to continue the story." She explained her encounter with the police and outlined why she had decided not to leave the box of gems or the DVD with them and concluded by saying, "In hindsight I think it was a good move but it didn't solve the problem of what to do with the box or the DVD.

"PC Harrison had also provided me with the name and address of the daughter of the last owner of the dressing table. This is another reason I haven't disclosed any of this to the policeman. PC Harrison should not have divulged her name and address to a complete stranger.

"I decided to go and pay the young woman a visit. It was agreed between us that she would come and stay at my house for a while until we found out what was happening. Then we would both have Bennie to look after us.

"We took Bennie for a walk along the canal towpath and I told her everything I could remember and one thing rang a bell with Rhoda, for that was her name,

Rhoda Huggard, she told me she had a set of drawers which matched the dressing table.

"We decided to go back to her house and check the drawers out and we found this." Jasmin opened her bag, took out the letter and laid it on the desk in front of Jacob.

Jacob read the letter and then passed it to Luther. Jacob and Jasmin waited in silence until Luther had finished reading the letter.

"Has your friend been to the solicitors with regard to the letter and key for the bank vault?"

"No, we only found that letter last night and Rhoda had to go to work early this morning. If I hadn't found the yellow box or DVD none of this would have happened. Since reading that letter it seemed even more important to try and find out what was on the DVD.

"Neither dare I leave these things at home in case I get burgled again. That's why I decided to come and see you, well not you really, I thought it would be your father sitting there. You seem to be a bit young to have such a reputation."

"My father died when I was ten years old and my mother went to pieces. I was taken into a care home for children only they didn't care much for children, and when I was fourteen years old, I ran away. I went in search of my mother but I couldn't find her. She had packed her bags and I never saw her again. I got in with a bad crowd, stealing cars, robbing houses, that sort of thing. Then one day one of the lads brought back a computer and it fascinated me.

"I found out all sorts of things, I hacked into other peoples' computers, got names and addresses and set up a con business. That's how I met Luther. I hacked into his computer and found out that there was already someone finding out confidential information on his computer. I approached Luther with this information and never looked back.

"Luther ran a very lucrative online business selling used computers. We got our heads together and set up this business. All legal and above board. We develop software for businesses that use sensitive material, all very hush-hush of course, but we thrive. I was only fifteen at the time when I first met Luther, and he was twenty-one."

"Are you in partnership with Jacob? I have not heard your name mentioned, and I have worked here for the past four months," Jasmin told him.

"As you can see for yourself, I don't have a face that instils confidence in people. Especially where confidential matters are concerned. I am a sleeping partner. Jacob is the face of the company and I am the brains," replied Luther.

"Why do you wear such bright clothes?" Jasmin wanted to know.

"It makes people stop staring at my eye," came the reply.

"Which eye?" asked Jasmin with a look of innocence on her face.

A smile spread across Luther's face, "The left one of course."

"I prefer the cat story myself," she told him.

"Me too, that's why I use it," he confirmed.

"Look, it's well past my lunch hour I must get back to my desk. Will you help me?" Jasmin asked.

"I will have a look into the evidence and get back to you, but I'm not promising you anything. Do you understand?"

"Thank you, that's all I ask." Jasmin stood up and left the room leaving all the evidence sitting on the desk in front of Jacob.

Jacob looked up at Luther, "What do you think?"

"I think you're a lost cause. You'll help her."

"I think you're right," agreed Jacob.

Chapter Five

Jasmin arrived back at her desk thirty minutes late. She was hauled into the supervisor's office and was asked for an explanation of why she had taken thirty minutes more than she was allowed. Jasmin explained that she had received a text message saying that her dog had escaped out of her back garden and she had to go home and find him.

The supervisor accepted the excuse but told her she would have half an hour deducted from her next wage and Jasmin was glad to be back at her little pod, donning her earphones.

Rhoda arrived at Jasmin's house at two-thirty after leaving work, and instead of doing her usual food and TV routine, she went straight to the back door and let Bennie in. He greeted her with his usual energetic welcome. After putting Bennie on the leash, she took him out and onto the canal towpath. It was a glorious day and once the canal path was reached Rhoda took Bennie off his lead and away, and he went. Rhoda followed at a leisurely pace and the sunshine, water and Bennie's enthusiasm lifted her spirits no end.

It was a pity that she didn't turn to look behind her or she would have seen two men following her, keeping the same distance behind her as she strolled along. After half an hour Rhoda decided to make her way back so she called Bennie. He did as he was told and came bounding back but instead of him stopping when he reached Rhoda, he carried on passed her and went to stand in front of the two men.

Both men were alarmed to see a rottweiler heading in their direction and they started shouting at Rhoda to call her dog back. "Bennie, come here," she ordered.

Bennie carried on and stood half a metre away from the two men watching and waiting for their next move. Both men stood stock still and waited for his next move.

Rhoda arrived at the scene and immediately took hold of Bennie's collar and attached it to the lead and dragged him away and the two men proceeded on their way with Rhoda's apologies ringing in their ears.

"What was all that about Bennie? You don't usually behave like that," Rhoda wanted to know.

Standing on the bridge over the canal was a man dressed in a dark-grey suit, bright pink shirt and scarlet tie. His one eye taking in the scene with much interest.

Rhoda and Bennie left the canal path and joined the main road, crossing the bridge that the one-eyed man was standing on. She passed him by without even seeing him but his back was towards her anyway so she would not have seen his face.

Once Rhoda and Bennie were out of sight, Luther went down onto the canal path and began walking in the same direction that the two men had taken. He wanted to know where they were going.

When Jasmin had left Jacob's office, it was decided between Jacob and Luther that they should do some digging without Jasmin knowing. The first thing they decided on was to find out about Rhoda. The daughter of a murdered man they decided, was the priority.

Luther went to see Mr Sackblock. He might know something about Rhoda that Rhoda hadn't told Jasmin. Luther had a face that didn't need threats to get what he wanted.

When he asked the shop owner for Rhoda's home address, he told Luther what he had told Jasmin. That he didn't know where she lived. He found out nothing that he didn't already know. Jasmin had told them that Rhoda worked at the petrol station on Chubb Lane and lived three doors down.

Luther decided to go to the petrol station and see if Rhoda was working and take a look at her. He was just in time to see a plump young woman leaving the kiosk and he heard a voice from inside shout, "See you tomorrow, Rhoda."

"Have a good shift, don't work too hard," was Rhoda's reply.

Luther followed her and saw her enter a house. Now he knew where she lived. He turned to go back to the office when he noticed two men who seemed to be watching her. They nipped into the bus shelter on the opposite side of the road when Rhoda disappeared into the house. He carried on further up the street and stood in the entrance to an alleyway, and he, in turn, watched the two men watching Rhoda's house, to see what happened next.

Rhoda came out of the house with a rottweiler on a lead and strolled down the street. The two men followed her. Luther followed the two men and stood on the bridge and watched as Rhoda and the dog went off along the towpath and the two men continued to follow her.

His position on top of the bridge gave him an excellent view of the towpath as the path ran in a straight line. Luther decided to stay where he was and see what happened. He was in a good position; he could run down onto the towpath if need be, but he didn't want to bring attention to himself.

Now Rhoda had left the towpath and was making her way back in the direction she had come, and with Bennie to look after her, Luther set off in pursuit of the two men that had followed her. He wanted to know where they were going.

To Luther's surprise, by the time he was down on the towpath, the two men had turned and were coming back towards him. There was nothing for him to do but turn towards the water and pretend to be looking down into the canal. If either of the men were to glance at him, they would see his good profile and hopefully not recognise him again.

The two men were so intent on what they were doing to give any attention to a man on his own looking into the canal and they went up the steps, onto the main road and were once again, standing in the bus shelter watching what Luther thought was Rhoda's house.

Luther took note of this and hurried back to the office and into the lift. He went straight into Jacob's office and related what he had witnessed.

"There's definitely something dodgy going on Jacob, I think the young lady should be told about the two men watching Rhoda's house before she leaves for home."

"I agree with you, there is something very dodgy going on and I think we need to take the two ladies under our protection until we know what this involves. It's turning out to be a very dangerous game, Luther. I managed to open the DVD whilst you were out. Take a look at this."

Jacob's fingers flew over the keyboard and a large screen lit the wall to the right of his desk. Luther turned and watched as the scene showed a riverboat docked at a mooring along a river neither could identify. The scene moved from the riverboat and followed a long immaculately cut lawn that led up to a house of no mean size. Again, neither of them knew the place.

The scene then became a flagged path leading away from the boat, making a large sweeping path that looked like a back-to-front letter C. It stopped when it reached a glass-encased structure that was a luxurious conservatory.

Out of this conservatory came two men in their mid to late twenties. They started along the curved path and down to the riverboat. Both disappeared into the boat's cabin. For a few minutes, there was no other movement. Then, a frogman appeared on deck, sat on the edge of the boat, leaned backwards and dropped into the water. Bubbles started to appear then they vanished, the water was still.

The second man came up on deck and stood at the boat's side near the mooring rope looking down into the water. He dropped a length of rope into the water and waited. Then the man on the deck began to haul the rope back into the boat and when the end of the rope appeared again, it was attached to a big black package about the size of a large suitcase.

As the package was landing on the deck, the frogman climbed back onboard. They looked at the package and shook hands. The screen went blank.

"Do you know either of them?" Jacob asked.

"Nope."

"Smuggling?"

"Yep."

"This is what the burglars are looking for wouldn't you say?"

"It doesn't need someone with half a brain to work that out. I agree with you. I think the ladies might be in great danger," Luther remarked.

"We need to get them to safety. I'm going to email Jasmin before she goes home and tell her to go home and get Rhoda and you will pick them up. First, we need to have a plan. I'll pull up the map where Jasmin lives and let's see if there is anywhere near where we can get them into the car without anyone seeing. If this is what we think it is, these two men will still be watching her house."

Luther sat and listened to what Jacob had said. He rubbed his chin and remarked, "Jasmin, you called the young woman Jasmin. I can't remember her telling us her name."

"Pod five. Jasmin Ward, not been living in Glaston very long. Worked in the office of a solicitor in Tanbrook before coming to work here."

"You've been into her personnel file?"

"Of course. Are you surprised?"

"Damned right I'm surprised. Never known you to take that much interest in a woman for a few years now."

"Interesting, isn't it?" said Jacob with a smile on his face.

"Trouble ahead from more than one direction then. Better pull that map up."

The map showed up on the large screen and they both put their heads together and found, heading back into town from Jasmin's house an alleyway that ran between a row of terrace houses and came out along the main road into Glaston. When the alleyway came to an end the main road was a one-way street but parking was allowed to the left of the alleyway where there was a layby, ideal for what they needed.

Jasmin glanced at the clock on the wall and saw it was ten minutes to five. It had been a long day but the next ten minutes were going to be the longest. Then her computer pinged, and an email arrived.

On opening it she saw it was from Jacob Firth, she looked around guiltily before she went on to read:

We need to meet. Get Rhoda as soon as you get home and go along the alley that takes you down between the row of terraced houses you pass going into town. Hurry (even run) down this alley and turn left. There will be a black saloon car parked in a layby waiting for you both. Just get in and do not look back. Nobody must see you get into the car. Try to be at the car by six o'clock. Jacob.

Jasmin's hands began to sweat, she wiped them down her thighs before she deleted the email and glanced at the clock. Five to five, she closed down all the screens she had open on the computer and turned it off. Other office workers were already collecting their belongings from the desks and beginning to head for the stairs leading down to the ground floor.

Jasmin tried not to be too eager to leave the building so she waited until a few of her fellow workers were out of the front door before she joined the queue. It took her all her reserve not to run and twenty minutes later she was opening her front door and Bennie was delighted to see her.

"Rhoda, thank goodness you are in. We have to go out straightaway. I'll explain on the way. I'll just go and change my clothes then we are straight out."

"What's going on?" Rhoda asked, following Jasmin upstairs.

"I don't know. I went in to see Jacob Firth in my lunch hour and told him all. I have left all the evidence with him. I didn't know what else to do or who else to go to.

"Only it wasn't Jacob Firth senior I encountered, it was Jacob Firth Jr. I'll tell you all about it when we are on our way. We have to be at the bottom of this alleyway at six o'clock. We'll take Bennie with us; it will seem if we are being watched, that we are just taking Bennie for his evening walk.

"When we get to the car, I will jump in the back with Bennie, and you jump in the front as quick as you can. Goodness knows what will happen next, but I do want to see what he has found out. Don't you?"

"To be truthful Jasmin, it's all beginning to freak me out. I took Bennie out for a walk along the canal towpath after work. Then this weird thing happened, I called Bennie back to go back home and he went charging passed me. Two men were walking along the canal towpath behind me and Bennie just went and stood in front of them looking threateningly at them.

"I had to pull him away, it was so unlike him. The two men weren't very happy at having a rottweiler standing staring at them. I had to apologise to them. I wish I had taken notice of their faces now. I was too busy seeing to Bennie to look at the men. Besides, I don't look at men, when I see the disgust in their eyes because of my size, I'd rather not see it. What if they have something to do with this business and Bennie sensed it? I wish I had never heard of Clive Huggard and even less about precious jewels and spooky DVDs. The only nice thing about this is, meeting you and Bennie."

Jasmin zipped up her jeans and smiled across at Rhoda, "It's been nice meeting you too Rhoda. It's good to have a bit of company. Ready?"

"As I'll ever be."

Jasmin put Bennie on his leash and following instructions they walked at a leisurely pace heading for town.

"I think I know why Bennie stood facing these two men on the canal. When I was walking home from work, I had to pass the bus shelter on the opposite side of my house and two men were standing under it. It was the same two men that were standing at the bus shelter across the road from your house.

"When we passed it just now, Bennie was pulling on the lead and looking towards the bus shelter. I glanced across the road to see why. He was looking at the two men standing at the bus shelter. I bet they followed you from work and saw you enter my house, so they are watching my house now. When you took Bennie along the canal, they will have followed you. Bennie sensed the danger," Jasmin told her.

Rhoda looked across at Jasmin as they walked towards the alleyway, "What's going on Jasmin? This is really scary," Rhoda said.

"I don't know, let's hope we can find something out tonight. I agree, this is really scary," Jasmin nodded.

When the alleyway was reached, they turned into it and Jasmin said, "Run Rhoda."

Rhoda set off running. Not having done any running for a few years, her stride was ungainly, but she made headway with Jasmin and Bennie following. Bennie was delighted at this unexpected activity. The alley was not very long and they were soon exiting at the other end. They turned left and found the black saloon waiting for them.

Rhoda opened the front door and jumped in. Jasmin did the same with the back door and Bennie jumped up onto the back seat and Jasmin climbed in beside him and pulled the door shut as she did so. As soon as the car doors were shut the driver indicated and he eased the car into the stream of traffic that was slowly moving out of town.

Two men appeared at the end of the alleyway and looked left and right, no sign of the two women and a dog and traffic was flowing. They turned and went back up the alley.

Rhoda, once she had got her breath back glanced at the driver and saw his profile. No eye. Panic set in and she held her breath.

"Don't worry, I have another eye and I can see perfectly well with it," Luther told her.

Rhoda was silent for a minute then she said to him, "I had a friend who had a lump in her breast and she had to have it removed. The doctor reconstructed her breast for her but he'd had to take her nipple away. They tattooed another nipple on her breast for her."

"Are you saying I should have a nipple tattooed on my eye?"

Laughter was heard coming from the back of the car and Rhoda glanced back and shot Jasmin a look of disapproval.

"I'm sorry Rhoda, it was the picture Luther conjured up of him walking around with a nipple on his eye."

"She's right you know; I would look a right Charlie. Besides, that would bring more attention to the eye than it already gets, especially if the tattoo is a nipple."

"I didn't mean that you should have a nipple tattooed on your eye," Rhoda said.

"Really! What then? Have you got a nipple fetish?

"No, I have not," Rhoda snapped.

"It's all right by me if you have, I don't mind talking about nipples," Luther turned his head for a second, met Rhoda in the eye and winked at her.

To change the subject Rhoda asked, "Is your name Luther? That's the name of the devil, isn't it?"

"Yes, Luther is my name, and you could say I'm a little devil. I like talking about nipples," Luther informed her.

Jasmin's shoulders shook as she sat in the back of the car with her arm around Bennie and lapped up the conversation in the front of the car.

"It's you that's the sex freak," Rhoda glared at Luther.

"Well, I like that. There I am innocently driving the car and all of a sudden you throw nipples at me, and you accuse me of being the sex freak?"

The car pulled to a stop at an impressive set of double wooden gates and waited for them to open. Open they did and through the gate and up along driveway went the car which came to a halt at a modest-looking bungalow.

Jacob appeared from inside the bungalow and as they emerged from the car, he asked Luther, "Have you explained things to them?"

"Hell no, we had a more interesting conversation in the car than smugglers."

Jacob looked at Jasmin and there was no mistaking the amused delight that shone back at him.

"Had I better not ask?" Jacob asked her.

"Nipples," Jasmin replied.

"I'd better not ask," decided Jacob.

Holding out his hand to Rhoda he said, "You must be Rhoda."

"I am, and please do not believe anything he has to say about me," Rhoda inclined her head towards Luther.

"I learned not to believe anything Luther says many years ago Rhoda, have no fear about that."

Then turning to face Bennie, Jacob planted his feet slightly apart placed his hands on his hips and said, "And who might you be young man?"

Bennie finding himself the centre of attention gave two delighted barks.

"You may take him off his lead, we are perfectly enclosed here, he will not be able to leave the property," Jacob told Jasmin.

Bennie was set free and he used his freedom by demanding a pat from all present, then he went on a sniffing expedition by himself.

"Are you sure he won't be able to escape?"

"Perfectly sure. Come on in, we have a lot to talk about." Jacob led the way inside the bungalow.

It was moderately decorated, neat and clean and surprisingly small for the length of drive they had to travel to reach it.

"Have you had anything to eat before you came here?" Jacob asked.

"No, by the time I got home from work and got changed, it was time to go and meet the car at six o'clock," Jasmin told him.

"As I thought. Come into the kitchen."

Like the rest of the bungalow they had seen, it was of small proportions but neat and clean. A small kitchen table was laid with a range of cold meat, pork pies and salad.

"Please take a seat and help yourselves," Jacob indicated the food and went to put the kettle on.

"I hope Bennie is all right. Would you mind if I went and called him? He might panic when he can't find me." Jasmin looked at Jacob.

"Take a seat and I'll attend to Bennie," Jacob smiled at her and left the room.

An ear-splitting whistle made them all jump and not thirty seconds later Bennie was following the smell of food and found Jasmin sitting at the kitchen table.

"Thank you," she said to Jacob,

"My pleasure," Jacob replied and took his seat at the table.

When they had all filled their plates with food Jacob said, "It looks like you have tumbled into a very dangerous situation without knowing it. I have managed to retrieve the information on the DVD and as far as I can tell, it involves smuggling. Drugs would be our guess.

"We, Luther and I, discussed it at length and it was decided that both of you must stay here until it is sorted out. This is for your own good. I think the smugglers think you have something they want and I don't think they will stop until they get it. Seeing the DVD, I think they are right, you do have something that they are after.

Now by doing what we have just done, fingers and everything else crossed, nobody is going to know where you have gone, and it is imperative that it stays that way."

"Stay here! I can't possibly stay here. I am on morning shift this week, I am needed at work," Rhoda told them.

"They will just have to manage without you I am afraid. I think it would be best if you were to text your boss and tell him you had to go unexpectedly up to Scotland because your mother had been taken ill." Jacob insisted.

"But I'll lose my job. For one thing, they know my mother is dead. They will know I am lying. How long are we going to be here?" Rhoda asked.

"That, I cannot tell you, for we do not know what is going on. We do not know who is involved, but what we do know is that whoever it is that's doing the break-ins, will stop at nothing to protect their cover. These are very dangerous and desperate people; according to Jasmin, you told her your father had been murdered for one thing. There has to be a connection."

Bennie went and laid his head on Jasmin's knee and she looked down at his bonny face, he was hungry.

"Lord, I had forgotten Bennie. I didn't bring any food for him. But then again, I didn't know I would be staying here. Will we be able to go to the shops to get him some food?" Jasmin asked.

"No, neither of you are to leave these grounds, I will attend to Bennie's food. For tonight, Bennie will have to make do with any sausage rolls and pork pies that are left over from our feast. It's not the ideal food for dogs but one night on a food binge will not do him any harm," Jacob told her.

"Now we've got Bennie sorted, you left that letter with us telling Rhoda about the solicitors holding a letter for her along with a key to a safety deposit box in the bank. Have you been in contact with the solicitor about that letter yet, Rhoda?"

"No, I had to take Bennie for a walk, that's more important than any old letter or safety deposit box," Rhoda told him.

"Did the solicitor not come to see you at the time of your father's death?" asked Jacob.

"Yes, of course, he did, but he didn't give me any letter with a key inside," Rhoda told him.

"That's one mystery that needs to be sorted out. Luther will ring the solicitors tomorrow and see what he can find out. Who are the solicitors?"

"Holmes, Holmes and Summers on High Street in Glaston," confirmed Rhoda.

"Next you both need to see what's on the DVD. See if either of you recognise either of the men on it," continued Jacob. "But we will need to go down to the house because that is where our secure computer is. If we invite people here, we always use this bungalow. There are very few people besides Luther and I that know of the existence of Low Valley House, where our computer room is. I am putting my faith in both of you not to divulge its whereabouts."

"In that case, I'd rather not see it if you don't mind Jacob, then I won't let it slip," Rhoda told him.

"I'm afraid you don't have an option. You must see the DVD if we are going to clear this up. After all, it was you that came to me for help."

"No, it wasn't, it was Jasmin's idea."

"But it is your father that has landed us all in the predicament, is it not?"

Rhoda had no reply to this so she remained silent.

"I am going to show you the secret way to Low Valley House, so again, I am putting my trust in you both. Because I don't know either of you, I am putting both Luther and myself at risk," Jacob said.

"Is there no other way?" asked Rhoda.

"Of course, there is, there's a path that leads from here to the house, but it's a long way round. This passage is in a direct line to the house. Better in bad weather too.

"When the DVD is inserted into a computer, we have to use our undetectable one in Low Valley House. Once the DVD has been handed over to the police, things should get back to normal. But until we know what we are dealing with and who we can trust, this needs to be kept between the four of us."

"You are starting to scare me," Rhoda told Jacob.

"Good," came the reply.

Rhoda looked at Luther and he asked her, "Would you rather we talked about nipples?"

Rhoda couldn't stop herself from laughing, "All right, I get the picture. You have my word; I will not divulge what I see to anyone else."

They all looked at Jasmin, "You have my word too."

"Then let's go."

Jacob led them all out of a side door in the kitchen into the integral garage. The front door to the garage was locked and bolted from the inside. Going to the back of the garage, Luther pulled a workbench away from the wall and stepped on what looked like a small pedal. An opening appeared at his feet.

Luther stood to one side and Jasmin was the first to move forward and peer down. A faint light showed a set of steps leading down, she moved forward and began to descend. Rhoda followed with Bennie tagging on at the back. Jacob waited on the top step until Luther had pulled the workbench back into position before he closed the sliding door and made it secure, then they followed the two ladies and the dog along the dimly lit passageway.

Jasmin felt the pathway beginning to slope downwards, then right and then the gradient began to get steeper. She carried on for a further few minutes until she came face to face with a solid wall. She could proceed no further.

"On the floor by your left foot Jasmin, you will see a small pedal. Press it down with your foot," Jacob told her.

Following the instruction, the pedal was pressed and what appeared to be a slab of rock face, came a few centimetres towards her then glided silently to the right. Jasmin stepped through the opening and found herself in a splendid bright hall. The curving staircase that led up to what could only be described as an elaborate top landing, looked like an art gallery. It put all the art galleries Jasmin had frequented to shame. She couldn't take her eyes off it.

Rhoda stood beside her, the splendour of what she saw left her feeling insecure and insignificant.

"This is beautiful," exclaimed Jasmin.

"All Luther's doing, he is the one with an eye for art," Jacob told her.

"Well, he certainly put his one good eye to good use," Rhoda remarked.

Luther looked back at Rhoda, "It doesn't miss much." He pointedly looked her up and down.

Rhoda felt embarrassed and utterly stupid, ugly and overweight.

Bennie on the other hand didn't give a fig for the opulence, there were different smells to discover and another adventure to pursue.

"Why the cloak and dagger stuff? Why did we have to go along that tunnel?" Jasmin asked Jacob.

"This house stands on slightly lower ground than the bungalow, that's why it's called Low Valley House, and from the bungalow, it can't be seen. This is our private home; Luther and I share the property. The house is large enough to enable us to do so. We have four bedrooms each, two with en-suite, two bathrooms each and two kitchens each. A room each, dining room and library. The computer room we share. Security is paramount, the less anyone knows about it, the better.

"There is also a second bungalow at the rear of the house and Luther's sister Sally lives there. She keeps house for us. As there is only the two of us, we usually stick to one kitchen at meal times," they were told.

Jacob led them through into another room with all four walls wainscoted. The room appeared to be a small office with a medium-sized desk standing in the middle of the floor. A television, to the right of the room, stood on top of a glass table with two shelves. The second shelf housed what looked to be a DVD player. There was also a black leather three-seater sofa.

At intervals, the wooden panelling had roses delicately carved into the wood, they were most impressive. Jacob took hold of one of the roses and turned it. A wooden panel glided to one side and a light came on to reveal the computer room.

Once inside the room, the panel was closed and the two ladies found themselves surrounded by computers.

Luther pulled two chairs out and nodded to Jasmin and Rhoda to take a seat. The computer facing them lit up and came to life. A few seconds later Jasmin and Rhoda were watching the same images that Jacob and Luther had seen in Jacob's office.

When the clip was over Jacob asked, "Did you recognise either of the two men?"

Rhoda said, "No, I've never seen either of them before. What are they doing?"

"Smuggling by the looks of things," Luther told her.

Jacob looked at Jasmin's stunned face, "Jasmin?"

"I know both of them, but they are not who I expected to see. Can I have another look at it?"

Jacob played the scene again and at the end of it, Jasmin said, "The frogman is a policeman, his name is PC Harrison, and the other man is Marley Burton."

"You know both men?"

"Yes, these are the men I was telling you about when I came to see you in your office. The frogman is PC Harrison and the other gentleman is Marley Burton who lives opposite me on North Lane. It's an odd carry-on."

"Right, there is further footage on the DVD, watch this," Jacob told them.

He started the DVD playing again and after a few seconds the black screen lit up again and there were people at a party on what looked like a boat. The action was centred on three people, two men and a woman and they were sitting at a table watching the other guests enjoying themselves.

When the footage ran out, Jasmin said, "That was Marley, PC Harrison and the woman at the second-hand shop. When I saw Marley and that woman driving away from their house, I should have realised something that didn't occur to me at the time. Bennie, it was Bennie that should have alerted me. He didn't bark at the intruder; he didn't bark because he knew him.

"It was Marley that broke into my house, what an idiot I am. That's why Marley wanted to go upstairs to check if there was anybody still prowling about. He wanted to retrieve his gun. What are we going to do now?" Jasmin wanted to know.

"I'll show you to your rooms so you can make yourselves comfortable and Luther and I will make some enquiries tomorrow and go from there," Jacob informed them.

"I don't want to stay here. This place is too grand for me it makes me feel uncomfortable," Rhoda said.

"Would you feel better staying up at the bungalow? You will be quite safe there. Nobody can get in through the gate and if they do, they will trigger off the security alarm and all you have to do is go into the garage and make your way down the tunnel. You will be quite safe here.

"We have a photographic camera installed that has taken both your photos and you will now be allowed to enter the house. Anyone trying to get in that has not been authorised by either Luther or myself will set off an alarm and all doors and windows will be locked. We have the best security system money can buy. Luther created it and installed it, it's unique. He might only have one eye, but his brain is intact."

"You could have fooled me," Rhoda murmured.

Luther grinned at her.

"All right, I'll stay in the bungalow if Jasmin and Bennie will stay with me. Anyway, I think Bennie would be more comfortable there, we can just open the door and let him out."

"What about you Jasmin, is the bungalow all right with you?" Jacob wanted to know.

"Of course, but we have no change of clothes and no food. Then there's Bennie, he needs proper dog food,"

"Don't worry your head over trivial things like that. I'll see to a change of clothes for you and Rhoda and I've already told you I will sort some food out for Bennie. You will find plenty of food in the fridge at the bungalow, Sally fills it up regularly, always has, nothing to do with your presence. Just stay inside the walls of this estate and nothing harmful will happen to either of you.

"Try not to use your mobile phone in case your number is traced. Not that I think the smugglers know either of your numbers, but the least used the better. I don't want to spend the day worrying about you and Rhoda. You will have each other for company so you should not be lonely," Jacob told them.

Jacob and Luther took them back to the bungalow and made sure they were happily settled in before leaving them to their own devices and going back to their house.

Jasmin looked at her new friend and said, "It's safer here than at home. Both of us are at threat. You because of your father and me because I bought that dressing table. It's pretty obvious that your father was seen taking those videos and had time to put them on the DVD before the smugglers caught up with him.

"I bet they forced him to tell them where the DVD was before they killed him. But I don't think he told them about the compartments because the burglars only pulled out all the drawers, so they found nothing. That's the reason they keep coming back. Not a pretty thought is it? Marley on the heels of the dressing table and that woman I saw in the second-hand shop must have told him I had bought it.

"I wonder why Marley was living in that house? Was it because he knew all your father's stuff had been sold to Mr Sackblock? But I think it was just a coincidence that he happened to be living there. It had to be because Marley was living in that house before I bought the item."

"What am I going to do about my letter from the solicitors? I wonder why he didn't give it to me in the first place when he came to see me?" Rhoda asked.

"I think we should leave it up to Jacob and Luther, they seem to be handling everything all right so far.

Come on, let's go to bed it's been a long day. I'll just go for a little stroll with Bennie before I retire for the night," Jasmin told her.

"I will come with you, I am getting used to taking Bennie out and if I have to be honest, my waistband isn't as tight as it used to be," Rhoda lifted her blouse and showed Jasmin the waistband. "And that's only after a couple of days, at the end of the month at this rate, I'm going to disappear."

The two ladies and Bennie walked out of the house and into the darkness without a care in the world.

Jacob and Luther on the other hand were sitting in two armchairs facing each other with a glass of whisky in their hand.

"What now?" asked Luther.

"Tomorrow, you have a word with the solicitor regarding the missing letter with the key inside, and let's go from there. I don't know about you but I'm dead beat, I'm off to bed."

"I'll drink to that," said Luther finishing off his whisky. "See you in the morning."

Chapter Six

The first thing Luther did when he arrived at the office the next morning, was to telephone the solicitors.

The phone rang and a woman's voice said, "Good morning, Holmes, Holmes and Summers, how can I help you?"

"Good morning, can I speak to the solicitor who is dealing with the estate of Clive Huggard please?"

"What is it about please?"

"I may have a claim on the estate."

"Please hold the line."

Luther said, "Thank you," and waited with the phone to his ear. After thirty seconds a male voice said, "Mr Metway speaking, how may I help you?"

"Mr Metway, I am a friend of Rhoda Huggard, and she tells me that you are holding a letter for her from her father. For what reason is the letter being withheld?" Luther asked.

"I cannot discuss a client's case with a complete stranger. If Miss Huggard wishes to speak to me, please tell her to call at the office," replied Mr Metway.

"Mr Metway, you are withholding information from the beneficiary of a will. I find that very suspicious, why was she not given the letter? If the newspapers were to get hold of this, I don't think it would do your business any good. And if I don't get any satisfaction from this phone call, I am going to advise Rhoda to go to the police and see what they have to say about it," lied Luther.

"You won't get very far with the police. It was a policeman that came to see me, and I gave him the letter. So do your worst, friend of Rhoda. If you contact me again, I will call the police myself."

"Before you go, what was the name of the policeman whom you gave the letter to?" Luther asked.

"Police Officer Coltley, please give him my name and tell him to contact me. I will tell him how you tried to blackmail me into giving you information you are not entitled to." Mr Metway hung up.

A satisfied smile spread across Luther's face as he got up from his desk and walked into Jacob's office.

"I've just finished talking to the solicitors about Rhoda's letter. Guess what? PC Coltley's got it," Jacob was informed.

"Has he now."

"We need to get PC Coltley onboard I think."

"I think you're right."

"How are we going to get to him though, that's the problem. I think the smugglers will be watching him."

"I think you're right."

"Well, I'm glad we are in agreement, but a bit of positive input wouldn't go astray."

"OK," said Jacob. I think PC Coltley's being set-up."

"I think you're right."

"We need to get him here with us."

"I think you're right."

"Well, I'm glad we are in agreement, but a bit of positive input wouldn't go astray."

They looked at each other and started laughing.

"What about getting Sally to do a bit of house-to-house leaflet dropping? There's a musical on at the Odeon, it wouldn't take long to print a dozen or so leaflets off and get Sally to start at the top or bottom of his street and drop the leaflets through the letterbox.

"She could wrap a throwaway mobile phone in one of the leaflets and drop it through PC Coltley's letterbox," Luther suggested.

"We don't know where PC Coltley lives, do we? But I must admit Luther, that is one of your better ideas," said Jacob impressed. "You get the mobile phone sorted out and I'll see to the leaflets,"

"I'll ring Cliff first to see if he can find out PC Coltley's address for us before we start buying mobile phones and printing off leaflets. Just hang fire a moment," Luther told Jacob.

Jacob waited patiently while he listened to Luther's side of the conversation with Cliff and was pleased to see Luther making a note on the writing pad.

After passing the writing pad over to Jacob, Luther went on his way and Jacob set about the task of designing a leaflet for the musical. When Luther returned, the leaflets were sitting on the edge of Jacob's desk. Luther picked one up and said, "What do you call these? I could have done a better job than this."

"No matter, it's a bit of free advertising for the musical and they will serve their purpose. I doubt whether the smugglers will ever see them. After all, they aren't on the lookout for a young woman delivering leaflets, are they?"

"It's nearly lunchtime, let's go back home and see Sally and the girls. Tell them what we have planned," Luther said.

"Missing Rhoda?" Jacob lifted an eyebrow at him.

"Don't talk ridiculous," snapped Luther.

Jacob just smiled and picked up his car keys and went to the back exit and down into the car pound with Luther at his side. They climbed into a small red four-door car and drove slowly out of the car park and into the traffic.

It wasn't long before they were stationary at the large wooden gates waiting for them to open. It was Bennie, out in the garden that heard the car engine first and stopped what he was doing. Jasmin and Rhoda were sitting at a picnic table on a veranda at the back of the bungalow when they saw Bennie looking towards the drive.

Jasmin and Rhoda looked at each other and went around the corner of the bungalow to see who had managed to breach the security system. It was with much relief that they saw Jacob and Luther getting out of the car.

Bennie bounded over to them and was dutifully made a fuss of before the two men set off in the direction of the two ladies. They all sat at the picnic table and Jacob said, "Luther has been in touch with the solicitors regarding Rhoda's letter and PC Coltley has it. We need to get PC Coltley over here and see what he has to say. But the problem is, we think he may be being watched."

After Jacob explained the plan to them, he went on to say, "Once Sally has delivered the phone, she will ring either one of you and let you know. Then either you Jasmin or you Rhoda will make a call to PC Coltley. When he connects, and before he can say anything, I want you to say something like, *'Don't say a word PC Coltley, just listen. We want you to go to the public toilets in Winkson's superstore and there, you will be met by a man with a holdall. There will be a change of clothes in there for you to get changed into, then put your own clothes in the holdall and hand it back to the man who gave it to you. Go straight out of the store, turn right and at the traffic lights, take a right turn again, and it will bring you to a car park. There you will see a black car waiting for you, the dip lights will flash so you don't get into the wrong car then leave the rest to us.'*

"Instruct him to wear a white handkerchief in the top pocket of his jacket so he will be easy for Luther to recognise when he goes into the toilets in Winkson's.

Or words to that effect, to get him out of his house and into the car without being observed."

"I'll never remember all that. Jasmin will have to do it," Rhoda told him.

"It might be better if I did phone him. I can tell him who I am, he might cooperate better then. Who is Sally?" Jasmin wanted to know.

"She's my sister," Luther informed them. "She keeps house for us and does anything else that crops up. In fact, you had better tell her what size clothes you need and she will go and buy you a change of clothes to wear whilst you are here. She is the one that keeps your fridge filled up."

"Oh yes, I remember you telling us, she lives in a bungalow at the back of Low Valley House," said Jasmin.

"Hey, just hang on a minute," Rhoda told him. "You might have money to splash about but I don't. In fact, if it wasn't for the fact that my mortgage is paid off, I would be out on the street by now. I can't just go buying clothes willy-nilly like the rest of you."

"Away with you lass. You are nearly as rich as Jacob and me. But there is a fund we keep separate for just such emergencies that is tax deductible. It won't cost you a penny," replied Luther.

"If I live to be a hundred, I will never be rich. I don't know where you get that from," Rhoda informed him.

"There is a yellow box lying in Jacob's safe with the crown jewels in it, and you say you're not rich? Also, when your father's estate has been worked out, you will be amazed at how rich you are. I think your father will have made a lot of money from his chosen profession," remarked Luther.

"They aren't my jewels. Jasmin bought the dressing table and what was in it, so they must belong to her."

"Don't talk daft. It states clearly in the letter from your father that they are yours. They are not stolen so you have no need to have a guilty conscience about them. I don't think Jasmin would want to keep something that she knows belongs to you," Luther told her.

"Let's go and find Sally and get this show on the road, we are wasting time," Jacob said standing up and going into the bungalow and into the passage that leads to their house.

Sally entered the sitting room and was surprised to see the two ladies perched on the sofa. "Sally, this is Jasmin and Rhoda, the two young ladies I was telling you about last night," Luther told his sister.

Sally was of small stature, with long blonde hair, pale complexion and dark, nearly black eyes, "Hello," she said.

Jasmin and Rhoda both smiled at her and said hello back.

"Sally we have a little job for you," and Luther proceeded to explain what they wanted her to do.

"When you've done this, try to ring his doorbell then ring Jasmin and let her know the phone is delivered. Make sure you have the special credit card with you that we use for miscellaneous items because you need to go on a spending spree.

"Rhoda and Jasmin need a change of clothes. They will give you their sizes, so go and have fun. Jacob and I will have to get back to the office now, so we will leave it in your capable hands. Oh, and don't forget some dog food, Jasmin will tell you what Bennie eats.

"Phone me to let me know when you are setting off to deliver the leaflets and I will make my way to Winkson's superstore, and hope PC Coltley turns up. You will find the mobile phone and leaflets in this bag along with PC Coltley's home address.

"The mobile phone number is in there also. Better make a note of the number Jasmin, if it's you that is making the call." After handing Sally the bag, Luther and Jacob went back to the office.

When the two men had left the room Sally said, "This is certainly a change to my usual routine. Right, give me your mobile phone number and dress sizes and I'd better get going if I am to get all this done before the end of the day. Can you have a meal ready for when the men come home? I don't think I'll be back in time to make anything."

Sally encountered nothing that warranted special caution. West Lane was practically deserted. Before she set off, she rang Luther to let him know she was on her way to deliver the leaflets. When she reached number fourteen, she selected the bottom leaflet, making sure it was still wrapped around the mobile phone before she slipped them both through the letterbox.

She placed her hand at the side of the doorbell and pretended to shake a stone out of one of her shoes and at the same time she pressed the doorbell as hard as she could.

She took out her mobile phone and rang Jasmin to let her know the phone had been delivered, whilst she carried on delivering the leaflets to the end of the street. Walking across the road, and into town, Sally dropped the remaining leaflets into a waste bin as she passed it by and went in search of the shops.

Hearing his doorbell chime, PC Coltley went to see who was at his door. As he approached the front door, he saw the mobile phone lying on his doormat half covered by a leaflet. He bent down and picked it up and turned it over in his hand to see if there was anything written on it. There was not. He then checked the leaflet. Nothing on that either.

He was about to open the front door when the phone rang. He pressed the green phone on the screen and was about to say hello, when a voice at the other end said, "PC Coltley, this is Jasmin Ward. Please don't speak, just listen. We know you are being set up. We need your help so please listen carefully…" and Jasmin gave him the instructions as laid down by Jacob.

PC Coltley cut off the call and went up into his bedroom. He opened the wardrobe door and felt in his old jeans pocket and took out an official-looking letter. He put on his jacket, then taking a handkerchief out of a drawer he tucked it neatly into the top pocket of the jacket and put the letter in the inside pocket and walked out of his house.

Walking at a leisurely pace, PC Coltley walked into town and Winkson's superstore and made for the gents toilets. Standing at a sink washing his hands was a one-eyed man. The man picked up a canvas bag from the floor and handed it to PC Coltley.

Going into one of the booths, PC Coltley proceeded to take off his jacket and trousers and don the jeans and zip-up fleece. Then he placed a black cap with a long peak on his head and pulled it forward hiding most of his face. He placed his clothes in the canvas bag and leaving the toilet stall he placed the canvas bag on the floor next to the one-eyed man and waited to see what happened next.

The one-eyed man picked up the canvas bag and held up two fingers indicating to him to wait a couple of minutes before leaving the toilets.

PC Coltley proceeded to wash his hands and after taking his time to dry them in the airflow machine, he sauntered out of the superstore, head slightly down and chewing on some gum he had found in the holdall. Turned right at the traffic lights, then right again, and the police officer walked into the car park and saw a black car flick the lights on and then off. He walked over to the car, opened the back door and jumped inside.

The car began to move instantly out of the car park and into the moving traffic before he could fasten his seat belt.

"Welcome PC Coltley, Luther's the name."

"Never been so pleased to meet anyone as I am to meet you, Luther."

"Let's hope it stays that way," remarked Luther.

Phil was bored, he'd read the newspaper from front to back at least three times. He had worked for George InGuesty for just over two years. An advert in the window of his local newsagent told of a vacancy for a car mechanic. He had applied, and at the interview, he had been told that there would be no record of his employment as it would be cash in hand.

At the time, Phil was all for it, with no income tax to pay and any overtime that came his way would be tax-free. The job was for a mechanic to look after two luxury cars as well as chauffeuring duties when and if required. Or any job that needed to be done because the mechanic's services would be few and far between.

He had grabbed the job thinking it was a clever move, but after two years he realised that it had been a big mistake. There was no record of him having worked for two years and if this kept on there would be no government pension at the end of it. He was on call twenty-four seven and he slept in an attic room over the garage that housed the two luxury cars. He was not allowed to have any friends in the garage so his life had become a lonely one.

Most days he was not required at all, he spent the day washing and polishing the two cars. Now here he was sitting in a bus shelter watching a house that a policeman lived in and under instructions to follow the policeman if he left his house and provide George with a detailed log of where the policeman went, who he met with, and at what time.

Someone came to take over from him when George felt inclined to send someone. So far after three days of sitting, watching and waiting, the policeman had not left his house. But things were about to change, the door he was keeping an eye on, opened and out stepped a gentleman that Phil took to be the policeman.

Phil followed and watched him go into Winkson's superstore. Keeping a discrete distance Phil followed the policeman into the superstore and saw him entering the gents toilets. Phil positioned himself in an aisle of men's clothing and pretended to be searching the rails. He was rewarded by the toilet door opening and a man in a dark grey-suit came out. The man only had one eye; he was not the man he had seen coming out of the policeman's house.

Phil went back to going through the clothes rack. A couple of minutes later the toilet door opened again and a youth, chewing gum, wearing jeans, a fleece and a baseball cap, sauntered out. Not the policeman, so he went back to searching the clothes rack. After waiting and watching the toilet for a further five minutes and nobody else came out, panic set in. Phil decided to go into the toilet and see what the policeman was up to.

The toilet was empty, Phil kicked each toilet door open and every cubical yielded no policeman. What was George going to say to this? He wasn't going to be very pleased with him. He had been on the receiving end of George's fist on more than one occasion. He knew what to expect.

Chapter Seven

Instead of turning into the driveway that led to the bungalow, Luther carried on for another four kilometres then turned up a country lane and travelled for another two and a half kilometres. A set of double, high wooden gates opened up, and this driveway led straight up to Low Valley House. The first person they encountered was Sally. Luther introduced PC Coltley to her and they shook hands. The officer kept hold of Sally's hand just that little bit too long and it didn't go unnoticed by Luther.

Luther cocked his eyebrow at Sally and she had the grace to blush. She turned away when the door opened and in walked Jasmin and Rhoda. They shook hands with the police officer but introductions were not necessary.

"I was pleased to get your phone call, Miss Ward. It is the best bit of news I have had for the past six months," PC Coltley told them all.

"Sorry about the cloak and dagger business, but Sally stepped in and helped us out of our predicament, and she did a perfect job as usual. She is the one that dropped the mobile phone in your letterbox. Jacob should be here shortly and we can get down to business."

"Did you manage to get something ready for dinner?" Sally asked.

"You two been busy in the kitchen?" Luther wanted to know looking over at Jasmin and Rhoda.

"We have prepared a meal like you asked, it just wants the oven lighting, it will only take thirty minutes to cook. We don't expect to be waited on hand and foot, but we don't want to interfere in Sally's kitchen either. If Jacob is on his way I will go and put a light under the veg," Rhoda told Sally ignoring Luther.

"I appreciate that. While the meal is cooking, come and collect your clothes." Once the vegetables were on the way, Sally led the way into an upstairs bedroom.

When the ladies arrived back in the sitting room Jacob had not yet returned, but ten minutes later they heard the door chime telling them that their wait was over, and Jacob entered the room.

"At long last," Luther said to his friend. "Jacob, this is PC Coltley, and this PC Coltley, is Jacob Firth."

"Pleased to meet you, Mr Firth," PC Coltley said.

"And I, you. Has Luther introduced himself? If he has, it will be a first. He takes it for granted that everybody knows him. I think it's his eye or lack of it, that does it. He uses it as an excuse for all sorts of things."

"Luther who?" asked PC Coltley.

"No, doctor," replied Luther.

"Doctor Luther?" asked PC Coltley.

"No, Doctor Who," replied Luther.

The three girls set off laughing and Jacob said to them, "For Christ's sake, don't encourage him." He looked at PC Coltley and said, "As you see, Luther likes his little jokes."

"I like his little jokes," Jasmin informed him.

"So, do I," agreed Rhoda.

Sally just looked at Luther with love in her eyes and a gentle smile on her face.

Luther, was more than satisfied, especially when he met Rhoda's eye and she looked away.

"Let's go into the kitchen and sit in comfort at the table while we eat and discuss what we have so far," Luther said.

"Why don't you tell us your part in the story, PC Coltley, then we might be able to piece some of this story together," suggested Jacob.

"Please call me Dan, PC Coltley seems very inappropriate. I don't think I will be a police officer for much longer, the evidence is building up against me.

"When I went to see the solicitor about Clive Huggard's will, he told me he had a letter for his daughter. I said I was going to see her later that day and I asked him if he would like me to deliver it for him. He snatched my hand off. I took the letter because evidence had been going missing at the police station and I didn't want the letter to disappear.

"A letter from Clive Huggard could be important information, it could tell us a lot. Besides which, my signature was being used regarding missing evidence. I had never been near some of the evidence boxes that had my name on. Somebody in that police station was forging my signature. I decided to keep the letter quiet and pass it on to Miss Huggard when I went to see her that afternoon. But before I could get the letter to her, I was suspended from duty.

"I went out one day with the intention of calling on Miss Huggard and spotted two men across the road from her house, they were acting suspiciously. So, I decided not to call on her. That is why I still have the letter in my possession. I know I am being watched because I saw this man sat reading a newspaper in the bus shelter across from where I live.

"I kept an eye on him and two buses came and went but he was still sitting there, reading his paper. Then I saw another man join him in the bus shelter. I had seen the second man before, he works on a riverboat. In my own time, I have been doing a bit of undercover work as a taxi driver, and I had dropped a few fares off at a boat along the river.

"I'd seen the second man greeting people as they boarded the boat. He works for a man called George InGuesty. I have been trying to find out who George InGuesty is and I think this has led to my suspension. So, I think your cloak and dagger business was well founded."

"What did it say in the letter from the solicitors?" asked Rhoda.

"I have no idea; I haven't opened it. It is not my letter. I did think about dropping it in the post-box, but I could feel the shape of a key through the envelope and I didn't want it to go missing in the post. Better safe than sorry. I have been trying to think of a good plan to get the letter to you without putting you in any more danger from InGuesty's men than you already are. They are a hard lot." Dan took the canvas bag Luther had passed to him when they had got out of the car, and he took the letter out of the jacket pocket and handed it to Rhoda.

Rhoda took the envelope and tore it open. She withdrew a sheet of paper, then tipped the envelope upside down and out dropped a small yale key.

The letter read:

My dear Rhoda

This key is for a safety deposit box at the Chapel Bank on High Street in Glaston. All you have to do is go into the bank with some ID and give the password 'Connie'. I have left instructions at the bank telling them that if someone with the name of Rhoda Huggard wants access to the vault, so long as she has the password, it is all right for her to have access. They will show you to the vault and the code number you need to open the box is 1448. Be very careful when you open the box, make sure there is nobody else in the vault with you when you open it.

There is, at my flat, a matching set of dressing table and drawers. There are some little brown buttons at the bottom of the hinges that hold the mirrors to the base at the back. Two similar buttons can be located at the back of the chest of drawers. Try pressing them in and they will be self-explicit.

Good luck Rhoda

I hope you find happiness; it always eluded me.

Your loving father, Clive Huggard.

"That's a good one, he signs it, *your loving father* if he was a loving father, I wouldn't want a bad one," Rhoda said with disgust handing the letter to Luther. When he had finished reading it, he handed it to Jasmin.

Jasmin said, "If Rhoda had received this letter when the solicitor called to tell her about her father, none of this would have happened. All Rhoda had to do was take it to the police and let them deal with it."

"Well, I'm glad I didn't receive the letter. If I had done so I would never have met all of you," Rhoda told them.

The letter was handed round and after they had all read it Sally asked, "What now?"

"We need to see what is inside that safety deposit box. I don't think it's a good idea for Rhoda to go to the bank just in case she is spotted," Jacob said.

"I doubt there will be anybody watching the bank, I can't see that anybody apart from us is aware of the letter or the safety deposit box. But if InGuesty has men out looking for either Jasmin or Rhoda and Dan, for that matter, it looks like another job for Sally," said Luther.

"But I don't look anything like Rhoda and it says in the letter to take some ID. I'd look a right idiot turning up and showing them my ID when they will be expecting someone called Rhoda Huggard," protested Sally.

Jacob just looked at Sally with a raised eyebrow.

"All right, so a false ID showing me as Rhoda Huggard is not a problem with the skills you and Luther possess," Sally told him.

The next morning found Sally approaching the counter of the Chapel Bank where she showed her ID. The cashier checked her computer and asked, "Do you have a password please?"

"Connie," replied Sally.

"One moment please, I will get someone to take you to the vault." The young woman stood up and disappeared.

A door to the side of the counter opened and another young woman smiled at her, and Sally was in.

She was shown into the vault and the young woman helped her to find the box she was looking for, then turned and left Sally on her own. With her heart pounding, she opened the box and was shocked to see the amount of money that was stuffed in there. Sally looked around her with a guilty look on her face, to make sure she was alone, and then she took two of the bundles of money out and put them in her bag.

Next, she saw a stack of invoices held together with a rubber band. She lifted these invoices out of the box and placed them in her bag too. Under the invoices lay a USB. This joined the money and the invoices and it was a struggle to close the bag. Feeling like a thief, all she wanted to do now was escape. She had the USB and for the moment it would have to do. She wanted to get out of there as quickly as she could.

Sally closed and locked the box and slid it back into the slot that it had come out of. Then she went and knocked on the door. Sally was soon out of the bank, onto the street, and into the car park. She climbed into her car, pressed the button that locked the car doors, and drove home.

It was lunchtime before Sally arrived home and she found all five of them waiting for her, "Sally welcome back. Did everything go to plan at the bank?" Luther asked.

"Yes, no problem. I was in and out in half an hour. My bag bulging with this," and she picked her bag off the floor and proceeded to take out the money, invoices and USB and place them on the table.

Rhoda looked open-mouthed at the two thick wads of bank notes sitting next to a pile of papers held together with a rubber band. "How much is there?" she whispered.

"I have no idea, I just grabbed a couple of wads and threw them in my bag. But I can tell you this, there is a small fortune still in the safety deposit box. I brought these two bundles in case you need some money. I was terrified of having my bag snatched off my shoulder when I left the bank, thankfully that did not happen. I am glad to be rid of it all."

"What's on the USB?" Luther asked.

"No idea, we haven't had time to look," said Jacob.

"What's all that paperwork about?" asked Luther.

"No idea, we haven't had time to look," said Jacob.

"I can see this conversation is going nowhere," Luther remarked.

"Well, you shouldn't ask stupid questions," he was told. "Here," Jacob threw Luther the USB. "Work your magic on that."

Luther caught the USB and went over to the computer with Dan following him.

Jacob picked up the invoices and flicked through them. Sally, Jasmin and Rhoda sat and watched.

"These are invoices with payment receipts attached, for all the precious stones by the looks of things. It will be easy to confirm this by going to the jewellers and checking with them. This is good Rhoda, if these invoices turn out to be kosha, you are a very rich woman," she was told.

"This is all too much for me, I want to go back to my quiet life. I miss my crisps," Rhoda complained.

"Don't worry about your crisps, I'll see to them," Luther called from his computer.

Laughter echoed around the room and the tension eased.

"Any luck with the USB yet?" asked Jacob.

"What's does USB mean?" Rhoda wanted to know.

"You should beware," replied Luther.

"You should beware. What of?" asked Rhoda.

"Me," countered Luther.

Once again laughter filled the room and Jacob said, "He's only teasing you, Rhoda. USB means Universal Serial Bus."

"I'm not you know," Luther told him.

"That's for the two of you to further. We have more important things to sort out than your love life," Jacob replied.

Rhoda was left speechless. How had asking what USB meant, turned into her having a love life? She remained silent.

"Here we go," Luther said.

They all went to stand behind him to see what secrets the USB held. It held a lot.

The first thing that appeared on screen was a picture of Marley and underneath was written:

George InGuesty, also known as Marley Burton. The police are looking for this man in connection with distributing drugs that have been smuggled into the country.

The second photo beneath George InGuesty was that of PC Harrison and the information was:

Police Officer Gary Harrison, second in command to George InGuesty. Stationed at Glaston Police station and a font of information. Harrison is trying to get rid of InGuesty to take over from him. He is a very dangerous man to know.

The third photo was that of a woman. Jasmin recognised her as the woman from the second-hand shop:

This woman is the wife of InGuesty. Goes by the name of Valerie, beautiful but lethal. A three-way triangle here. Married to InGuesty, having an affair with Harrison. Not advised. If InGuesty finds out, it's goodbye Harrison.

The fourth photo was that of the rear of a large house, taken from the river's edge:

InGuesty owns a rather large house on the river four kilometres north of Glaston. Tree House is the name. Taken I should imagine from the dense trees that obscure the building from the roadside. This is where InGuesty keeps his riverboat moored. Difficult to approach from both front and rear without being seen.

This caused my problem; I think I was spotted taking this photo. I must get all this information down before they catch up with me.

George InGuesty does not smuggle drugs into this country, he is the distributor. Once the drugs have landed, a time is arranged for the drugs to be left on the riverboat and InGuesty is always somewhere else when this occurs.

A barge chugs slowly up the river and once it nears Tree House, a frogman leaves the barge and takes the drugs to InGuesty's riverboat that is on its mooring and attaches the contraband to the underside.

A couple of days later, Harrison will dive under the riverboat and retrieve the drugs. Parties are held along the river, and this is how the drugs are disposed of. It is so well planned. There is someone else at Glaston police station, informing George, it is known, by the police, when and where the party is taking place. So, they change the venue.

InGuesty is on my case. Not be long now before he catches up with me. At least I might be responsible for the downfall of InGuesty and the closing down of the syndicate and my daughter might have something to be proud of me for.

Once again, Rhoda, I warn you to be very careful, these are desperate men. Choose your friends carefully.

I would advise you to take all this evidence to the police, but I don't know any police that are not bent. Tread carefully.

Clive.

"This is excellent stuff. Some of the best evidence I have seen in any of the cases I have been involved with. We need to be very sure who we show this evidence to, there might be more than Harrison involved in this from Glaston police station," Dan told them.

"I think, you and I Dan, should go and see Cliff Broadman," said Jacob after giving the matter some thought.

"Cliff Broadman, you mean, Chief Constable Broadman?"

"Yes, that's the one."

"You will never achieve it. You will have to get past a barrage of police officers before you get to see Broadman."

"Oh, ye of little faith. Get a good night's sleep we have a 160-kilometre journey in front of us tomorrow," Jacob told him.

"Aren't you even going to ring Barrow police station to see if they will let you see him?"

"No need. He will see us. Besides which we don't want anybody knowing anything about this until we have had a word with Cliff."

"You seem confident about that."

"I am. Sally will show you to your room when you are ready. I have a couple of things to see to before I retire. I'll see you at breakfast, six o'clock sharp, I want to be off by seven."

After Sally had shown Dan to his room, she joined Luther, Jasmin and Rhoda in the sitting room.

"I am going to make my way back to the bungalow now if you don't mind Sally. I know Bennie has been in and out of the garden all day but he needs a good walk.

I am going to walk back over the fields with him instead of using the shortcut along the passageway. He might settle down for the night then. Are you coming Rhoda, and you too Sally? You will be more than welcome," Jasmin told them.

"I think I will pass this time if you don't mind Jasmin, I need a bit of time to think about what all this means," said Rhoda.

"Of course, I don't mind. What about you Sally?"

"Thank you, that is very kind of you but I need to get a few things done. I've been neglecting my duties these last couple of days."

"Luther, if you are not going back to work, you are also invited to join Bennie and me," Jasmin told him.

"No, I don't think I will go back to work, I have had enough for today. I think I might escort Rhoda back along the passageway, make sure she doesn't get lost."

"You don't need to do that, I know the way by now," Rhoda told him.

"I know I don't have to, but I want to."

Rhoda tried to think of something to say to this and she failed. She found herself walking the dimly lit passageway with Luther.

"You are a very special young woman, do you know that, Rhoda?"

"Are you being sarcastic?"

"No, why would I be sarcastic?"

"Because I only have to look in the mirror to see I'm not special, that's why."

"I only have to look in the mirror to see I am not a very handsome man. Only having one eye puts most people off. You wouldn't believe the names I have been called because of it. Yet here we are, walking along a dim spooky passageway and not a thought in your head about cyclops or a one-eyed monster.

"The only thought in your mind was to defend yourself to me. I think you might be the victim of other young women who can be very cruel at times. Your size is not important, to be honest, I find you very, very attractive. I lay in bed thinking about you and when our eyes meet, I get the strangest feeling in the pit of my stomach."

Again, Rhoda could think of nothing to say so she did what she usually did and kept quiet.

They had reached the bungalow by this time and Luther said, "Let's not waste this little bit of time we have together Rhoda. Jasmin will be back shortly and I don't know when we will get the opportunity to be alone together again. Nor do we know where this mystery is going to take us. Let's use this moment for ourselves, let's live a little you and I."

Luther walked towards Rhoda and took her in his arms. She did not complain. Nor did she complain when his hands went under her jumper and undid her bra.

She felt his hand moving around and under the loose bra and he cupped her breast in his hand. He waited for her to object. She did not. His finger found her nipple and ran lightly over it. Her nipple decided it liked it.

Luther and Rhoda were both sitting innocently on the sofa drinking coffee when Jasmin walked in. Bennie made a charge over to the sofa and placing his head on Luther's knee, he demanded attention. Luther gave it to him.

After a few pleasantries, Luther went back home. When he arrived, Jacob was nowhere to be seen. He sat down at his computer, signed onto the private email programme and proceeded to type. If an investigation was to take place by the police, into who sent the email, it would lead them nowhere.

Chapter Eight

George InGuesty was working on his computer when it notified him that he had received an email. He had had this one-room building added onto the back of the garage where he kept his limousines, nine kilometres up the road from Tree House. It was his private office.

There were too many visitors to Tree House and when he was absent from home, he didn't want anybody gaining access to his office. Nobody was allowed into this room, not even Valerie.

Phil had been told by George, not, under any pretext, was he to enter the office and that he would know if Phil had defied his orders. Phil knew he had better not attempt it.

George pressed a few keys and his email box opened. Scanning the emails there was nothing of interest except an email that was entitled: From a friend.

George studied the email before he opened it. He was no idiot; he knew if he pressed on open, all sorts of nasty things could happen to his computer if someone had sent him a virus. But he knew he had quite a few anti-virus programmes installed on his computer too. Should he risk it and open it? It was the subject heading that decided it, 'From a friend'. He didn't have any friends, not what you can call a friend, the friends that he had would as sooner place a knife in his back than support him. To hell with it, he clicked on open. The email read:

I thought you were a clever and shrewd man Mr InGuesty, but it would seem you are not. For some time, word has it that Gary Harrison is trying to get rid of you and become the head of your smuggling syndicate. Your wife seems to have enough confidence in him to achieve his goal. As you will no doubt be aware, many a man has tried to capture the attention of your wife, without success. It would seem Harrison has achieved what no other man has. For three months now passionate encounters have been played out between them. I am sure you have the intelligence to be able to confirm this information for yourself.

I would sign this off as a friend, but truthfully, I don't think you have any friends.

George read and reread the email. The more he read it, the angrier he became. It was a long time since George had felt anything much at all. His father used to beat his mother up, and him too if he didn't get out of his way in time. His mother was too frightened of his father to stop him from giving George the hiding of his life. George was not his real name, he was christened Marley Burton.

School had been difficult. His clothes weren't of the highest standard and not all that clean. He knew that he didn't smell like the other children. He started playing truant. This created more beatings from his father and then, his mother disappeared. She was there one day, gone the next. He never knew what happened to her and if truth be told, he didn't want to know.

In the end, he disappeared too. He stole some money from his father's trouser pocket and caught a bus. He had no idea where the bus would terminate and he did not care. The further away the better. He alighted from the bus at a place called Furbridge where the bus terminated.

Furbridge was a very small town on the edge of a river and night was beginning to close in. He wandered along the river's edge for a while before he came to a wooden building with two large wooden doors, closed and padlocked for the night. Marley could tell it wasn't a house so he went around to the back.

No windows or doors there, no way to gain entry, but under his feet, there was what looked like a trapdoor. This door even provided a brass ring, so he lifted the brass ring and pulled. The trapdoor began to rise and Marley was looking down at a set of wooden steps.

He descended the steps and the further down he went the darker it became. At the age of ten, Marley had become a smoker, and by the time he decided to run away from home at the age of thirteen, he was practically a chain smoker. Getting hold of cigarettes had been no problem. When his father was in a drunken stupor his pockets were raided and money taken out along with cigarettes and transferred into Marley's own pockets.

Marley fished in his pocket and found his cigarette lighter and flicked it on. He was in a cellar among many different coloured tins of paint and stacks of boxes piled high. Standing on a wooden table that looked like a butcher's block, he found a paraffin lamp and lit it. It was some sort of storeroom. He decided it would do for him to sleep in for the night. At least it was free, warm and dry. He went back up the wooden steps and pulled the trap door closed.

The next morning, he was woken by the sound of footsteps descending the wooden steps. He stood up and hid behind a stack of boxes and he heard a male voice say, "Things all right, Bert?"

"They've been better."

"Yes, for me too. Had a bit of a scare this time when I was disembarking from the ship. Customs were checking some of the passengers and I hoped and prayed they wouldn't search me. As luck would have it, me and the next passenger were let through. Could have been because of our age.

"The other passenger was older than me by the looks of him, but who knows, looks can be deceiving. It's bad enough for me just passing these cigarettes on. I'm glad it's only cigarettes and booze I smuggle in for Trevor Crast. I refuse to touch drugs. I have decided to pack it in, that was too close for comfort."

"But Clive, will Trevor let you pack it in? Clive Huggard is a well-known name. You are high up on Trevor's list of employees, he's a hard man to shake off."

"I'm going to give it a good go. I might be high up on the list but I am of no use to him if I am in prison. The authorities will get suspicious sooner or later with all the trips I'm doing and when they do, it will be a case of, cross Trevor Crast, or do a stretch at her Majesty's pleasure. Hobson's choice.

"There, that's my last load delivered, over to you now, Bert. Good luck," said Clive Huggard and he turned and mounted the wooden steps.

Bert was to find out later that, Clive Huggard had stopped being a courier and was no longer smuggling goods into the country. But Trevor Crast would not let him go. He said that he knew too much about the operation and so, Clive became the organiser for the distribution of the illegal items, and it turned out he was very good at it.

Marley heard a second set of footsteps on the wooden stairs and when he heard the trapdoor close, he ran up the stairs and pushed up the trapdoor. With his head poking out, Marley was just in time to see Clive Huggard get into his car and drive off. He heard the wooden doors to the front of the building sliding open so he hopped out, dropped the trapdoor shut, and went around the front to see how the land lay.

It turned out to lay very flat for Marley. On entering the building, he saw it was a boatshed and the owner was busy checking under a boat that had been lifted onto dry land.

"Hello Bert," said Marley, and at the age of thirteen, his entry into smuggling had begun. He never returned to school. Bert did not have a problem with that. Marley lived in the boatshed and Bert was happy to have him. Unpaid labour was hard to find.

He had started working in the boatyard but Marley soon became involved in the smuggling. When he was eighteen years of age, Trevor Crast vanished, and he was never seen or heard of again. Marley Burton also vanished and George InGuesty was invented, and George InGuesty was now the head of the smuggling ring.

He was twenty-one when Valerie Jones had appeared on his horizon: beautiful, clever and very assured. George hadn't stood a chance. Three months after meeting Valerie, they were married. And together, George and Valerie InGuesty were a formidable force.

George had seen on the news that the police were looking for Marley Burton in connection with Clive Huggard's murder. PC Coltley had gone missing and so had Jasmin Ward and Clive Huggard's daughter. How this was possible, was a problem that George could not figure out. He had his best men on the job, watching all three of them.

George had been on the riverboat with Gary Harrison collecting the contraband. When Gary had dropped over the side of the boat, out of the corner of his eye, George had seen a flash across the river from where the boat was moored. Someone was taking photos. George went down into the galley and taking up his binoculars, he searched the opposite side of the river. Standing next to a tree stood Clive Huggard, with a camera in his hand. George's blood ran cold. He must get that camera at all costs.

His best man had been put on the job and four days later, Clive Huggard was shown onto the riverboat. George told the man who had brought him on board, to go outside and keep watch. George was left on his own with Clive. It was a good job the riverboat was isolated for the screams that came from below deck carried a long way. It didn't take long to extract the information he had wanted out of Clive. Once George was satisfied, he had learned all he needed to know, he opened a drawer in his desk, took out a gun, aimed it at Clive's head and the screaming stopped.

The next day Clive's body was found floating in the river. Unfortunately for George, some of the information he had extracted from Clive, was false information and now he had no idea where the camera that he had seen Clive holding was. He was told that the camera was in a shed at the back of a house in Beech Avenue. When the shed was searched there was no camera.

Clive had told George that he had hidden a DVD in a dressing table at his house with information about the syndicate. This created a problem for George, he should have asked what the dressing table looked like, there could have been more than one dressing table.

But as luck would have it, Harrison had come across a letter Clive had started writing to Rhoda, telling her to look in the dressing table with three mirrors, whilst the police were searching Clive's house after he had been found dead. Harrison had sneaked the letter into his pocket when nobody was looking.

That caused another problem for George, the police were all over Wayward Avenue. The only ace George had up his sleeve was Gary Harrison. He needed to know where Clive Huggard's daughter lived. Another job for Gary.

PC Coltley was getting a bit too close to the smugglers' ring, this information was also provided by Gary. Gary Harrison was a bonus that George had come across unexpectedly at one of his parties onboard the riverboat. A policeman with gambling habits. Easy prey.

Life had come full circle for George. Harrison was trying to do to him, what he had done to Trevor Crast. The only difference was, he now has prior knowledge, Trevor Crast had not. George had felt no guilt when he used his gun for the first time. Trevor Crast had been a stumbling block to higher things, and George was aiming high.

Clive Huggard had crossed him, he could no longer take the risk of having him as an employee. He had taken care of him but had not reached his goal. The camera was still missing and so was the DVD. He did not know where they were or what information they held. He was pretty certain that he had been photographed retrieving the contraband along with Harrison.

George had intended to keep the information from Gary. But then he changed his mind, he needed help to retrieve the camera and DVD and Gary was the best man for the job. He admitted to himself, that he had taken Clive Huggard out, but had not checked the information he had been given was correct before he had done so.

It had been a big mistake, if word got round, it would show him up as incompetent. As head of the syndicate, he could not be seen to have any faults. Alas his need for the camera and DVD was greater than his ego.

The above email could of course be someone wanting to make mischief for him with Valerie. But he didn't think so. She was the only vulnerable spot in his makeup. Everyone was aware of this; Valerie was his property and woe betide anybody that tried to take her away from him.

Again, he had to admit to himself, that this email confirmed the suspicions he had started to notice. Things were taking on a new slant with Valerie and

Harrison. Nothing he could put his finger on, just the odd look between them that sent alarm bells ringing in George's head. It was by choice that he had ignored the signs, he didn't want to believe what he was seeing. He couldn't ignore them any longer.

Who had sent him this email? It was not an easy task to get into his computer, so he replied to the email asking how the sender knew this information. The email was returned, unable to send. Another mystery. It no longer mattered. Time for him to act.

He picked up the phone and dialled a number. When the phone at the other end was answered George said, "Phil when I leave work, I want you to come home with me tonight. We will leave in my car, leave the limos here. I want you to climb in the back and keep your head down when we enter Tree House, I don't want you showing up on the CCTV.

"I want you to sleep in the car tonight. Then in the morning when I come down to the garage to leave, I want you to drive the car away. If the CCTV is checked when the car leaves Tree House in the morning, it will only show the back of your head so you won't be recognised. Drive a few kilometres away, and find a large car park, so the car mingles in with the other cars. Wait until I ring you before you bring the car back. Is that understood?"

"Yes, Sir. You want me to come home with you, sleep in the car overnight, then in the morning drive the car away and wait for your phone call," confirmed Phil.

"Good man. I'll be in the garage in ten minutes." George hung up.

He turned off his computer, opened a drawer in his desk and took out a gun. He was on his way.

Over dinner, George said to Valerie, "I have an appointment with a client tomorrow, so I will more than likely be away all day."

"Oh, do I know the client?"

"No, neither do I. A lead from Nigel Worth. He thought it might be beneficial to us, but who knows? I'm going to check it out, you never know. I will be setting off early, around seven, because the meeting is over in Richtown and that's a good fifty kilometres away."

"What time do you think you will be back?"

"No idea, depends on how the meeting goes and whether I think I can trust him. If I like him, I might be away all day. If I don't like him or what he has to offer is no good to us, I could be home by lunchtime."

"Fine, I'll arrange dinner for six o'clock this evening. If you arrive early, you can take me out for lunch."

"Deal," George confirmed.

After kissing Valerie goodbye the next morning, George made his way down into the garage. He found Phil sitting in the car and already in the driver's seat. No words were exchanged and Phil sat and waited until George had opened the garage doors before he turned the engine on and eased the car out of the garage. He moved slowly down the drive. If anyone was watching from the house window, they would have seen Phil's hand appear out of the driver's side window and click the automatic garage doors shut.

After pulling the bolts across the garage door so it was locked from the inside, George went over to a cupboard at the back of the garage, opened the door and took out a folding chair, opened it up and placed it to the side of the garage window so he could watch the drive. His patience was rewarded an hour later. He observed Harrison's car pull up outside his front door.

Going over to a panel on the wall, George opened the front to reveal a series of buttons. His fingers moved over the keyboard and a computer screen lit up and the inside of his house appeared, it was an image of his hall. It was empty. Not for long, the front door opened and the security alarm was disconnected.

Harrison had a key to his home. He had not given Harrison a key to his home. Harrison had the alarm code to his house, he had not given him the code to stop the alarm from going off.

By pressing buttons on the keyboard George watched as Gary took the stairs two at a time, along the top landing and into his and Valerie's bedroom. George used the keyboard again and the screen showed the inside of their bedroom.

Valerie was laid on top of the bed, naked apart from a brightly coloured pink feathered boa scarf that started between her legs obscuring her vagina. The feathers continued up over her left breast, round her neck and down to cover her right breast. Her legs were slightly apart.

Gary stood at the foot of the bed taking in the scene. He slowly took off his jacket and let it drop to the floor. Next, his hands went to his throat and the tie joined his jacket.

George had seen enough. He went over to another security panel on the opposite wall, he pressed a few more buttons and every door and window in the house was locked. No escape.

He took his gun out of his jacket pocket and left the garage by the integral door and walked leisurely up the staircase and into the bedroom.

Gary was now naked and lying next to Valerie with the feather boa in his hand. They both lay perfectly still, frozen at the sight of George returning their gaze. The look they saw on George's face left neither of them in doubt of what was going to happen next.

George did not disappoint, he raised the gun, pointed it at Gary and pulled the trigger. The hand holding the boa went slack and lay still upon the lady's vagina. Two seconds later, Valerie could no longer feel the weight of Gary's hand upon her she would never feel anything ever again.

Job done. George packed a suitcase and left the bedroom. He went into his home office, took some documents and money out of the safe and put them in a briefcase. Then he went out of the back door making sure it was closed and locked before walking along the curved path and down to his boat.

He left his suitcase and briefcase on the path before he went on board. He collected all the spare gas cylinders that were stored around the boat, taking them down into the galley. Next, he collected some paperwork out of a drawer, went up on deck and pulled open a narrow door attached to the back of the cabin. It revealed a fold-up pushbike.

He took it out of the cupboard and onto dry land. After placing the paperwork, he had taken from the riverboat in his briefcase, he opened up the pushbike, kicked the stand down so his hands were free to hang the briefcase on the handlebars and fasten his suitcase onto the rack at the back. Climbing back onboard, he went into the cabin, turned on all the gas cylinders then lit the gas ring.

Calmly closing the cabin door behind him and jumping down onto dry land, he straddled the bike, kicked the bike stand up and started peddling along the riverbank. George was still in hearing distance when a loud explosion took place. A satisfied smile appeared upon his lips as he pedalled slowly along.

Phil, still sporting a black eye, sat in the car and waited for his phone call. It did not come. The newsreader on the car radio informed its listeners that an explosion had occurred on a riverboat on the River Raybarn. The riverboat was moored at a property called Tree House.

Investigations were being carried out to see if anyone was onboard at the time. Phil switched on the car engine and returned home.

Chapter Nine

Jacob and Dan made good time. The motorway was pleasantly light of traffic and their destination was reached in less time than Jacob had expected. He pulled to a halt at the back of Barrow Police Station and switched off the engine.

"This is going to be a waste of time, you do know that don't you? To travel 160 kilometres without checking first to see if the chief constable will see us is madness," Dan told Jacob.

"He'll see us," confirmed Jacob.

They entered the police station and approached the front desk. A glamorous, young policewoman with her hair tied tightly back into a bun at the nape of her neck smiled sweetly at them and asked, "May I help you?"

"We have come to see Chief Constable Broadman," Jacob said.

"Do you have an appointment?" she asked.

"No. Just tell him Jacob Firth is here to see him."

"I'm sorry Sir, but the chief constable is a very busy man and unless you have an appointment with him, I cannot disturb him."

"Chief Constable Broadman is a servant of the people is he not?" asked Jacob. "I am one of the people that the chief constable is a servant of. I too am a busy man, and I need to see the chief constable."

"He is a servant of the people, but you will still need an appointment to see him," came the reply.

"All you have to do is tell the chief constable that Jacob Firth is here to see him and if he says he does not want to see me then, I will go quietly. No pun intended," said Jacob.

In the end, the young lady in reception made the call and two minutes later a side door opened and out stepped Chief Constable Broadman, "My God, this is a turn-up for the books. I couldn't believe my ears when I was told Jacob Firth was in reception. Come on up." He held the door open for Jacob and Dan to step through then he said to the receptionist, "Have tea and biscuits sent up." He led the way up to his office.

"Sit down man and tell me what brings you here."

"First let me introduce you to a fellow police officer, PC Dan Coltley, from Glaston police station," said Jacob.

"Pleased to meet you lad, always nice to meet a fellow officer. You must be the police officer who Luther rang me about. Wanted to know your address. Wouldn't give that information out normally, but I knew it must be important if Luther was asking. How is Luther by the way?" Chief Constable Broadman wanted to know.

"Same as ever," smiled Jacob.

Once the tea and biscuits were delivered and the young policewoman closed the door, Chief Constable Broadman said while he poured tea, "Call me Cliff while we are in here, not to be used when others are present." He looked pointedly at Dan.

"Point taken Sir," said Dan.

Jacob started his story, "I had an unexpected visitor a few days ago. A young woman who works for me sneaked her way up to my office. Well, curiosity won the day and I allowed her in. Because of the information she came to me with, and because of the circumstances Dan has found himself in, and how things have accumulated and escalated, the only person I am prepared to share this information with is you. So here we are."

Jacob proceeded to tell Cliff Broadman the story and he produced the DVD, USB, letters, invoices and the yellow box. They all piled up on the chief constable's desk, just like they had on his desk when Jasmin had related her story.

"Can I access this DVD?"

"Of course, Luther made you a copy. Not encrypted. Likewise, the USB. The letters are self-explicit."

"So, evidence is going missing at Glaston Police Station?" Cliff asked looking at Dan.

"Yes Sir, and my name has been falsely ascribed to it. As Jacob told you, I am on suspension because of it," confirmed Dan.

"In that case, let's have a look at this lot and see what we can do about it." Cliff picked up the DVD and inserted it into his computer drive.

Phil could not sit still so he decided to drive past Tree House and see what was going on. When he got there, four police cars were parked on the road outside the grounds of Tree House, so he returned home. He tried calling George's mobile phone, no answer. He tried calling Valerie, but the same applied, no answer. He tried calling Harrison. No reply.

He sat down and switched on the TV. The TV confirmed there had been an explosion on the river Raybarn at a place called Tree House, but it was not known if there were any fatalities.

Up in the attic of the garage, Phil hoped and prayed that there were fatalities, and it involved InGuesty. If it did, he was going to vanish. Get out of the life he had landed himself in, once and for all.

He switched off the TV, went downstairs and into the little laundry room that was attached to the side of the garage, and filled a bucket with hot water. Picked up a sponge and went outside to George's car and began to get rid of all evidence that might be on or in the car that could lead the police back to him. He decided to be prepared to take off as soon as he knew what had happened.

By the time it was eight o'clock at night, Phil had made his decision. Having worked for George InGuesty he was aware of all the escape paraphernalia that was scattered around in case George needed to disappear in a hurry. He was going to disappear and he was going to use the tools that were to hand.

Phil went over to a metal cabinet and took hold of a set of false number plates, there was more than one set but he didn't care which set he took. The original number plates came off George's car and were replaced with the false set.

Next, he went over to the same metal cabinet and took out a crowbar. He made his way to the back of the garage block and set about jemmying the office door open. It took longer than he had anticipated but the rewards merited his hard work.

Going over to the desk he rifled the drawers, lots of loose money, notes and coins now filled his pockets. That was all he took, money. There was a safe but Phil knew it was of little use trying to open it, so he left it well alone. For one thing, he couldn't carry anything large and he was more than satisfied with what he'd accumulated. He would be able to start a new life with what was in his pockets. That's if he managed to pull it off.

There was no way that he could clean all his fingerprints off the limos and garage. The police would eventually find the garage and would then have his prints on record. He had decided to leave the country. He had cleaned George's car of all his fingerprints so when the car was abandoned and the police eventually found it, there would be no trace of him, hopefully, he would by then, be out of the country.

Putting on his gloves to avoid leaving fingerprints in the car, he picked up his bags, and stowed anything he thought he could carry into the car. He then went into the garage and picked up two five-litre cans filled with petrol, and he emptied one can into the car's petrol tank and he placed the other inside the car, on the floor behind the passenger's seat.

He would drive the car as far away as the petrol in the car would allow. Where he would end up, he did not care. Life had taken on a new meaning for Phil and he intended to take it. He no longer cared if George was alive or dead. He had decided to get out anyway. He headed for the coast. He would get the first ship leaving England and hope he could succeed to make good his escape.

Glaston Police Station had received a phone call informing them of the explosion, and the procedure was started. Police officers were sent to the location, as was the fire brigade. When the services arrived at Tree House, they found their progress blocked. They could not gain entry; the security system was on and there was no way they were getting in through the gates.

The river police were called in but when they got to the mooring at Tree House there was no sign of any riverboat. The odd piece of debris was found floating on top of the water but other than that, nothing. The riverboat had been obliterated.

The police were taken down the river by the river police and they approached Tree House from the river. But once again their progress was hampered by the security system. They had even tried breaking the glass on one of the windows but that too blocked their progress. It would seem the glass was bulletproof. They would have to get in touch with the security company that installed the system. That too foiled them, they could find no maker's name, address or contact details anywhere on the security box.

Luther sat at his desk, and the TV in the corner of his office was switched on the local news channel. Police were swarming all over Tree House grounds but according to the news reader, access had not been gained. No information had yet been received about the explosion that had triggered the police presence. The owners of the property could not be contacted. A satisfied smile played on Luther's lips as he turned the sound down and got on with his work.

Jasmin and Rhoda were walking Bennie around the grounds of Low Valley House when Rhoda said, "Yesterday when you came in from walking Bennie, Luther and I had just had sex."

"But you've only known him a couple of weeks."

"Don't you think I know that? Are you disgusted with me?"

"Who am I to be disgusted with anybody? Was it good?"

"It was amazing. The pervert started by playing a tune on my nipples, and I didn't want it to stop."

Jasmin burst out laughing, "You don't really think he's a pervert, do you?"

"No, he's the most wonderful thing that has happened to me. Look at me, I never thought any man would want to take me to bed and here I am, after a couple of weeks into knowing someone, I let them play a tune on me. But Jasmin I don't care, I am glad it has happened. All sorts of things have gone through my head since then.

"One thought struck me, I'm not on the pill. What if I end up pregnant? I really panicked then because I don't have any money. How the hell am I going to afford a baby? Then I remembered all that money I have that Sally gave me from the safety deposit box and she said there was plenty more. Now I hope I am pregnant. These are all ridiculous thoughts. How many people get pregnant after having sex for the first time?"

"More than you imagine I suspect."

"Luther said when he was leaving, '*keep it where it is, I'll be back for more.*' What do you think that meant? Keep what where it is."

"You are asking the wrong person here Rhoda. Like you I am not into the way men think, but I should imagine he meant, keep your vagina where it is. He must have enjoyed it too if he's coming back for more."

Rhoda looked at Jasmin, "I feel so stupid, he's a good-looking man he can have anyone he wants. I bet he's disgusted with me for letting him have his way with me, but it just happened. There I was one minute, walking down the passage with him the next I'm in bed with him. God, I can't believe I did it myself."

"I thought you enjoyed it."

"I did."

"Then why do you feel stupid? I have not slept with a man so if you are looking for answers, you have come to the wrong place. I know we have only known Luther for a couple of weeks but I don't think he's the sort of man to take advantage of a woman, he seems to be a very kind man. The very first time I met him and we shook hands, he covered mine with both of his. It was such a kind thing to do at the time. It brought tears to my eyes. He is certainly funny. I like him very much."

"Are you still a virgin?"

"I am."

"But you are beautiful. I thought all the boys would be after you."

"Well, you thought wrong. Maybe it's me that gives the wrong signals out, I don't know. What I do know is every time I come into contact with a man, I see my father. It puts me off."

"Was your father cruel to you?"

"No, just the opposite. He was gentle, kind and loving and then he suddenly died, he had a heart attack, and I was devastated. It might be because I don't want to feel like that again, that I dare not put my trust in a man. In case he up's and leaves me just like my father did."

"What about Jacob, does he remind you of your father?"

"For some weird reason, no, he does not."

"Are you going to sleep with him?"

Jasmin burst out laughing, "I don't know, I hadn't thought about it. Now you've put the idea into my head, I guess it's going to take some shifting."

"I haven't seen Luther since sleeping with him. What am I going to say to him when I do?"

"Like I keep telling you Rhoda, it's no good asking me this sort of question because I don't know the answers."

"I don't know what's going to happen when all this is over but I do know I am glad it has happened. I am so pleased to have met you Jasmin, Jacob, Luther and Sally."

"Then that makes two of us. I am pleased to have met you Rhoda, Jacob, Luther and Sally, too. But there's someone you've missed out," Jasmin said.

"Who?"

"Bennie."

Rhoda grinned, "Bennie is my favourite new meet."

"In that case, let's give him a run for his money. Let's set off running back the way we came, he'll come bounding after us, he'll love the chase."

"As you saw in the alleyway, I do not run. I am very ungainly."

"I thought we were friends?"

"We are."

"Then I don't care what you look like, it will be good for you and for me. And Bennie will not care what you look like either, he'll love the chase."

Rhoda said, "Let's go then."

Bennie off on his sniffing excursion glanced back to make sure he still had Jasmin in his sight, and he saw their flight. The chase was on.

Cliff Broadman switched off his computer and looked at Jacob and Dan and said, "This is pretty damning stuff."

"We know, that's why we are here."

Cliff thought for a few seconds then he picked up the phone and called Glaston Police Station, "Inspector Longreen please, this is Chief Constable Broadman."

In the silence that followed, Dan's heart missed a beat, Inspector Longreen was his superior officer at Glaston Station.

"Hello Reg, how are you?"

"Hello Cliff, long time since we spoke. Hope you are well."

"Yes, yes I'm fine. I have this investigation that has landed on my desk regarding smuggling at a place called Furbridge. I believe that's near you, isn't it?"

"It is, in fact, there is an ongoing incident that has captured the interest of the press. Damned inconvenient. Have you seen it on TV?"

"No, I have been pretty busy trying to come up to scratch with the smuggling. Tell me."

Silence filled Cliff's office as he held the phone to his ear and listened to what Inspector Longreen had to tell him.

Cliff replaced the receiver and picked up the TV remote control and switched the news channel on. All three sat and watched and listened as the news was relayed over the air.

When they had heard it all, Cliff switched off the TV and said, "What the newsreaders don't know yet, is that entry into the house where the explosion took place has been foiling our tech boys. Also, your partner Gary Harrison hasn't turned up for work and he is not answering his mobile phone."

"We'd better get back." Jacob stood up.

"I'm coming with you, I'll follow behind. I take it you have a spare room still available at your place?"

"Always Cliff, even if Luther has to sleep on the floor."

The comment made Cliff smile, Luther on the floor. He'd like to see that.

Travelling back to Glaston in the car with Chief Constable Broadman following behind, Dan asked, "What makes you so close to the Chief Constable?"

"I had a few close shaves with Cliff before I saw the light. Stealing computers, taking them to pieces and reassembling them so they could not be traced. I had heard that Luther was a whiz with a computer so I thought it would be a good idea to see if I could find out what it was that he did to earn such a reputation.

"Unfortunately for me, or fortunately for me depending on which way you look at it, Luther caught me trolling through his computer. It didn't take him long to trace where the hack was coming from and he came to see me. Because we were both computer freaks, he suggested we join forces so we did.

"His computer business, now ours, took off. I admit that at first, I did a bit of hacking into different company computer databases and found their weak link. Luther would invent an anti-virus programme and show the companies the error of their ways and sell them our programme designed to make it very, very difficult for someone to hack into their computers.

"Our reputation grew and soon, we were being asked to design computer software for all kinds of companies. No need to do anything illegal any more, our reputation went before us and the IT International Company was founded and Luther and I became millionaires.

"It hasn't been as easy as it sounds, there have been a lot of mistakes made and money wasted on projects that have not taken off. But most of the business we projected turned our hard work into well-earned money. We have no complaints.

"We had the property we now live in built especially for us and Luther designed and manufactured our own security system. It is unique and very, very reliable.

"About two years before I met Luther, I bumped into Cliff Broadman, he was a sergeant then, but he had caught me a couple of times trying to break into someone's property. He had given me a good talking to, leaving me in no uncertain terms, if I didn't mend my ways, he would see me behind bars. But we became good friends.

"So, whilst he was still a sergeant, Luther and I came across Cliff one night while he was trying to escape from some very nasty men whom he had caught breaking into a warehouse. There were four of them and only him. Had they caught him he wouldn't have stood a chance for they knew he had seen their faces.

"It just happened that Luther and I had been out for a drink and when we left the pub, I went to the gents and Luther went to bring the car round. I came out of the pub and Luther had just pulled to a halt. Before I got into the car, a man came running round the corner with four men in pursuit of him. I recognised the man. It was

154

Sergeant Broadman, I pushed Cliff into the car and told Luther the get the hell out of there.

"Cliff came back to our place until he felt it was safe to return to the station. That's when Cliff found out about our computer business. He stayed about two hours then we drove him back to the police station. As you know, the car park is at the rear of the station and before Cliff had time to climb out of the car the four thieves set about us. They had been waiting for him to return.

"Four of them, three of us, but Luther and I had some experience of looking after ourselves and in the long run, the four robbers were overpowered and arrested. It was a high profile case at the time, the police had been looking for these men for some time. Not only in Glaston but up and down the country.

"That is how Luther lost his eye. One of the men hit him on the side of the head with a crowbar so hard that his eye ruptured and there was nothing the doctors could do for him except remove the eyeball.

"It was the case that set Chief Constable Broadman on the road to the top. There has been the odd time when Cliff became frustrated with how the law works. If he needs something looking into that was beyond the capabilities of the law, Cliff knows where we are and vice versa. Cliff is the only policeman we know that we would trust with our lives. He's a good copper, a hard man but also a fair one. Look how he let me off being arrested when I was younger.

"I asked him once why he had done that. If he had arrested me, it would have been even more credit to his police career. He told me that he saw a young man with potential and he didn't think sending me to prison would have helped me mend my ways. So, he befriended me and helped me to become who I am today.

"I trust you not to repeat what I have just told you, for Cliff's sake, not mine. People that know me well, know my background and I feel you are a man I can trust not to spoil the reputation of an excellent keeper of the law in Cliff Broadman."

"You have my word I will not repeat any of this to anyone. I am glad to have heard it though. I respected Chief Constable Broadman before any of this. I respected the way he had started off as a simple PC to become chief constable. After your story, I respect him even more now," Dan told Jacob.

"Good," said Jacob.

Chapter Ten

Jacob pulled to a stop in the car park behind the IT International building and waited for Cliff to join them and all three went into the building and up to the third floor.

They found Luther hard at work as they entered his office without knocking.

Luther looked up and as soon as he saw who was entering his office he stood up, went to the front of his desk and gave Chief Constable Broadman a crushing bear hug, "Good to see you, Cliff,"

"Likewise Luther, likewise. Been stirring things up again I gather," Cliff beamed.

"Not me this time, trouble landed at Jacob's door and of course, I was dragged in."

"Wouldn't expect anything else."

"Have you heard the latest?" Luther asked.

"If by latest you mean the explosion on the river, yes, we have. Have you heard the latest, Harrison is missing and he is not answering his phone?" Jacob told him.

"Really, no I haven't heard that," said Luther innocently.

"Have you heard that the police can't gain entry into Tree House because of the security system and shatterproof glass?" continued Cliff.

"No, I haven't heard that either," admitted Luther. "Let's go home and update the ladies."

"Home it is," agreed Jacob.

As they were making their way down to the car park Cliff remarked, "What's got into Luther? All the time I have known him you have to drag him away from his computer."

"The pull of the skirt," Jacob told him.

Cliff looked at Luther and said, "What?"

Luther replied, "It had to happen sometime."

"Whoa," was all Cliff could find to say. Then he had an afterthought, "I can't wait to see her."

"You keep your eyes to yourself pal," Luther told him.

When introductions had been made and they were all sitting in the kitchen enjoying a sandwich and coffee, Cliff said to Dan, "What's your story lad, how did you get involved in all this?"

"Quite by accident. I had run out of coffee at home. I was on days and when I called into the newspaper shop for a paper on my way to work, I purchased a jar of coffee. I put the coffee in my desk drawer and forgot all about it. It wasn't until I got home, I remembered the coffee. I would have had to go out to the shop to buy more coffee, so I decided to nip back into work and get the coffee out of my desk.

"Gary and I share a desk, as I was passing Gary's side of the desk to get to my own, I saw a sheet of paper lying in his tray. I glanced at the letter. I saw it was not signed, nor was it addressed to anyone. I assumed it was an anonymous letter so I thought as we share a desk the letter could have been meant for either of us. I read the contents and was surprised at the information on it. It said there was to be a drugs party on a riverboat called *Valerie* tomorrow at three-thirty at a place called River Bend. I collected my coffee and went home.

"Gary was already at his desk the next morning when I arrived at work and I mentioned the letter to him. He denied having seen any letter. I decided to do some investigating in my own time. I looked River Bend up on the map and saw it was on the river Rayburn, not many kilometres from here. I went there at three o'clock. There was no sign of any riverboat. Next day I went into Inspector Longreen's office and told him about the letter. He said, no letter, no boat, no party. He dismissed it.

"It niggled at me, so in my own time again, I checked to see if I could find out if there was a riverboat called, *Valerie* and I discovered there was. It was owned by George InGuesty. I tried to find out who George InGuesty was. There was no trace of him. I had come to a dead-end. I took to walking along the riverbank until one day I was approaching River Bend and there it was, a riverboat called *Valerie* and people were boarding the boat, so I joined the queue.

"Once on board, I tried to keep a low profile by standing behind a pillar that was near the cabin door and it was there that I overheard a conversation between two men who were standing in front of me. It went something like this:

'How's it going Huggy?'

'Shite, absolute shite. I wish I could find a way out of this life but InGuesty's got me by the balls.'

'I know the feeling, he has me too.'

"I left the boat and waited until all the people onboard came ashore and hoped this Huggy would be one of them. He was. I followed him to his car and wrote down the registration number. It was easy for me to find out his home address and I went to see him.

"I told him if he helped me to get some proof of who George InGuesty was and any of the men that worked for him, I would try and get him immunity from being arrested and see about getting him into witness protection. He agreed, and he said he would get some photos of some of the top men in the syndicate. Unfortunately, with disastrous consequences.

"To be honest, it was just a bluff on my part about smuggling taking place onboard the riverboat, I had no proof, nor had I seen any evidence of drug selling or taking whilst I was on the riverboat. Huggy just assumed I knew what was going on."

"You did the right thing lad. It's not your fault that Huggy was murdered. You didn't pull the trigger, nor were you doing any smuggling."

"What do you know about this Huggy?" Cliff wanted to know.

"Not much, Clive Huggard had been found floating in the river with a bullet through his head, execution style. If he was dead, he couldn't be arrested and therefore questioned. He could not defend himself, nor could he lead us to George InGuesty. When he was found he had a gun in his pocket. If that gun turned out to be the same gun that shot a lady after another break-in, again he could not be questioned. The killer of that lady might be walking around free to kill again. Clever, don't you think?"

"Very clever," agreed Cliff.

"I'm sorry that you have to listen to all this Rhoda, but it's better for us to try and piece all this together," Jacob said kindly.

"Don't bother about me. I knew my father was up to no good before I ever met any of you. Carry on, I want this finished just as much as the police," replied Rhoda.

Jasmin said to change the subject, "We saw it on the news about the explosion at Tree House, just before you arrived."

"That's about all we know too. The boat has been blown to kingdom come and the police are having difficulty getting into the house. Can't crack the code. There's no maker's mark or anything on the box to indicate who installed it, so they can't ring the company up and ask them for the code," Cliff told them.

"Have they tried 1448?" asked Rhoda.

All eyes turned on Rhoda and colour rushed to her cheeks and she cast her eyes down and concentrated on her food.

Cliff looked at Luther who nodded his approval. Cliff took his mobile out of his pocket and looked up a number then put the phone to his ear, "Jack it's Cliff, are you still at Tree House?"

"Yes, looks like I'll be here all night. We've tried every combination we can think of and still trying. This is some security system," Jack replied.

"Try, 1448."

Cliff took the phone away from his ear and folded it up and placed it back in his pocket, "They are in. 1448 turned out to be the code. How did you know that?" Cliff asked Rhoda.

Not being used to being in such exalted company, Rhoda stuttered, "I, er, I thought, it was something my father wrote down. It was er, the number to the safety deposit box at the bank. I wondered at the time why he chose that number. Then I heard you saying about not being able to crack the code to the security system it was just a thought that went through my mind. You know, code for security box, why that number?" She trailed off and carried on eating.

"I didn't think you had such good taste, Luther. A lady with brains," Cliff told him.

"She sure has, brains as well as beauty," confirmed Luther and he winked at Rhoda.

Rhoda felt her stomach churn, and she looked down at her plate to hide her embarrassment. She couldn't eat anything as there was nothing left on her plate to eat. She needed comfort food.

Jasmin glanced over at Jacob and she met his eyes, now it was Jasmin's turn to turn bright red.

"Oh, for God's sake, have I interrupted a love nest or what?" asked Cliff.

"Might have," confirmed Luther.

Sally said, "Shall I go and get some wine from the cellar? I think we all deserve a drink."

"I'll come with you," offered Dan and he stood up and followed her out of the dining room.

"What love nest?" asked Rhoda.

"All this eye contact business and blushing. Now Dan has buggered off down to the cellar with Sally," Cliff told her.

"Who's been blushing?" asked Rhoda.

"Besides you, Jasmin for another."

"Jasmin! I haven't seen Jasmin blushing. Why would Jasmin blush?" Rhoda persisted.

"Eye contact with Jacob," said Cliff.

Rhoda looked with disbelief at Jasmin, "You and Jacob? When did this happen?"

"Apparently since Chief Constable Broadman arrived," said Jasmin innocently.

"As the Chief Constable, I have been trained in such matters," he told her.

Rhoda digested this and then remarked, "I don't believe you."

Jasmin was spared any further embarrassment when Cliff's mobile phone started ringing.

"Hello, Chief Constable Broadman speaking."

"Hello Sir, Jack here. On doing a search of the house we have come across two bodies. Mrs Valerie InGuesty and PC Gary Harrison. Both laid naked on the bed, well almost naked, the woman has a pink feathered scarf thing, covering her best bits."

"Pink feathered scarf thing, eh? I hope there's a better description in the file notes, Jack."

"Well, I don't know what it's called. I'm not into all this kinky stuff," Jack said in his defence.

"I think it must have something to do with the air around here Jack. What about InGuesty?"

"No sign of him, Sir."

"Keep me informed."

"They've found InGuesty's wife and Harrison in bed together, both single shot to the head. InGuesty is missing. I don't think even Rhoda would have difficulty in working that one out," Cliff told them.

"Hey, don't bring me into this, I didn't shoot them, I've been here all the time. Jasmin can vouch for that."

"Rhoda my dear, I am very pleased to have met you. No wonder Luther has fallen head over heels in love with you. I might have taken a fancy to you myself but Luther got there first," replied Cliff.

Rhoda could find nothing to reply to that, so she kept her mouth shut and glanced at Jasmin. To her surprise, Jasmin and Jacob were doing that eye contact thing and she had no doubt then, as to what Cliff had been referring to.

Down in the cellar, Dan asked Sally, "Are you attached to anyone?"

"No," replied Sally.

"Any chance when this case is over you might think about becoming attached to me?"

"I think I would like that."

"Good, then that's settled. But just to let you know, I don't know whether I will be out of a job at the end of this case, so I won't expect you to commit yourself until we know the outcome."

"Luther will give you a job if you want one."

"Will he? Let's wait until things are sorted out, shall we? I'm not really into computer stuff, although I am willing to learn if the need arises. But how do you fancy trying out a bit of kissing before we join the others? There are always people around upstairs and after all, you might not like kissing me."

"It works both ways, you might not like kissing me."

"In that case, we don't have much choice, do we? We will just have to go ahead and try it out," He opened his arms to her and she walked into them.

When Sally and Dan joined the others in the dining room Cliff remarked, "Where's the wine?"

It was Sally's turn to be embarrassed and to hide her embarrassment she turned and scurried back down to the cellar.

"Been up to no good down in that cellar lad?" Cliff asked Dan. "It would seem I am playing the wallflower here, after all."

"Pity Bennie's not a Bella, or you would be sorted out," remarked Luther.

"I've had worse companions to deal with than a dog," countered Cliff.

"I've had a thought," said Rhoda.

"Have you my dear, I would love to hear it," Cliff told her.

"The house that my father lived in belonged to a Valerie InGuesty."

"Did it now," said Cliff. "And how did you know that?"

"The solicitor told me. He said I had to remove all my father's belongings out of the house by the end of the month, or I would have to pay rent on it. I don't get a lot of money from working at the petrol station.

"I couldn't afford to start paying monthly rent that's why I had to go to see the second-hand shop owner and ask him if he would do the house clearance for me. But all the same, I still had to pay a month's rent before the house was cleared out."

"And what would the address be where your father lived?" he asked.

"Seventeen, Wayward Avenue, Glaston. I thought George InGuesty if he is still alive, might go to one of his wife's houses and because Wayward Avenue, is empty and has been a crime scene, it might occur to him that it would be the last place the police would look for him," he was informed.

"Let's go PC Coltley." Dan and Cliff went out to the car.

Dan was behind the car wheel and Cliff took out his mobile phone, "Jack, send two of your men to seventeen, Wayward Avenue, Glaston. I'll be waiting there for them."

Chapter Eleven

Dan parked the car on Wayward Avenue, but further down the road from number seventeen, so as not to be too obvious. Cliff pulled his mobile out of his pocket and rang Jack. "Instruct your men no sirens Jack, and no lights flashing either. We are in an unmarked black Ford Mondeo Estate, I will get out of our car and go and tell them what I want them to do, as soon as they draw to a halt."

When the police car pulled up behind Cliff's car, Cliff jumped out and went over to it, "We are targeting number seventeen, I want the two of you to go round to the back and if someone tries to escape through the back garden, I want them arrested. Is that clear?"

"Yes, Sir."

"Good, then we will wait five minutes to give you time to get in place before we knock on the front door. If you hear a commotion, come to the front. I'm sure I don't have to elaborate, use your common sense."

The two officers got out of their car and made their way around to the back of the house. It was a row of terrace houses so before they went around to the back, they counted the doors from the end of the row to make sure they were watching the right house.

Cliff gave Dan the nod and they too climbed out of their car and made for the front door of number seventeen. Cliff rang the bell and they waited. The door was opened by George InGuesty. The look of surprise on his face told its own story. He recognised PC Coltley.

"Hello, Mr Burton. Or should I say George InGuesty?" PC Coltley asked.

"How the hell did you find me so quickly?" George asked.

"Let's just say, we got lucky. Will you come with us please, Mr InGuesty? You are of course, under arrest, you do understand, that, don't you?" PC Coltley asked.

"You got lucky, my luck has run out." George held his hands out, but PC Coltley told him to place his hands behind his back. When this was done, Dan fastened them together with a pair of handcuffs.

Cliff took out his mobile phone and called Jack, "Jack, we have InGuesty in custody. Your two men are at the back of the house in Wayward Avenue, can you get in touch with them and ask them to go to the front of the house and stay there until you can arrange for the house to be searched and made secure? They will find the front door unlocked."

When Sally had returned with the wine Jacob, Luther, Jasmin and Rhoda, were all sitting on a semicircle, cream-coloured, five-seater sofa, with a glass of wine in their hand. Cliff and Dan had already left.

"Why did you go down to the cellar for more wine when there is plenty up here?" Rhoda asked.

To change the subject Jacob remarked, "I wonder if InGuesty learned about Harrison and his wife having an affair, and that set this turn of events to take place?"

"Yes, very interesting. If someone did inform InGuesty regarding the situation with his wife and Harrison, they saved the taxpayers a lot of money, no court cases, no life stretches at her Majesty's pleasure, to name but a few," agreed Luther.

"Who do you think it could have been?" asked Rhoda.

"I shouldn't ask that question more than once if I were you, Rhoda. I guess we will never know the full story and to be honest, I don't want to know, and neither do you. Ten years ago, I would have loved this intrigue and would have been enjoying every minute of it, but now, I have more important things to think about," Luther told her.

"Such as?" asked Rhoda.

"Nipples and crisps," Luther replied.

Jasmin laughed at the shocked look on Rhoda's face and she said to her, "You ask too many questions, Rhoda."

"Well, I want to know what's going on. I never get the answer to my question that I expect."

"Come on," and Luther stood up and held out his hand to her, "let me explain nipples and crisps to you in more detail. By the time we get back to the bungalow, if you are still puzzled by my answer, I'll just have to demonstrate."

Rhoda looked at the other people's faces sitting around the sofa and felt her colour heighten, but the temptation was too great so she put her hand in his and walked by his side out of the room and Luther closed the door softly behind them.

"Blimey," said Sally. "I've never seen Luther like this over anyone before, he's certainly got the hots for Rhoda."

"I haven't seen you have the hots for anyone for a long time before Dan came on the scene. Now you can't even remember a bottle of wine," Jacob teased.

"I must admit, I like him a lot. But he says he might be out of a job soon so he's not committing to anything yet. I told him Luther would give him a job if he did get dismissed from the police force, but I don't think he was very impressed by the idea."

"There's no need to worry about his job now Sally, he's back on the case and with the chief constable too," Jacob told her.

"I am so pleased to hear it, now there is something for me to look forward to," Sally told them.

"I think we have all found what we are looking for in these past weeks. Look at Jasmin and me. Who would have thought it?" Jacob told her.

Sally looked from one to the other, "Chief Constable Broadman was right then?" she asked.

"Of course," confirmed Jacob.

"This is all news to me," put in Jasmin.

"Lying does not suit you, Jasmin Ward. You know very well we are going to find out one another's little secrets and that's going to start right now. Beat it, Sally, you don't want to watch what's going to happen next," said Jacob.

"I bloody well do," she responded.

"You can tell she's Luther's sister, can't you?" Jacob asked Jasmin.

Jasmin laughed but did not comment.

"Go find some pots and pans to wash Sally," Jacob's voice did not invite conversation.

Sally stood up and said to him, "Spoilsport," as she went out.

Sitting in an interview room at the police station, Chief Constable Broadman said for the benefit of the tape, "Those present at this interview, Chief Constable Broadman," then he looked over at Dan.

"Police Officer Dan Coltley."

When George refused to comment, the chief constable said it for him, "Also present is George InGuesty, also known as Marley Burton, suspected murderer, who refuses to confirm his name. Let the interview begin."

"Mr InGuesty, you are in custody because we have reason to believe that you shot your wife and PC Gary Harrison. Do you have anything to say?" PC Coltley asked.

"There's not much I can say is there? You have the evidence of me shooting my wife and her lover Harrison, on my CCTV system. What do you want me to say, I didn't do it?"

"You were aware that the shooting was being recorded then?" asked PC Coltley.

"It's my security system, of course I knew it was being recorded."

"Why would you record it?"

"I thought once you saw my wife and her lover dead and see the CCTV footage of me pulling the trigger, you would jump to the conclusion that I had blown myself up along with my riverboat, out of remorse.

"I thought that the police would spend time trying to find my body amongst the wreckage of the boat. I was under the impression it would take you days to crack the security code so you could enter my house. That would give me a few days to organise my assets over here and go abroad and no one would know I existed.

"Maybe have a facelift and change my name. I could come back to Glaston and live in Tree House, let everybody think I had bought it and carry on as before under the new name. It had worked before so I don't see why it couldn't work again."

"When you say it worked before, are you referring to calling yourself George InGuesty?"

"Yes, I am."

"Why would you want to change your name Mr InGuesty?"

"I don't know if either of you have heard of Trevor Crast, well, I killed him too. When I first met him, he was the head of the drug distribution and smuggling ring. I intended to take the syndicate over, and Trevor was in the way so, I shot him. I changed my name to George InGuesty and let Marley Burton lie low for a while.

"When things got a bit too close for comfort for George InGuesty, I became Marley Burton and vice visa. It worked brilliantly, it had the desired effect. While I was Marley Burton, the police could find no George InGuesty. He was the first you know, Trevor Crast. Your lot never found his body, vanished without a trace."

"If Trevor Crast was the first, who was the second?"

"Clive Huggard. I spotted him taking photos from across the river when Harrison and I were collecting a load of smuggled dope that had been delivered the night before. I saw he had a camera. I wanted that camera. I had him brought to me at the boat. I made him tell me where the camera was and what he knew.

"I was surprised at the amount he did know. He rented one of my wife's properties so we could keep an eye on him. Obviously, it didn't work. Anyway, I shot him and dropped him in the river which was a huge mistake. I should have checked out what he had told me before I shot him. It never entered my head he would lie to me. I never did find the camera. Have you?"

"That is none of your business. Where is the body of Trevor Crast?"

"He's buried in the wood at Tree House. He'll be just a set of bones by now."

"You have no regret at killing these four people?"

"No, why should I have? They were either in my way or double-crossing me. I have done you a great service by taking Harrison down. He was a bad cop and an even worse friend. He was planning to get rid of me and take over my business and also my wife. I could live without the wife but my business, that's a different matter."

"You do realise that all this you are telling us is being recorded, don't you?" asked Chief Constable Broadman.

"Not much point in denying it is there. I have been caught and you have me shooting Val and Gary on CCTV, so I am going down whichever way you look at it. You, PC Coltley, have been a pain in the arse from the beginning. I wanted to waste you months ago but Gary said it would be best if we frame you so he set about doing the evidence log thing at the station.

"He was a good forger was Gary. He was working on a set of plates so we could print off a load of twenties. It would have worked too if he hadn't gotten greedy. He said he'd had the plates stolen. I didn't believe him. Mind you, it could have been Valerie who manipulated him, she was good at that. She knew how to seduce men. She also knew what would happen to her if she crossed me. End of story."

"Your home address is Tree House. How did you come to be living on North Lane?"

"It's a house I use on occasions, I own it. It's been empty for about twelve months so I go there for a few days here and there, just to let people think someone is living in it," George replied.

"So, you are saying it was a coincidence that you happened to be living there when Miss Ward purchased the dressing table?"

"That is correct," confirmed George.

"Just one other thing Mr InGuesty, about the gun that was found on Huggard's body, was that yours?"

"No, I didn't know he had a gun on him. It never entered my head to search him."

"You already know we found the gun you used to shoot Huggy with, under Miss Ward's dressing table. Where is the gun that you used to shoot your wife and Harrison with?" Dan wanted to know.

"Your men will find it at, Wayward Avenue, while they are doing a search. That's if they do their job right. It's not hidden. I didn't think I needed to hide it. You would have thought I knew better, wouldn't you? They will find more guns in different places, in different locations. In my line of work, you can't have too many guns," confessed George.

Chief Inspector Broadman ended the interview for the night and George InGuesty was taken back to the cells.

"Well lad, it's been a long day, what say we head back to Jacob's? I'm ready for my bed."

"Does this mean I'm reinstated?" asked Dan.

"I have already told your inspector that you are working on the case with me, the paperwork should have gone through by now. No stain on your character and I am putting a bravery award request in for you, you've done a good job. Time to go PC Coltley."

When Cliff and Dan arrived back at Jacob's the security gates opened up for them to pass through and Dan asked the chief constable how he knew how to operate the security system. Cliff explained he had known Jacob and Luther for many years and they had given him an electronic key fob to access the property, he opened his hand and Dan saw the little black device.

When they entered the house there was no sign of anybody. Cliff went off to bed and Dan searched the downstairs rooms. He found what he was looking for in the kitchen, she was taking clean plates out of the dishwasher.

"Hello," he said.

Sally looked up, put the plates down and ran to him.

He opened his arms and the kissing continued where it had left off.

After Dan came up for air he said, "I wanted you to know that I am now a fully-fledged police officer again. The suspension has been lifted and I am back at work."

"That's good for us, isn't it?" Sally asked.

"That's very good for us Sally. I can now court you like I wanted to do the very first time I laid eyes on you. But you'll have to get used to me dashing off to work at all hours of the day and night if I am needed. Working long hours and weekends and holidays. I thought I'd warn you before we get attached to one another and we both get hurt."

"It's too late for that Dan, I think we are both already attached to each other. But if you come home to me, I can put up with the inconvenience of odd hours and nonstandard holidays. After all, that's what my life is now anyway. I can't say I'm a partygoer or a Friday night at the pub sort of girl. I'm pretty boring really."

"You've not been pretty boring since I met you. You've been a bogus leaflet deliverer and an impersonator to gain access to a security box in a bank that doesn't belong to you, and that's only in the three days since we've been acquainted."

"That's because Luther asked me to."

"Do you do everything he asks you to do?"

"No."

"But you did this time?"

"Yes, I could see it was important."

"Well, I'm glad you did. It has helped me prove myself innocent of the charge laid against me. That means we are good to go, Sally, you and me."

"Yes Dan, we are good to go."

Jacob lay in bed with Jasmin's head on his bare chest and his arm tightly around her, "Can I hear Bennie scratching at the door?"

"He usually sleeps with me. He'll be wondering why he's been locked out."

"I'd better let him in then." Jacob threw off the duvet and walked naked to the bedroom door and Bennie bounded into the bedroom and jumped up onto the bed.

Jasmin watched with approval as Jacob walked back towards the bed, her heart missing a beat.

Luther's one eye was closed and there was a look of contentment on his face.

Rhoda lay beside him watching him while he slept. She couldn't take her eyes off him. She never thought she would experience the touch of a man's hand roaming over her body. Even less she never expected to feel the passion that engulfed her while Luther was demonstrating what nipples and crisps meant. The thing was, Luther was not asleep and he could feel Rhoda's eyes on him.

"Can't believe your luck eh, Rhoda?" Luther asked, his eye still closed.

Rhoda turned onto her back and said, "You certainly live up to your name, Luther. How the devil did you know I was watching you?"

"I could feel your eyes on me."

"What's your surname?"

"Deeman."

Rhoda was silent for a moment then she asked, "Your name is Luther Demon?"

"Something wrong with that?"

"I don't believe you. You're having me on again."

"On my sister Sally's life, I swear my second name is Deeman."

"I shall ask Sally tomorrow," Rhoda told him.

"I am cut to the quick to think you don't believe me."

"No mother would call her son Luther Demon."

"Alas, my mother was madly in love with my father and it did not matter one hoot to her that his surname was Deeman. I don't suppose she even considered what it would mean to any children that she bore. Love blinds all faults."

"I don't believe you; I don't care what you say. Your name is not Luther Demon."

"You only asked me what my surname is, I didn't say that my first name is Luther."

"I didn't need to ask you for your first name because I know what it is."

"No, you don't."

"All right then, what's your first name?"

"Wilfred."

"Wilfred Demon?"

"Wilfred Deeman," confirmed Luther.

Rhoda thought this through then she said, "I prefer just Luther."

"So, do I," Luther agreed.

"How come you go by the name Luther?" Rhoda wanted to know.

"You like asking questions, don't you?"

"I want to know. Anyway, I find it interesting."

"In that case, if you find it interesting, I will tell you how I became known as Luther. It's not very interesting though, so you might be disappointed when you hear the story."

"No, I won't, I want to know."

"Very well. When I started school, I was, and still am christened, Wilfred Deeman. But like you, everybody that went to school with me thought my surname was spelt D-e-m-o-n and as no doubt, you will be aware there is always the comedian that likes to take the micky out of others.

"The comedian in my class was called Darren Mitchell and he had a field day at my expense. Darren, thinking my surname was spelt D-e-m-o-n started calling me Luther and the nickname stuck. Everybody in school started calling me Luther, and I have become attached to the name myself, so I let everyone think my name is Luther. Not many people asked for the surname, so I am just Luther."

"How do you spell your surname?"

"D-e-e-m-a-n."

"I also had a comedian in my class at school. She nicknamed me fatty."

"Yes, there's always one."

"I haven't got the excuse you have, like being called Luther because your surname is Deeman whichever way it's spelt. I am called fatty because I am fat. I too have learned to live with it."

"You have a choice, Rhoda. As do I. You can go on a diet and lose weight, or you can stay as you are. Either way, I will adore you. You have no need to lose any weight for me, just stay as you are. I have a choice to revert back to my birth name if I want to. I don't want to; I like being called Luther."

"I don't like being fat."

"Then make the decision, go on a diet. But do it for yourself, not because of the cutting remarks made by an immature, childish and cruel classmate. It's your life and you have to make the decisions that you want. You are a very wealthy young woman now, you can buy a crisp factory if you so wish."

"I don't feel very wealthy."

"Jacob gave your box of gems to Cliff, along with the invoices that Sally retrieved from the safety deposit box, and he is going to have them checked out. I don't see that there will be a problem with them, he has proof of purchase with the invoices and receipts. When he returns the box to you, your money worries will be over.

"Apart from the gems, Sally said there is a lot of money in that safety deposit box at the bank. Did you count how much there was in the two bundles that Sally brought home for you? As my wife, you will be a millionairess, so either way, you are a wealthy woman."

"What do you mean as your wife?"

"You are going to have to marry me now, to make an honest man of me. I don't usually go around sleeping with someone who I have only known a few weeks. That is your fault for being so endearing. I can't keep my hands off you. And now Cliff is eyeing you up, I am making my claim on you. He'd better not try to muscle in on you."

"What about you taking my virginity? I think it's you that has to make an honest woman of me."

"Yes, that's another reason why you have to marry me, I know you have been saving yourself for me, and boy did I feel great when I realised it was your first time. Made me feel special, you gave me your virginity and I took it. A marriage made in heaven."

"You think so?"

"I know so."

"Not much good putting up a fight then?"

"Nope."

"But what am I going to do with all that money?"

"What would you like to do with it?"

"Set up a refuge for dogs."

"Then that is what you do with your money. Nothing to stop you, it's your money, do some good with it. I'm sure the needy dogs will appreciate it."

"Bennie was a stray you know."

"Was he? He seems to be happy now."

"He is, and I love him."

"Is he the only one you love?"

Rhoda smiled and said, "No, there's a guy called Luther, I seem to have found a soft spot for him."

"Glad to hear it. We are getting married, aren't we?"

"I would love to marry you, Luther, more than anything."

"Then that's settled."

"But where will we live?"

"Either here in the bungalow or in the big house. Up to you, I don't mind either way."

"What about my house?"

"We can go and live there if you want to. So long as we are together, I don't mind where we live. Or you can always sell your house and buy some dog food for all your strays."

"What about Jacob and Sally? If we live in Low Valley House, where will they live?"

"Don't you have eyes in your head woman? Jacob and Jasmin and Sally and Dan. Although it looks like Sally will be living with Dan once this little farce is over. But as you already know, she has a bungalow at the back of Low Valley House, she does not live in the house. Low Valley House is large enough to house six families. We have separate apartments already Jacob and I, and still, plenty of rooms to house all our kids."

"Why do you build such a big house with all that security system?"

"Once our IT business took off, we were making so much money we didn't know what to do with it so we built Low Valley House. We do a lot of secret work here Jacob and I, that is not listed at IT International and we needed a secure place to do what we are doing. Hence our computer room and the security system. You would be surprised how many people would love to get their hands on some of the work Jacob and I do."

"What did you mean about the kids?"

"Enough of the questions my lovely, do you need an explanation, about kids, or do you want me to demonstrate?"

"I think I would like you to demonstrate."

"Your wish is my command."

The next morning Cliff went down to breakfast and he was the first one to appear in the kitchen. Sally was busy at the hotplate making sure the bacon wasn't burning and she turned and smiled at him, "Good morning Chief Constable."

"My name is Cliff when I am with friends, please call me Cliff."

"Thank you, I will, I have to get used to the idea first, of calling a chief constable by his first name."

"It's only a job title Sally, nothing to be frightened of."

All the occupants of the house appeared one after the other and during breakfast, Cliff's mobile phone rang and he answered it, "I see, thank you for the information, goodbye."

"You will be pleased to hear Rhoda, the boys back at the station have checked your box of glass out, and it is confirmed that they are precious stones and the receipts are genuine. Your father bought the gems legally so I will have the box and the receipts returned to you in due course. You will have to get in touch with Her Majesties Revenue and Customs for tax purposes. The only thing they didn't find out about them is the value. You will have to have them valued yourself to be able to declare them for probate," he told her.

"God, it's one thing after another. How am I going to get in touch with the customs people?"

"It's called inheritance tax. There is a limit to what you can inherit before you are taxed on it. But the amount of money the gems I saw in that box, will generate far more than what the tax man will take from you."

Cliff's phone went off again and after he had completed the call he said, "That was Jack, he's had the results back on the gun that was found on your father and it was not the gun that shot Valerie InGuesty and PC Harrison, but we knew that anyway. What we didn't know was that the gun was used to kill a woman who lived on Beech Avenue, in Glaston."

"Beech Avenue," said Dan. "That's the house that I attended when there had been an alleged break-in. Because she lived alone, we weren't able to confirm if anything had been stolen. We received a phone call from an anonymous caller saying she hadn't been seen for over a week. When we got there, we found her dead. We found the kitchen window had a hole cut out of it and the front door was shut but not locked.

"We assumed it was a break-in because of the method of entry. I had seen this entry and exit method, prior to this but nobody was hurt. She was forty-five years old; she had no children. Her name was Glenda Stanton."

"I wonder how my father got that gun?" Rhoda commented. "Please don't tell me he's a murderer as well as all the rest."

"Here we go again with the questions. You should employ Rhoda as an interrogator Cliff, the poor buggers who she interrogates, wouldn't know what had hit them," Luther said.

"What poor buggers?" Rhoda wanted to know.

"The prisoners of course," Jacob replied.

"I'm not going to work for the police. I'd be terrified sitting in a little room with criminals," Rhoda informed them all.

"You are putting a brave face on sitting in the same room as Luther," Cliff said.

"Luther is not a criminal, he's a very kind person," Rhoda jumped to his defence.

"Only because I haven't been able to find proof of any misconduct yet. But I am on the lookout for any, so he had better watch his step," Cliff informed her.

Rhoda looked from Cliff to Luther and she then realised that Cliff was only joking and she started laughing.

"I wonder if the yellow box holds any other information. After all, none of us took the gems out of the box. You never know, there might be a false bottom to it, my father seems to have had a fancy for false bottoms. If he secreted all this other information away, he might have done the same about the gun and told how he came by it," Rhoda piped up.

"We don't know if the gun did belong to your father, it could have been planted on him after he died to make it look like he killed this Glenda Stanton woman. We are keeping an open mind," Dan told her.

"When can we go home?" Rhoda asked.

"I don't see why you can't go home now. George InGuesty is now safely under lock and key and PC Harrison is no more. I don't think you are in any danger now," the chief constable said.

"I wonder if I still have a job," remarked Rhoda.

"Me too," Jasmin said.

"You won't be going out to work ever again," Luther told Rhoda.

"Nor will you Jasmin. You have already been replaced at IT International," Jacob said.

"But I have a mortgage to pay," explained Jasmin.

"I can pay your mortgage off for you," Rhoda offered.

"That's a very generous offer Rhoda thank you, but I would prefer to do so myself. I don't like being beholden to anybody," replied Jasmin.

"What is it going to take for the two of you to get it through into your brain, you are both betrothed to millionaires?" Jacob asked.

Rhoda looked at Jasmin, "I want to go home."

"So, do I. This is going to take some getting used to," Jasmin told her.

"I'm afraid, you are not betrothed to a millionaire," Dan smiled at Sally.

"No, but you are," Sally smiled back at him. "Same difference."

Silence fell upon the kitchen and Luther said to Jacob, "Looks like we've got our work cut out."

"Certainly, looks like it," agreed Jacob.

"While you lot are working out who is a millionaire and who is not, Dan and I are going to the police station to collect Rhoda's yellow box and bring it back here. I think she might be onto something, after all, she was the one that helped us solve the InGuesty business without even getting into a sweat over it. So, I would appreciate it if you would both stay here until Dan and I return.

"It's been an interesting couple of days but I really must be getting back to Barrow Police Station, my work is piling up. But I am intrigued to see if Rhoda's instincts are right though and there is something else in the bottom of the yellow box," Cliff told them.

After Cliff and Dan had left, Jacob said to Jasmin and Rhoda, "You may stay here you know, there's no need for you to leave."

"I want to go home," Rhoda told him. "It's been enjoyable and so different to what I have ever known but it's also been stressful."

Jasmin and Rhoda went back to the bungalow and sat outside on a garden bench to wait for the return of Cliff and Dan with Rhoda's yellow box.

Jasmin said, "I have something to tell you, Rhoda."

Rhoda looked at Jasmin with unspoken interest in her eyes, "Go on then, the suspense is killing me."

"Yesterday, when you and Luther left the room, Jacob took me to bed."

"Bloody hell. Was it good?"

"Never known anything like it."

"Same as me. I am so pleased about that Jasmin. Now I don't feel so bad about jumping into bed with Luther after such a short acquaintance."

"I know exactly how you feel, I'm glad it happened to me too, but like you, I need some space to come to terms with all this. It has happened too fast; I am afraid it won't last."

"Tell me about it," replied Rhoda.

Chapter Twelve

It was midday before Cliff returned to Low Valley House to find Jacob and Luther working on their computers but there was no sign of the ladies.

"Taken Bennie for a walk, they shouldn't be long as they are back. Any news?" Jacob asked.

"No, Dan has stayed at the station, he's going back through the files to see if anything has been missed with regard to the shooting of Glenda Stanton. A couple of police officers went knocking on the doors along Beech Avenue to see if they could find anything out about Glenda. They did not. It seems she kept herself to herself, not very sociable according to the neighbours.

"But you know, I don't think InGuesty had anything to do with the shooting of Glenda Stanton. He had no hesitation in admitting he had killed his wife, Harrison and Clive Huggard. He even volunteered the information regarding a man called Trevor Crast. We have never heard of Trevor Crast, there is no record that the man ever lived, and our lads can find no trace of him.

"Marley told us where to look for the body, so some of our men are digging up the garden at Tree House as we speak. If they do find him, you never know we might get lucky and get a trace of DNA from him. I can't see

Trevor Crast being his real name because we can find no record of his existence. The DNA might lead to us solving some of the old unsolved crimes.

"If Marley had no conscience about the other killings, I don't see why he would have any hesitation in admitting killing Glenda, had he done so. He is the worst narcissist I have come across. He thinks he's God. Heaven help him in prison," Cliff told them.

"It sounds like the ladies are back, well Bennie at least," smiled Jacob

"Taken a fancy to the dog as well as the owner then?" asked the chief constable.

"Nothing not to like about him," replied Jacob.

"Only the size of his teeth," countered the chief constable.

The ladies followed Bennie into the home office and sat down at the same desk as Cliff.

"Now Rhoda, here we are, invoices back and little yellow box back. Let's see what we have inside," said Cliff passing the yellow box across the table.

Rhoda opened the box and tipped out the gems. Then after examining the inside of the box, she put her fingernail between the side of the box and a piece of card laying on the bottom and gently lifted it out. They all leaned forward and looked inside. What they saw was a thin square piece of white card. Rhoda took it out of the box and turned it over. It was a photograph.

The photo consisted of a young woman holding a stick of candy floss and a tall thin young man at her side.

The caption on the white margin at the bottom of the photo, under the woman's feet, read, *Glenda Stanton,* and under the young man's feet it read, *Peter Squires.*

"Anybody recognise him?" asked Cliff.

"I think he's my next-door neighbour," said Jasmin.

"You've certainly been unlucky with your neighbours since you moved into that house," commented Jacob.

"You don't have to tell me that. I have only seen him once since I moved in. He works away on some oil rig or other. He's put a bit of weight on since that photo was taken and his hair is a bit thinner on top but I'm sure it's him. And my neighbour's name is Peter Squires."

"Well, well," said the chief constable.

"I've had a thought," Rhoda told them.

All eyes turned to Rhoda and she felt self-conscious, but her confidence was growing.

"Please feel free to share your thoughts with us, my dear," Cliff said.

"I wish you'd stop calling her my dear. She is not your dear, she is my dear," Luther told him.

"You can decide who's dear she is later. What is your thought Rhoda, we would all like to hear it?" Jacob told her.

"I wonder who owned the house Glenda Stanton was living in?"

Cliff pulled out his mobile and rang Jack, "Jack, Chief Constable Broadman here. Can you check with the land register who owns five, Beech Avenue, Glaston, and call me back? Yes, that's right, the house that Glenda Stanton lived in. Ring me back."

"Who's Jack?" Rhoda wanted to know.

"Sergeant Jack Webster. We were mates back in the day. Cops on the beat together. We kept in touch," she was informed.

"Jacob, did you keep a copy of that DVD with the shot of the people on the riverboat?" Jasmin asked.

"Of course."

"Can we see it again, please?"

They all sat and watched the screen and waited until the image of George, Valerie, and Harrison appeared, and Jasmin asked him to freeze the frame.

Going over to the screen, Jasmin pointed to a party sitting at a table to the right of InGuesty and said, "There, isn't that Peter Squires sitting at that table?"

"I believe you're right Jasmin. He looks a bit older there than in this photo but I would say that's Peter Squires," agreed Cliff.

"Do you know where he works?"

"No, just that he works away on the oil rigs, or so he told me."

"So, you will not know when he will be back at his house?"

"No, but if he is a murderer, I hope it's never."

"May I keep this photo, Rhoda?" asked Cliff.

"Be my guest, it's no good to me," Rhoda told him.

"I'll be getting off now and pass the information onto Dan to sort out. It's been a pleasure meeting you both again and I hope we meet again soon. Don't forget to invite me to the wedding. Luther keeps a good bottle down in his cellar. I won't miss out on that." With that, he took his leave of them.

After the chief constable had left Rhoda asked Luther, "Will you take me home?"

"If that's what you want, but you may stay here for as long as you like you know, you and Jasmin and Bennie of course."

"I need a bit of time on my own to think about this. It has happened so quickly and I have a job to go to. They will be wondering where I am. I have worked at the petrol station for six years. I need to go back home and sort everything out," she replied.

"As do I," chipped in Jasmin. "I too have a job, or should I say had a job. I can't believe we've been here a month."

"You will not be coming back to work for me. You are no longer employed by our company," Jacob told her.

"So, you said. I will have to start job hunting again, I can't afford to live if I don't work."

"You don't have any money worries from now on Jasmin, you can have anything you want. I will have a credit card made out in your name. The sooner you come to terms with that, you will feel much better," said Jacob.

"I can't do that Jacob. But thank you, it's not that I don't appreciate what you are offering, but we are not married yet and it seems inappropriate. Like Rhoda, I need to go back home and give all this some thought. She is right, it has all happened too fast. Not just for Rhoda and myself but for you and Luther. We have known each other for a month and here we are married with two kids. We need some space, all of us," insisted Jasmin.

"If the only thing stopping you from accepting the credit card, is the fact that we are not married, I'll arrange for us to get married by special licence," Jacob told her.

Before Jasmin could reply Rhoda asked, "Who's got two kids?"

"It was a figure of speech Rhoda, that's all," smiled Jasmin.

"Yes, but it's been the best four weeks I've had for a very long time." Luther winked at Rhoda.

"It's not been too bad for me either. Neither of you will escape us now, we will be keeping an eye on you both just to make sure you are safe, this affair might not be over yet. But I think I agree with you both, we all need a bit of space and time to think. The outcome will still be the same you know. We are all destined to be together, even Sally and Dan are a match made in heaven," said Jacob.

"Come on then, let's get you both home, Jacob and I need to get back to the office," Luther stood up and went to pull Rhoda's chair back for her.

"Before you go, take one of these each." Jacob went over to a wall safe and took out two key rings with a little black gadget on the end.

Giving the ladies one each he added, "These are to open the front gate if ever you need a place to hide. Just point it at the gate and it will open, but for God's sake don't tell anybody what they are for, or lose them, keep them safe."

"Before we go, there is something that I would like to say and do more than anything I have done before. This has been the best time of my life and also the most stressful, but I wouldn't have missed it for the world. I would like to remember it by having my engagement ring made from one of these stones from my father. Not only me, but I would like Jasmin to select one or two or even three, and have her engagement ring made from one or more of them. If Jasmin hadn't called to see me none of this would have happened and it's my way of saying, thank you. Please Jasmin, please accept my offer, it would mean so much to me."

"That is a lovely thought Rhoda, and thank you. I will enjoy going through them all with you and selecting the one I want. We'll do it before you have them appraised, the tax man will never know."

"When you have chosen which stones you want, Luther and I will have the stones made into engagement rings for you. I agree with Jasmin it is a lovely thought, but Luther and I never heard you mention selecting one before the stones are valued," said Jacob.

Luther dropped Jasmin and Bennie off first then carried on to Chubb Lane where he pulled to a stop outside of Rhoda's house.

"You will come and see me won't you Luther?"

"I finish work at five, I will be here at half past, have some dinner ready for me." He leaned forward and kissed her.

Rhoda got out of the car and watched it until it was out of sight. Then she went to unlock her front door, only it wasn't locked, the door had been forced open.

Rhoda went inside giving no thought to her own safety, she was furious. This was the second time her house had been broken into and it was getting beyond a joke. She went through the house but there was nobody to be seen.

The only room that had anything out of place was her bedroom. Her chest of drawers had been ransacked. Every drawer had been pulled out and all the lingerie was strewn all over the floor. Rhoda went to the window and looked out. The bus shelter was empty, with no sign of the two men that had been watching her house.

"Creeps!" she exclaimed and went to find her mobile phone to phone Jasmin.

"Hello," Jasmin said into her phone.

"Jasmin, it's Rhoda. I've been burgled again. Guess what, my chest of drawers is the only thing with anything out of place. Every drawer pulled out and all my knickers thrown all over my bedroom floor. Creeps, creeps, creeps."

"I'll come over and bring Bennie with me, are you OK until we get there?"

"Yes, I'm too mad to be frightened. If I get my hands on whoever is doing this they had better watch out. I was going to go over to the bus shelter and challenge those two men but they are not there."

"For goodness' sake Rhoda, don't go challenging anybody. I'll see you in a bit," said Jasmin and she rang off.

Fifteen minutes later, Jasmin was surveying the chaos in Rhoda's bedroom. "I wonder what they are still searching for?"

"I don't know, I thought that was the end of this fiasco when that InGuesty's stuff was sorted out. What the hell can my father have been into?"

"We've got to ring the police," Jasmin said.

"I want to ring Luther first," Rhoda told her.

"OK, ring Luther and see what he makes of it."

"Hello sexpot, missing me already?" Luther said into his mobile.

"Luther, I've been burgled again."

"The devil you have. Have you rung the police?"

"No, I didn't know what to do."

"Leave it with me and I'll get back to you. I want you to go to Jasmin's and stay with her until you hear from me."

"Jasmin is here with me now, I rang her."

"Then the pair of you lock up and go to her house, *now*."

"I can't lock my door it's been jemmied open, the lock's broken."

"Just pull the door closed and get the hell out of there. I will arrange for a new lock to be put on but get out of there right now. When you reach Jasmin's, lock the door behind you and don't open the door to anybody, do you hear me?"

"Yes, Luther, I hear you. There is something else I want to say to you."

"I'm listening."

"I love you." She rang off.

Rhoda looked at Jasmin who had a smile on her face.

"Well, I do love him and if I am going to get murdered in my bed, I wanted him to know before it's too late."

"I think it was a very brave thing to do. I love Jacob but I wouldn't dare tell him so."

"He knows, we all know. It's the way you look at him."

"Really?" asked a shocked Jasmin.

"Sure, no big deal. Luther says we have to go to your place and lock ourselves in and not let anyone in until we hear from him. He said right now, just to go and leave everything as it is. He's going to get my lock fixed."

"We'd better go then. But I must warn you, my house doesn't smell very nice. I was going to clean out my kitchen when you rang. Come on Bennie, we are going home."

"My house didn't smell very nice either when I came in. I opened the back door and left the front door open to let the smell out, that's why it didn't smell too bad when you arrived."

Luther picked up the phone and rang Dan, "Dan, it's Luther here, Rhoda and Jasmin have gone back home and when Rhoda went to open her front door, it's been forced open. Guess what, her chest of drawers has been searched again."

"I'll send someone round. I am going to ask your mate Chief Constable Broadman if I can have permission to take the box of evidence regarding Glenda Stanton's murder, out of the station and bring it to your place so that we can all go through it. Can you get Jasmin and Rhoda back there, they might be able to spot something we missed. I'll be in touch."

"Chief Constable Broadman here."

"It's Dan Coltley here Sir. I've just had a telephone call from Luther. Jasmin and Rhoda have gone home and when Rhoda got there, she's been burgled again. I was wondering if I could have permission to take the box of evidence regarding Glenda Stanton's murder over to Luther and Jacob's house and get the two ladies to go through the evidence with us. They might spot something that we have missed. Whoever it is that is doing these break-ins must be looking for something other than what we have already found."

"I'm on my way Dan, I'll call at the station and pick you and the evidence up when I get there. It might be the camera they are looking for; we haven't found that yet. Have the evidence ready to take out to the car but don't let Longreen in on this. Keep your mouth shut, this is between you and me. I want to be in on this."

Dan rang Luther back and told him what was planned and Luther said he would arrange for the ladies to be at Low Valley House when he and Cliff arrived.

When Rhoda and Jasmin arrived back at Jasmin's, they locked the front door, but the back door was left open to try and get rid of some of the smell.

"Our homecoming has been short-lived," Jasmin said.

"Yes, I was looking forward to having a quiet evening with the TV and my crisp packet," Rhoda moaned.

Jasmin laughed, "You have lost a lot of weight you know in the past few weeks. You don't want to put it back on do you?"

"Truthfully, no. I feel much better than before all this to-do, but I think that's a lot to do with Bennie. I like taking him for a walk, but I like my crisps, they were my comfort food when my mother was alive."

"I think Luther is your comfort food now, you don't need crisps any more. Not that you can't have a packet of crisps now and then, there's nothing nicer, just not three or four packets a day."

"We can't even take Bennie for a walk, Luther said we had to stay locked in until he comes to pick us up."

"No, but we can go and play with him in the back garden, can't we?" Jasmin asked.

"Good idea," Rhoda jumped up and Bennie followed her.

They had not been outside very long when Jasmin heard someone say, "Hello there."

Looking over the fence Jasmin was shocked to see her neighbour, Peter Squires, home from the oil rigs.

"Good afternoon. I didn't know you were back home."

"I arrived late last night."

"This is my friend Rhoda Huggard. Rhoda this is Peter Squires, my next-door neighbour."

Rhoda smiled but was rendered speechless, things just keep going from bad to worse.

"Anything of interest gone on while I've been away," Peter asked.

"I don't know many people on the street so my knowledge is limited. I only know that Marley Burton from across the road has gone back to live with his wife and as far as I know, the house remains empty. Apart from that, all I know is work and Bennie," Jasmin told him.

"I see you still have the mutt, I thought you would have got rid of him by now."

"No, Bennie is here to stay. No one came forward to claim him so he's mine now."

"Good guard dog I presume?"

"Oh yes, the best," confirmed Jasmin.

"Well, no doubt I'll be seeing you around while I'm here. Nice to have met you, Rhoda Huggard." With that, Peter went back inside the house.

"I don't believe this," Rhoda told Jasmin. "That's the man in the photo, isn't it?"

"It is. Strange he's turned up again and your house has been broken into."

"You mean it is him that's been looking at my knickers?" asked a shocked Rhoda.

"Could have been," confirmed Jasmin.

Rhoda and Jasmin exchanged looks and Rhoda said, "He's a creep, a bloody creep!" Creep was becoming Rhoda's favourite word.

"Let's get ready for when Luther picks us up, should not be long now," Jasmin told her.

Luther was true to his word, he pulled up in Jasmin's driveway and the two ladies locked up and got in the car with Bennie sitting in the back seat next to Jasmin.

"You all right, my darling?" Luther asked Rhoda.

"I am now you are here. You'll never guess who Jasmin introduced me to this afternoon," Rhoda told him.

"I'm listening," Luther said.

"A murderer."

"And who would that be?"

"Peter Squires."

"Your next-door neighbour," Luther looked at Jasmin in the mirror.

"Peter Squires has turned up. Rhoda and I were in the back garden and he appeared over the garden fence. But you need to have a word with Rhoda and tell her she is not to go and speak to these men that have been standing in the bus shelter watching her house," Jasmin told him.

Luther glanced over at Rhoda and she turned round and said to Jasmin, "Tell-tale," then she looked back at Luther. "When I saw I had been burgled again I was so mad I was going to go over to those men at the bus shelter and ask them if it was them that had broken into my house. But they weren't there so I couldn't."

"That would have been a stupid thing to have done. These men are dangerous. But I think all danger is over now Marley has been arrested, I think the syndicate has been broken up and moved elsewhere. I don't think either of you have anything to be frightened of now. But all the same, for a few weeks you will both have to be vigilant and keep your eyes peeled for any strangers hanging about," Luther told them.

"After you rang me, Rhoda, I rang Dan and had a word with him. He said he was going to try and get permission from Cliff to bring the Glenda Stanton file to Low Valley House so we could all go through the evidence and see if we could spot anything the police had missed that might tell them who shot Glenda. I don't know whether he managed it or not for he hadn't arrived when I left to come and collect you two."

When Luther and the two ladies arrived at Low Valley House, Bennie went off on his own while the others went in search of Jacob. He was found in the computer room along with Dan and the chief constable.

"Good afternoon, ladies. We will have to stop meeting like this, it's playing havoc with my workload," Cliff told them.

"You should be in my shoes," Rhoda told him.

Jacob went over to Jasmin and took hold of her hand and stood holding it while the others exchanged pleasantries.

"Right, now we are all here let's get this show on the road. Each take a stack of paperwork and read through it, see if anything jumps out at you. Let's see if we can spot what it is that is so important that the thief or thieves are risking getting caught for." Cliff started handing out piles of paper to each of them.

After an hour of solid reading Rhoda piped up, "Is this of any interest?" She read from a notebook she held in her hand: "'G.H came today, one-thirty left seven-thirty. God, I am knackered.' G.H could be Gary Harrison."

"What's the book?" asked Luther.

"I think it's a diary because a few pages back it said—" Rhoda flicked back through the book and when she stopped, she read: "'Huggy appeared again today, *told him nothing. He is becoming a regular visitor. I wonder why?'* Huggy is my father, Clive Huggard.

"Wait a minute before you say anything there is also this." When she found what she was looking for she read:

" *'GH has been here again, third time in a month, and insists I've got them. I haven't. Next time I see Huggy I am going to ask him if he's got them. He's the only other one that could have got them if GH hasn't. Then PS turned up. He also wants them, I'm not going to get beaten up by PS to save GH, he might have hidden them himself and is just saying they have been stolen. I've seen and felt PS's handiwork. If Huggy has taken them, I wish he had taken GH instead. GH is insatiable, he has an abnormal sex drive, I hate him.'"*

"That is extremely interesting Rhoda, good work. I think you are onto something there, G.H is Gary Harrison. Huggy is Clive Huggard and PS is Peter Squires. There's the connection, whatever it is they are looking for, these three are involved. Harrison and Huggard are both dead, that leaves just Squires," said Cliff.

"And guess who turned up today?" Luther asked.

"Peter Squires?" asked Cliff.

"The very same, he turned up in his back garden while Jasmin and Rhoda were in her back garden playing with Bennie," nodded Luther.

"There is something that has been niggling at me since our interview with InGuesty," Dan said.

"Out with it, lad, let's hear what you have to say," Cliff told him.

"InGuesty told us that Harrison was an excellent forger. That he had been working on a set of plates to print money off. There were no plates found at Harrison's house, or InGuesty's," Dan replied.

"You are dammed right Dan, I remember him saying so myself. I think you've hit on it; Squires is looking for the counterfeit plates," confirmed Cliff.

"But how can Squires know anything about the counterfeit plates? He works away on the oil rigs," Jasmin told them.

"By the sound of it, the notebook tells us Glenda was entertaining all three of them. Who knows what they talked about? But I think Rhoda's right, she been right about all the other things, you know, codes and house owners, they are all connected. It's worth looking into. We've got nothing else unless any of you can offer anything better," Cliff said.

"I've had another thought," piped up Rhoda.

"Have you my dear, we are all ears," Cliff smiled at her.

"We need to ask Sally what was in that safety deposit box at the bank. If my father is involved in this, he might have come by the counterfeit plates and stowed them away in the bank safe."

Dan jumped up and said, "I'll go and find her." Off he went.

Cliff said watching Dan's back disappear behind the closing door, "Contrary to the saying *'a policeman's lot is not a happy one,'* sometimes it has its perks."

Ten minutes later Dan and Sally appeared in the computer room and Cliff explained to Sally what they wanted to know.

"Sorry, I didn't look. As soon as I saw the USB, I grabbed it along with a couple of rolls of money. When I found the USB, I decided to get the hell out of there. There could have been anything in the bottom of that box."

"That means Rhoda is going to have to go and take a look in that box. Dan and I will go with her as backup, show our badge and make sure she is let into the vault. If it's the same bank employee that served Sally, there might be a problem for Rhoda to get access.

"I think we had all better stay here tonight and set off for the bank first thing in the morning. The sooner we see what's in that safety deposit box, the better," Cliff told them. "Dan and I will go back to the station and sort some things out. We had better take this box of evidence back too. Make sure it doesn't get lost, or that Longreen finds out we've taken it from the station. We'll be back later."

"I'll be glad to stay here for the night, I don't fancy going home or sleeping at Jasmin's, after all, she does have a murderer living next door to her," said Rhoda.

"We don't know that he is a murderer yet Rhoda. You might be doing the man a great injustice," Luther remarked.

"Of course, he is. He was on InGuesty's riverboat, he was having an affair with Glenda, what more do you want? And he's been in my drawers," Rhoda told them.

"The devil he has," Luther growled.

Jasmin laughed and Luther said, "It's not funny."

"Oh yes, it is. It's all right though, nothing for you to be jealous of, Rhoda thinks he's a bloody creep," Jasmin laughed.

Chapter Thirteen

Nine o'clock the next morning found Rhoda, Dan and Cliff at the window of a bank employee. Rhoda showed her passport as ID along with the solicitor's letter confirming that she was the beneficiary of Clive Huggard's will.

The cashier said there was paperwork to be filled out and she was shown into a private side room and a supervisor took all the details and told Rhoda that before she could get access to the box, she would have to produce Clive Huggard's death certificate as well as a copy of his will, then all his assets could legally be put into her name.

Rhoda explained the two gentlemen she was with were policemen and that they needed to take a look inside the safety deposit box now. All the other legal stuff could be done another day.

The supervisor said she couldn't allow this without the proper paperwork if Clive Huggard was dead.

Rhoda popped her head out of the office door and signalled to Dan and Cliff to join her in the office.

Rhoda explained to them about the paperwork and Cliff pulled out his warrant card and handed it to the supervisor. "We still need the correct paperwork to give you access to private information," she said handing his card back to him.

It was on the tip of Rhoda's tongue to tell the supervisor that Sally had not had this problem when she had been here a few days ago. But the bank had not known then that Clive Huggard had passed away. She didn't want to get anyone into trouble, so she kept her mouth shut.

"I came prepared for this complication." Cliff handed over a search warrant and the supervisor had to relent.

"Do you have the password?" the supervisor asked.

"Connie," confirmed Rhoda.

The supervisor stood and said, "Follow me."

They were all shown down into the basement and into the vault and told where to look for the numbered safety box.

When the supervisor had left, Dan pulled the safety box out and placed it on the table. Rhoda handed him the key and reminded him of the code number. Dan lifted the box lid.

What they saw left Rhoda open-mouthed. She had never seen so much money in her life.

Dan took all the money out and placed it on the table then looked at the bottom of the box, and there, wrapped in bubble wrap were two blocks of metal. "Bingo," said Dan.

"We are going to have to take these Rhoda," Cliff told her.

"Please do. What do I want with them? They have caused me enough trouble as it is. Once it is known that you have the counterfeit plates in your possession, let us hope that is the end of this nightmare. When did you get the search warrant?" Rhoda wanted to know.

"I made arrangements for it when we went back to work last night. I thought we might need it," Cliff said.

"What are you going to do with all this cash?" Dan asked.

"I have no idea. Put it back in the box. I will have to think about it. I have never had any spare money in my life before, so I am going to have to ask Luther what to do with it, he'll help me."

Cliff took charge of the counterfeit plates and Dan put all the rolls of money back into the safety deposit box, locked it and placed it back in the hole it had come out of.

They dropped Rhoda back off at Low Valley House before returning to the police station. Dan decided to have George InGuesty back in the interview room. Sitting opposite him with the recording machine set in motion, Dan asked, "What can you tell me about Peter Squires?"

George looked at Dan and asked, "How the hell do you keep doing this? How have you come by Peter's name so quickly?"

"So, you do know him then?"

"Of course, I do."

"A bit more information is required than *'of course I do'*."

"I don't suppose it matters now; you will find out soon enough if you have Peter's name. He was my accountant."

"We were informed that he worked on the oil rigs."

"There were a lot of red herrings to take you down the wrong path. And down the wrong path, you went. Now all of a sudden, you seem to be coming to the correct conclusions. Why is that?"

"I hope that is something you will never find out," PC Coltley told him.

"I should have taken you out when I wanted to instead of listening to Harrison. If I had, I might still be free to lead the police down another wrong path," George told Dan.

"Would your wife and Harrison still be alive to help you take my colleagues and me down the wrong path?" Dan asked.

"Hell no. They had to go; you had no hand in that. Their decision to cross me. They knew what would happen if I found out about them. You reap what you sow PC Coltley. Valerie and Harrison were planting the wrong seeds. I enjoyed the look on their faces when they saw me standing at the bottom of the bed. It made it all worthwhile. There is not much that I enjoy these days, but I enjoyed that. Something to keep me warm in my cold cell."

"Did Peter have anything to do with the shooting of Glenda Stanton?" Dan asked.

"Of course, he did, he was the one that shot her. He couldn't find what he was looking for, so in a fit of temper he shot her."

"That would be because he was asking the wrong person," Dan told George.

"Was he now."

"You were looking for the same thing I imagine. Unlike Peter Squires, you were asking the right person for the information you were seeking, but you were given the wrong information and fortunately for us, you chose to act upon it."

"It sounds as if you have found what we were looking for."

"And what would that be Mr InGuesty?"

"If you aren't telling, neither am I."

"All right, let me ask you a different question. Was Peter Squires on the lookout for Clive Huggard?"

"Huggy! He was not only on the lookout for him, he was the one who found him. Peter Squires is my best man or was my best man. I set Peter the task of finding Huggy, and he did. He brought him to the riverboat and stood guard while I interrogated Huggy.

"The irony of it is, when Huggy went missing, Peter went to stop at two Mains Street, one of the houses owned by me, where Huggy lived. He knew it was only a matter of time before Huggy turned up. All his belongings were there, we knew he would turn up sooner or later, and he did.

"Peter was staying at the house where the dressing table was but he never found any DVDs or the camera and believe me he did more than one search. Then it was too late the police were all over the house. We assumed there must have been a secret drawer in the dressing table or chest of drawers because they had already been searched but nothing found."

"So, Peter Squires was with you when you questioned Clive Huggard about the photos he had been taking of you?"

"He was."

"What did you do when Clive Huggard revealed the location of what you were looking for?"

"I shot him. Peter saw to it that his body would be found floating in the river. I saw Peter put something in Huggy's jacket pocket before he tipped him over the side of the riverboat. I didn't see what it was, and I didn't care. But when we were having a drink later that evening, I asked Peter what he had placed in Huggy's pocket. He told me it was the gun he had shot Glenda Stanton with.

"He knew the police would soon find out that it was the gun that had been used to shoot Glenda, and not being very bright, the police would automatically come to the conclusion that because Huggy had the gun that was used, it was Huggy who had shot her. Pity things haven't worked out as we hoped they would, but we were bound to be caught out sometime.

"I'm just glad I got my revenge on Valerie and Harrison. The syndicate will have been closed down by now and restarted somewhere else, by somebody who was involved with the syndicate. I am happy to let it go and know that I am not being replaced by my wife and her lover. Good luck to whoever takes over."

Dan went in search of Chief Constable Broadman only to be told that he had gone back to Barrow Police Station. So, he then went in search of his inspector. He found him sitting at his desk, head bent forward studying some paperwork that was spread all over his desk.

"Inspector Longreen, sorry to disturb you but might I have a word please?"

"Of course, come on in and sit down."

"I've just had InGuesty back in the interview room and I have found out some interesting information."

"Go on then, tell me more. But I thought George InGuesty's real name is Marley Burton."

"Yes, Sir, it is, sorry. Marley tells me that Peter Squires was his accountant and that it was Peter that had shot Glenda Stanton."

"What do you intend to do now?" the inspector asked Dan.

"I was thinking about getting a search warrant for Peter Squires' house to see if we can find any evidence to corroborate what Marley has just told me."

"I think you need a bit more proof of the accusations against Squires before you go searching his house. The chief constable seems to have taken you under his wing and seems to have confidence in you to let you have your head on this case. So, I suggest you find more out about Peter Squires, then come back and see me about a search warrant."

"Very well, Inspector, thank you." Dan left the inspector's office and decided to head over to see Jacob and Luther.

Back at his desk, Dan glanced at the clock, three-thirty. He changed his mind and decided he would finish his shift in the office first, then go to Low Valley House. Kill two birds with one stone. See Jacob and Luther and spend the rest of the night with Sally. Dan had never been a lady's man but there was something about Sally he couldn't get out of his head.

When Dan had left his office, Inspector Longreen picked up his phone and rang Peter Squires, "Reg here, I am ringing to let you know the game is up. Marley has told Dan that it was you that shot Glenda. He is wanting a search warrant for North Lane; I can only hold off for so long. He will be heading for your house sooner rather than later." Reg hung up before Peter could comment.

Half past five saw Dan driving towards Low Valley House. He had been provided with an electronic fob to open the second set of gates that led straight up the main house. Dan aimed the fob at the gates, they parted and he entered the grounds of Low Valley House.

Dan got out of the car and rang the bell, but nobody came to answer it. He tried again, and this time, to his delight, the door was opened by Sally, "Dan, you know we don't lock the door, no need for you to ring the bell. Come on in. What are you doing here?" Sally opened the door for Dan to enter.

Without speaking a word, Dan walked into the house closed the door behind him and took Sally in his arms and he left her in no doubt as to what had brought him there.

"Does that answer your question?"

"I thought you had come to see Jacob and Luther or Jasmin and Rhoda," Sally said onto his shoulder.

"So, I have, but I am using them as an excuse to come and see you. I needed to see you and hold you, but if I came during work hours it would only be for a few moments. I waited until my shift was over so I could have a word with Jacob and your brother and spend the rest of the evening with you. I don't get paid to do this sort of thing you know. No, come back at work if they found out."

"I won't tell anybody."

"Good girl," Dan approved. "Are they here, Jacob and Luther?"

"No, not yet, they haven't arrived home from work, and Jasmin and Rhoda are over at the bungalow."

"I need to have a word with Jacob and Luther first before I say anything to the ladies. That leaves just you to entertain me. Got any suggestions?" Dan asked.

"I could mention a couple of things but as Jacob and Luther are due home any moment now, I had better keep them to myself."

"I like how your mind works. I will ask for further details later," and his lips found hers.

"Come into the kitchen with me Dan, I am in the middle of cooking dinner. Will you join us?"

"Thank you, I would love to join you all."

"Good."

While they were in the kitchen and Dan was sitting having coffee, he asked, "When this case is over Sal, will you come and live with me at my house?"

"I would like nothing better, Dan, I would dearly love a house of my own."

"Won't you miss this place? What will Jacob and Luther say if you tell them you are leaving? After all, they will have a problem getting someone to come and do what you are doing for them. They know they can trust you one hundred percent, you are going to be hard to replace."

"Question one: No, I will not miss this place. Low Valley House is not like a real home, it's more like an institution. Question two: Jacob and Luther will be over the moon to know I have finally met someone I want to be with. Especially, Luther, I think he feels responsible for me. He isn't of course, but you know what you men are like. As for replacing me, I think they already have, don't you?"

"You don't mind?"

"No, of course not. I like both Jasmin and Rhoda. I've not seen Luther so happy for a long time. He was engaged to someone before he had his eye removed. She soon dumped him when he came out of the hospital and saw how much his face had changed. It hit him hard. I only hope Rhoda doesn't hurt him by rejecting him."

"I don't think there's much chance of that, do you? We've all seen the way they look at each other."

Sally laughed, "Yes, not much guesswork there. As for Jasmin, Dan, she is welcome to the place. I want a home and family of my own."

"What's your story, Sally? We all have one."

"I was engaged, to someone who worked for Luther and Jacob. To cut a long story short, Luther found out he was selling IT International secrets to their competitors. End of my engagement. I came to hide my hurt here, away from prying eyes. That was two years ago. I'm over it now, have been for quite a while. It was easy for me to just plod along. Then you appeared and all my self-doubt vanished and now you've asked me to come and live with you, I can't wait. That's my story, now it's your turn."

"Not much to tell, history repeating itself really. I was engaged to a fellow police officer, woman police officer of course, and one day I called home during work hours to collect something, can't remember what now. Anyway, it's of no importance. I walked into the flat June and I shared and guess what, I caught her in bed with Gary Harrison. End of my engagement, except at the time, if I'd had a gun on me, I would have shot them both."

"He was your partner and he was sleeping with your fiancé?"

"He wasn't my partner at the time. That came later. By the time Harrison and I became partners, June had gone through most of my fellow officers in the department. Harrison did me a great favour, I ended up being grateful to him for showing me the light."

"Here, make yourself useful and set this cutlery out whilst I see to the dinner. I hope they aren't much longer or it's going to be spoilt."

"Just to make things clear Sal, you came to the door and opened it before you knew who was there. That's not very security conscious, I could have been anybody and here you are on your own in this vast place."

Sally went over to the wall and pressed a button and a panel clicked open. She pressed a few buttons and a screen at the side of the buttons lit up. Dan saw an image of the gates at the side of the property begin to open up and his car entered. The video followed his car up to the door and he watched as he got out of the car and rang the bell.

"As soon as the gates are activated the security system kicks in. You would never have got through the gates had you not had a fob key. If you had managed to get into the grounds, an alarm goes off, I would have pressed this button. It operates a switch on the porch entrance that slides a glass door across the front of the porch and the unknown visitor is locked in. The glass is bulletproof and the door can't be opened by the visitor. Caught in action as the saying goes. There are keypads scattered around the place so you can activate the panic button. I am quite safe here, as are Jasmin and Rhoda."

"Impressive," said Dan.

Before Sally could turn off the monitor, it buzzed again and they saw Luther's car coming through the gates with Jacob's car behind it.

Sally picked up her mobile phone and rang a number.

Jasmin picked up her phone and answered it, "Hello."

"Jasmin, it's Sally, dinner is on the table."

"On our way, thank you, Sally."

"Are you doing all the cooking for everybody?" asked an indignant Dan. "Aren't Jasmin and Rhoda helping you?"

"They have both offered but I like my kitchen to myself. Anyway, it's not all that much more work, just a few extra vegetables to do, that's all. They only come here for an evening meal and the odd other meal if something has got to be discussed. Mostly, they look after themselves in the cottage. I just fill up the fridge freezer for them when I go to the shop. It's no big deal, I enjoy shopping. If things work out as we planned, I'll only be cooking for the two of us in your own house. Won't I?"

"Guaranteed, Sally," Dan smiled at her.

Jasmin and Rhoda started back along the passage, "I hate this passage," Rhoda said.

"I can't say I enjoy the trip from bungalow to house either. That outside path takes twice as long. Bennie would enjoy it though," Jasmin told her.

"Do you know what Jasmin, I think I'm being brainwashed?"

"Brainwashed, what on earth are you talking about?"

"When I first came here, I hated the place. Now I don't feel safe anywhere but here. I felt safe at your house, but now that knicker creep has turned up, I'm not so sure."

"I don't think he was looking at your knickers Rhoda, he was looking for the counterfeit plates. Your knickers just got in the way. Once Squires finds out that the plates have been discovered, hopefully, all the danger will fade away and we can get back to normal."

"We'll never get back to normal. Everything has changed. Before I had money problems because I didn't have enough of it, now I have money problems because I have too much of it."

Jasmin and Rhoda had reached the house and emerged into the hall and made their way to the kitchen where they found Sally and Dan sat waiting patiently for them all to appear.

"Good, you are here. Jacob and Luther have just arrived so sit down and I will start serving dinner," Sally told them.

Over dinner Dan explained about having another interview with Marley and that he had told him that Peter Squires was his accountant.

"So, Peter did not work on the oil rigs as he told me," commented Jasmin.

"No, he didn't. The problem I have now is where did Squires live when he was absent for months at a time from the house next door to yours. My inspector tells me I have to find out about Squires before he authorises a search warrant for his house," Dan told them.

"Inspector Longreen, say's I have to get proof that Squires is responsible for breaking into Rhoda's house. After all, we only have Marley's word that Squires has anything at all to do with this enquiry. He's right you know. We don't have any proof that Peter is the accountant for Marley.

"That's why I have come to see if either of you two have any suggestions. Is there any way to find out where Squires has been living for the past six months? The thing is, this case is all about identity. How do we know that Peter Squires is his real name?"

"Have you tried checking with the banks to see if any of them have a Peter Squires on their books? Or if he has a credit card, and if so, where was the last location it was used? That might give you some idea," Jasmin said.

"No, I haven't had time to do any of that yet, but it's worth giving it a shot. I'll do a bit of digging in the morning and see if I can find anything out. It was late in the afternoon when I interviewed Marley and I have other cases on my workload as well as this one. I did a bit of overdue paperwork until it was home time and then I came straight here."

"You two had better stay here for the night until we can find out about Peter Squires," Luther told Rhoda.

"I'm game for that," Rhoda told him.

"Really? I thought you would object."

"I've been brainwashed," Rhoda told him.

"By whom?"

"Knicker creeps."

"Your own fault, you shouldn't wear such sexy knickers."

"How do you know Rhoda wears sexy knickers?" asked Sally.

"None of your damn business."

Jasmin laughed and said, "Right, I am going to see to these dishes then I am going to take Bennie for a walk."

"There's no need to see to the dishes, I'll just pile them all in the dishwasher, job done," Sally told her.

"Are you sure Sally, I feel guilty with you doing all the work? Rhoda and I will take some of the responsibility off your shoulders. After all, we are used to doing all our own housework at home."

"It's nice for me to have a bit of company Jasmin, there is nothing to feel guilty about, I like having you both around. You and Rhoda look after the bungalow, that's one job less for me to do. And Bennie, he likes my cooking and doesn't feel guilty when he's seeing off the last of the beef."

"In that case, I'd better take him for his walk and let him run off all that beef," Jasmin smiled.

"I'll come with you," Jacob said.

"What would you like to do now sexpot?" Luther asked Rhoda.

"I'd like you to take me along the path that leads back to the bungalow instead of going through the depressing tunnel."

"Nice night for a walk." He stood up and waited for Rhoda to do the same.

Left on their own Dan said, "I know something better to do than dog walking and pathfinding. Want to know what it is?" he asked Sally.

"I'd love to know what it is," she replied.

"It doesn't involve putting dirty dishes in the dishwasher so they are just going to have to wait."

Chapter Fourteen

Peter looked at his reflection in the cracked mirror over the sink in his bathroom. Fourteen North Lane, Glaston, had been his bolt hole when he needed some time to himself. Although the house belonged to Marley, for he liked to know where his workers were, it was a place to take a break. Working for Marley had been no mean task.

Gary had made some counterfeit plates and they had gone missing. Marley wanted those plates back.

Marley had set Peter the task of tracking the plates down. So, find them he must. If Marley did not get those plates, heads would roll, and his head was the head that was on the top of that list.

Peter had been just seventeen years old when he met Trevor Crast, and in all honesty, in the beginning, he had idolised Trevor. Trevor had picked him off the street one evening when he had indulged in too much beer at the Red Lion. Peter can't remember anything at all about that night, but the next morning, Trevor Crast inducted him into his smuggling syndicate, and he never looked back.

On reflection, his life now told a different story. Instead of it being the start of a new life for him, it had become a fight for survival. A fight he was now losing. Bad things were starting to escalate. Inspector Reg Longreen had kept him up-to-date with the George InGuesty case, now renamed Marley Burton case.

Marley in prison, Valerie dead, Harrison dead and Glenda Stanton dead. He had known about Glenda of course, for he had killed her. No big deal, no one would miss her and she had a crap life anyway, he had done her a favour.

She should have told him where Harrison had stashed the counterfeit plates. It never entered his head that Glenda didn't know anything about them. Peter knew that Harrison and Huggy were regular visitors to Glenda's, so therefore she had to know where the plates were. But even if she had told him, he would probably have shot her anyway. Dead people can't talk.

Plan two didn't do any better either. He had planted the gun he had used to shoot Glenda with on Clive Huggard, hoping that the police would automatically put the shooting down to Huggy. Reg Longreen informed him that the police knew that it was he who planted the gun on Huggy. There was only one person on this earth that knew he had done that, and that was Marley.

Marley was in prison, if Peter gets arrested himself, he hopes he is put in the same prison as Marley. Marley is not going to get away with grassing him up, not after all he had done for him. Peter would not rest unless he got his revenge.

Reg Longreen had also informed him that the counterfeit plates had been recovered by the police. So, no use trying to find them in the dressing table in the house next door. That is where Marley had told him to look, there, or in a set of drawers at Huggy's daughter's house. He had searched Huggy's daughter's place but had come up empty-handed.

After Reg had telephoned him and told him PC Coltley had been to see him and he wanted a search warrant for his house, he decided it was time to disappear. But before he did that, Inspector Reg Longreen and Marley were not going to get away with the parts they had played in this, Peter would see to that.

Peter cleaned his teeth, combed his hair and put on his best suit. He picked up his holdall, placed it on the table and looked inside. He was double-checking that he had all the account books that he needed. He had; they were all there. Then, picking up his suitcase and holdall he went out of the front door and closed it with a bang. End of an era.

He'd had a couple of them. An identity change was now required, he had done it before, he had taken a leaf out of Marley's book, and it had worked. He would give it another go and see if he could pull it off again. No harm in trying.

He was going to stop in Glenda Stanton's house in Beech Avenue until he was ready to disappear. He knew it would be empty and the police would have left weeks ago. A good place to hide while he went to the bank and took what he would need out of the safety deposit box at the bank.

He was going to need some cash before he set off. He also needed a bank book he had opened up under another name. Peter Squires was dead for now, but he might reappear in years to come. Marley had taught him well, he needed to be ready to disappear at a moment's notice, so he already had a passport in another name alongside the bank book in the safety deposit box at the bank. Standard practice.

He knew how the system worked, he knew Marley liked to keep track of his workers, that's why he bought houses and made his workers stay in them.

Being the accountant, Peter also knew, Glenda Stanton's house wasn't owned by Marley. That is the reason why he thought it would be a good place to stay for a day or two. Just long enough to sort his assets out. The police would be looking for houses owned by Marley, this one was not. Marley had not been satisfied with Peter just doing his accounts, he had sent him around the world, meeting drug dealers and setting up deliveries.

Dan entered the police station and the officer at the front desk said to him, "Morning Dan. Funny goings on if you ask me with that smuggler bloke."

"What do you mean by that?" asked Dan.

"That solicitor of his has been to see him every day since he's been locked up. I did tell Inspector Longreen, but he said never mind, there is no way the solicitor will get Marley off, we have too much evidence on him."

"How long does he stay?"

"Two, three hours. Sometimes twice a day. He arrived here this morning at quarter to seven, and he's still here."

Dan glanced at the clock on the wall behind the officer and saw it was fifteen minutes to twelve, "Five hours," Dan remarked.

The officer nodded but did not comment.

"Thank you for letting me know, Frank."

"No worries, Dan, I know it's your case."

Dan decided not to mention anything to Inspector Longreen, not much point if he already knew about it. He went and sat at his desk and got on with more paperwork. He would wait and see if Jacob and Luther had managed to find anything out about Peter Squires. He intended to go to Low Valley House that evening, straight from work.

Jasmin and Rhoda were doing their daily walk with Bennie when Rhoda said, "Luther says I have to make my own mind up when I want to do things."

"Such as?"

"You know, going on a diet. I have to do it because I want to do it not because I think other people think I'm too fat. Luther says it doesn't matter to him whether I am as I am or if I lose some weight. What do you think I should do?"

"I think Luther is right. If you do it because you want to, then it will make doing it a lot easier and make you feel proud of what you have achieved."

"I have lost some weight since meeting you, you know."

"Yes, I know you have, I am not blind. But I don't like you any better for losing the weight than I did before. You are the same nice, kind person now, as you were then. Only thinner."

"I still have those two rolls of money in my bag. I haven't even counted them, I don't know how much is in each roll and there are loads more in that security box in the bank vault. I bet I've lost this weight by worrying about that."

Jasmin laughed, "You have lost the weight because you have been eating the right food and taking a lot of exercise. All this walking with Bennie is doing you a lot of good."

"It's not just Bennie, Jasmin, it's having company as well. I don't feel the need to eat like I did and then there's Sally's dinners, I really enjoy them. She's been teaching me how to cook, I've enjoyed doing that too."

"Nothing to do with being brainwashed then?"

"Thinking about being brainwashed makes me want to eat. Take my mind off it. Trouble is Jasmin, I have come to like being here, not having to go out to work, to be able to take Bennie out for a walk whenever I feel like it. Then there's the money. I am coming round to the fact that I don't have to go out to work, not for a while anyway, I have plenty of money to tide me over.

"When we get back to the bungalow, shall we count the two wads of money and see what it amounts to? Then when this is over, will you come to the bank with me? I have to take my father's will and death certificate to prove I am the beneficiary of his will before they will transfer any assets he might hold at the bank, over to me."

"If that's what you want, of course, I will."

"Let's go back then and count the money before the men get back from work. Goodness knows what they will have in store for us this time. I tell you what Jasmin, I am staying here, don't care if I have been brainwashed, it's better than out there."

Jasmin laughed again and said, "Race you back," and she set off running with Rhoda not far behind, but Bennie, it didn't take him long to take the lead.

When they reached the bungalow, Jasmin and Rhoda were practically neck and neck, "If someone had told me a couple of months ago that I would be running and enjoying it I would have thought they were mad. I kept up with you."

"We will have to make it a rule, every time we take Bennie for a walk, we do a bit of running, it's good for both of us, not just you. Deal?"

"Deal," agreed Rhoda.

"I'll put the kettle on, you get the money."

"Deal," smiled Rhoda.

Sitting next to each other on the little leather sofa, Rhoda handed Jasmin one of the rolls of money and she kept one herself. Sliding off the paper ring they both flattened out the money on the coffee table and started to count it into one-hundred-pound piles.

Both ladies counted how many piles of one hundred pounds they had and it was an equal amount, twenty piles each. Each bundle consisted of two thousand pounds.

"That's four thousand pounds just in these two bundles. The safety deposit box was bulging with these rolls so heaven knows how much there is altogether. Then there is the money in the bank accounts, I have no idea how much there is or where to start.

"What am I going to do about declaring all this money to the government, you know, like Chief Constable Broadman said, that tax thing?"

"What money?"

"All this and what there is in the safety deposit box."

"What safety deposit box?"

"Are you trying to say, don't declare it?"

"Now, would I say a thing like that? What I am saying is, what money? I haven't seen any money and you haven't told me about any safety deposit box in the bank."

"But the government will know I have it."

"How? They didn't know your father had it. You will, of course, have to declare what you get from your father's assets that are in any bank accounts, the bank will, I think, do that for you for they cannot hide it. Don't take my word for it though Rhoda, to be honest, I am as ignorant as you on the subject.

"All I am saying is, if it were me, I would leave the money in the safety deposit box and take it out when I need it. But I have to admit that really, it is illegal, so you will have to make up your own mind, like Luther says, do what you do for yourself, Rhoda. If you feel uncomfortable about not declaring the money, then you have the option. Your choice."

"But Chief Constable Broadman knows about it."

"I don't think Chief Constable Broadman has you down on his hit list Rhoda. In fact, I think Chief Constable Broadman has that much on his mind, that your little stash of money is already forgotten. Just go and see the solicitor that made out your father's will and ask him to work the probate out for you."

"Do I tell them about the money?"

"Do you want to tell them about the money?"

"No."

"Decision made. You will have to declare the gems though Rhoda. You will have to get them appraised and give the information to the solicitors. Chief Constable Broadman took them into the police station and had them checked out. He had to, to make sure they weren't stolen. Too many people know about them to try to hide them.

"I think Cliff told you that you would have to declare the gems and inform the tax people, because he was covering your back, Rhoda. I don't think Cliff will be interested in a few banknotes. Nor do I think the tax man will try tracing the money in the safety deposit box for they do not know it exists, they will be getting plenty of money tax-wise from you when all your assets are worked out."

"God, it's never-ending."

"Better put all this money away somewhere until you need it, you never know what life has in store for you."

"You can say that again," Rhoda confirmed.

"What do you say to taking the long way back to Low Valley House along the path, it will give Bennie more exercise and we can practice our running skills?"

"I'm up for that, and I am also ready for one of Sally's dinners. I'm starving. But before we go, shall I get the box of gems and choose which one we want for an engagement ring? Select the ones we want before I give the box to Luther, and let him get them valued for me. I can't wait to have an engagement ring on my finger. Never thought it would happen."

"Go get the box Rhoda, I can't wait either," agreed Jasmin.

Dinner was over and they were all sitting in the large elaborate lounge with a glass of wine in front of them when Dan asked, "Did either of you find anything out about Peter Squires?"

Jacob replied, "No, I did a bit of snooping around one or two bank records, but I could find nothing out about Squires. None of the banks I checked had anybody on their books with that name."

"Luther?"

"No, I too came up blank. I tried looking at national insurance numbers to try and find someone with that name, I could find no Peter Squires registered."

"The thing is, Peter Squires has gone missing, he's no longer living at North Lane. I sent one of the police officers to knock on Peter's door on a pretend break-in enquiry and there was nobody in. The officer knocked on one or two other doors and he was told that Peter Squires had been seen leaving the house carrying luggage. What do you think we should do now?" asked Dan.

"What we need now, is a eureka moment from Rhoda," Luther said.

"Why bring me into this? I didn't know Peter Squires existed until I found out he had been in my drawers."

"I know, but you suddenly have a thought that turns out to be a first class lead. We could do with one now," Luther told her.

"Well, I had thought about the houses," Rhoda told them.

"Which houses?" asked Dan.

"All the houses that Marley's bad men lived in, were owned by his wife Valerie. What about that?"

Silence fell in the room as the men digested this thought.

Luther stood up and said, "Give me a minute." He went out of the room.

"Have I said something that means something?" Rhoda asked.

Jacob smiled at her and said, "We'll know when Luther comes back. Let's keep everything crossed you have said something that means something."

"There was an incident that cropped up at work today. The officer at the front desk told me that Marley's solicitor has been calling every day since he's been arrested. This morning he was there for five hours. Apparently, the officer at the desk reported it to my inspector and he said to let it pass, the solicitor cannot get Marley off because there is too much evidence against him.

"Makes me wonder why the inspector shrugged it off and lets Marley have so much of his own way. The solicitor has to be going to see Marley about something, especially for hours on end. It makes me nervous just thinking about it."

"When Luther comes back, I'll ask him if his solicitors will do the probate for me, at least I can trust them. If Marley's solicitor is creeping round the police station, I want nothing to do with him or any other solicitor I don't know. Do you think your solicitors will do the probate for me, Jacob? I will pay them of course; I don't expect it done for nothing."

"I don't see why not, they are solicitors after all."

The security screen sprang into life and the image of the side gates that lead up to Low Valley House opened up a car drove in and came to a stop at the front door. The car door opened and out stepped Chief Constable Broadman.

Sally jumped up and went to let the Chief Constable in.

"Good evening one and all, glad to see you all present, especially you Dan. Where's Luther?" asked Cliff.

"Just checking something out, he'll be back directly," Jacob informed him.

"Good. Any of that delicious-smelling dinner left Sal, I'm starving?" Cliff asked.

Sally went out and came back with a tray complete with a plate full of dinner and a knife and fork. Cliff smiled at her and reached for the tray. He placed it on his knee and made short work of picking up the knife and fork.

"Anything of interest Dan?" asked Cliff with his mouthful.

"I was telling everybody about Inspector Longreen allowing Marley to have as many visits from his solicitor as he wants, and for as long as he wants. Apart from that, we are still on the lookout for Peter Squires. That's where Luther is, checking on houses that Squires might have gone to ground in."

"Interesting, very interesting," said Cliff. "Sally that was delicious as usual, thank you very much, just what the doctor ordered." Cliff held his tray up and Sally vanished into the kitchen with it.

Luther appeared just behind Sally as she returned from the kitchen and he held out his hand to Cliff as he passed him and they shook hands.

"I wasn't expecting you tonight," Luther said to Cliff.

"No, I wasn't expecting it myself but something came up and I thought we should talk it through. I called Glaston Police Station before I came here to see if Dan was on the late shift but I was informed that he had already left. So, I came here to see if he was still chasing Sally's skirt."

Sally and Dan exchanged glances and Sally's cheeks became flushed. "Oh hell, here we go again with the blushing. Sorry, I mentioned it, but I guess I'm right, for here he is," Cliff commented.

"I came to see if Luther and Jacob had found anything out for me," Dan informed him.

"I believe you lad, thousands wouldn't."

"Find anything out?" Jacob asked Luther.

"Not much that we didn't already know. But what I did find out was that Glenda's house on Beech Avenue is the only house that is not owned by Marley. The houses on North Lane where Marley and Squires were living, are both owned by Marley. As does the house on Wayward Avenue, where Clive Huggard was living.

"I could not find anything out about Beech Avenue," Luther finished.

"I know who owns Beech Avenue," confirmed Cliff. "I had it checked out at work."

Jacob said, "I hope you are going to tell us."

"Ready for this Rhoda?" Cliff asked.

"Not my father?"

"Yes, Clive Huggard. He is the owner of Beech Avenue, or should I say, the house that Glenda lived in."

"Are you saying my father was a pimp as well as a smuggler and murderer?"

"No, I am saying that he owned the house that Glenda lived in."

"But she was entertaining all those men, doesn't that make her a prostitute?"

"She might have been employed by Marley to keep his workers happy, who knows, we might never know. Tell me again, what is the point of this investigation into who owns these houses?" Cliff asked.

"Squires is the man we are now looking for in connection with Glenda's murder. He has gone missing. It turns out that Squires was Marley's accountant. As well as being sought in connection with the shooting of Glenda, he is also wanted for questioning with regard to the smuggling syndicate.

"We can't find him. Rhoda had one of her thoughts, and it was, why was Valerie InGuesty the owner of all these houses where people connected to the syndicate lived? It turns out that Valerie was not the owner of these properties, Marley was, with the exception of the house that Glenda was living in. We think Valerie's name was used as a cover-up. More misdirection's for us to follow," Jacob informed him.

"When did this Peter Squires go missing?" Cliff asked.

"Sometime today. He lived in the house next door to Jasmin on North Lane. When he was home from the oil rigs that is. But it is looking more and more likely that he never went near an oil rig, he worked for Marley. He lived in seventeen North Lane, which belongs to Marley," Dan told him.

"Even more interesting. What's your next move?" Cliff asked Dan.

"Now I know that Clive Huggard owned the house where Glenda lived, I thought it might be a good idea to get a search warrant to enable us to get into that house to see if Squires has gone into hiding there. He might think it's the last place we'd look for him," Dan said.

"Good thinking. But isn't Rhoda now the legal owner of Beech Avenue? Or she will be once probate has gone through," Cliff asked.

"Well, yes, I suppose she is," agreed Dan.

"Do we have your permission to enter your house on Beech Avenue, Rhoda," asked Dan.

"If it helps bring this farce to an end, you may do anything you like at the house Cliff, with my blessing," Rhoda told him.

"Right lad, let's go," Cliff stood up.

"What, now?"

"Right now, we need to strike before anybody else that is involved in this case gets wind of the fact that we know who owns Beech Avenue." Cliff walked out of the room with Dan following.

"You're driving lad, you know the way." Cliff threw Dan his car keys.

The light was fading by the time they reached Beech Avenue, and Dan cut the engine and turned off the car lights.

"What's our best move, Sir?" Dan asked.

"I think our best move is to creep up to the front door and try it. See if Peter forgot to lock it behind him, thinking nobody was likely to go calling. Murder scene and all that. Then if the door is locked, we will have to take the matter into our own hands and try picking the lock. I don't think Rhoda will mind, do you? Mind, it's a long while since I picked a lock, so I might take longer than I used to. If I can't manage to unlock the door, we will have to call Glaston Police Station and get back up. But that's the last thing I want to do, involve Glaston Police Station. We need to keep this to ourselves if we possibly can."

"Then what?"

"If it's open, we go in."

"Peter Squires is a very dangerous man Sir,"

"So am I when I have to be. Are you up to it lad, or not?"

"Yes, Sir, I was just warning you to take care, he shoots people and thinks nothing of it."

"We had better be quiet then, just in case he is in the house and take him by surprise hadn't we."

"Yes, Sir."

"Let's go."

The car doors were closed gently to make no sound and Dan followed Cliff up the driveway and onto the porch. Cliff tried the door, it gave way. They stood in the dark hall not knowing which door to go through when they heard a door closing above them. Someone was upstairs.

Cliff pointed up the stairs and Dan took them one at a time, testing for creaks as he put his weight on them. He made it to the top of the stairs and waited until Cliff joined him.

The sound of running water told them that someone was in the bathroom, either running a bath or in the shower. The glass panel in the bathroom door was frosted and steamed up but it didn't obscure the shape of a man's head that appeared on the other side of the door. Nor did the shape on the other side of the door hesitate to open it and leave the bathroom.

Dan pounced on Peter Squires and Cliff made a dive for his legs. They buckled under the weight of the chief constable and Peter fell backwards hitting his head on the doorframe as he went down, and it knocked him unconscious.

Before Peter came round, Dan pulled out his handcuffs and handcuffed Peter's hands behind his back, Dan was taking no chances. Then he went into the bathroom and turned off the taps.

"Good work Dan, we had better find him some trousers before he's taken to the station. There might be passers-by when he's taken from the car. We can do without irate women screaming the heaven's down. Naked men and all that."

"Lucky it was Peter Squires, Sir, or we could have been in big trouble, molesting an innocent person," Dan said.

"Rubbish, even if it wasn't Peter Squires, this person would still have been in the house illegally This is Rhoda's house and they shouldn't have been in here, so no comeback on us," countered Cliff.

Trousers were found and they pulled them over Peter's hips and zipped them up and buttoned the waistband. That should stop them from dropping down.

"Is there anybody you can trust at Glaston police station to call and come and pick this man up and make sure he's safe in custody until tomorrow morning?" Cliff asked Dan. You and I need to stay here and do a search."

"There is an officer called Frank Boxer, I think he can be trusted. I'm not sure that Frank is very impressed with our inspector at Glaston. Only thing is, Frank will be off duty by now, I think he's on the day shift this week."

"Have you got his number?"

"Yes, on my phone."

"Ring him and ask him if he's up for a bit of overtime."

"Hello Frank, this is Dan. We have an arrest here, and we need someone to come over to Beech Avenue, you know, Glenda Stanton's place, and take the prisoner to Glaston Police Station and book him and make sure he's locked up tight. No mistakes, he's a dangerous man."

"You do know it's overtime, don't you? Inspector Longreen will never authorise overtime."

"It's not Inspector Longreen that's doing the authorising Frank, it's Chief Constable Broadman."

"In that case, we'll be there in half an hour. I'll ring Eddy. See you in a bit."

"He'll be here in half an hour," Dan told Cliff.

"Good. Let's take a quick look around and see what we can find while we are waiting. Is he safe to leave?" Cliff nodded at the inert body of Peter Squires.

"He's still out cold, but just in case he comes to, I'll try to find something to tie his legs together with so he can't run off."

When he was satisfied that Squires was going nowhere, Dan went downstairs to scout around and Cliff stayed upstairs.

It wasn't long before Dan came across a holdall which he opened and looked inside. There were four large ledgers and three smaller books that looked like diaries. Before Dan took them out, he took a photo of the holdall with his phone and also a photo of the books inside. Then he shouted Cliff down, he needed to see this.

They heard the sound of a car pulling up at the front of the house and Frank and Eddy appeared at the door, "Come in lads, good of you to come at such short notice. Dan will take you upstairs and show you where your prisoner is. You might have to get the duty doctor to have a look at him when you have him safely locked up."

"Very well, Sir, I will see to that. Do I need to get in touch with Inspector Longreen to let him know what's happening?" Frank asked.

"No, I will see to that. You just take this prisoner in, charge him with murder for starters, no doubt we will be able to add other things to the list, but for now, murder will do. Understand?"

"Perfectly Sir."

"Good, let's get on with it, then we can all go home. If Inspector Longreen questions you over it, tell him I told you not to trouble him this late at night. That should cover your back. If you find yourself in any trouble over it, let me know."

Chapter Fifteen

Cliff and Dan went back to Low Valley House taking the holdall with them. Dan produced a box of rubber gloves and they all took a pair and put them on. Cliff told them that they had to take care when handling the books, he didn't want anyone leaving any fingerprints on them. Then he took out the four ledgers and three dairies and placed them on the coffee table. "Take your pick," he said.

Jacob, Luther, Dan and Jasmin, all took a ledger each and then Cliff, Rhoda and Sally selected one of the diaries. They began to read.

Half an hour into the reading Rhoda said, "Listen to this," and she began:

" *'Friday the thirteenth of July, Huggy called, said there was hell on at Tree House. Harrison has had his counterfeit plates stolen. Marley is in a rage. Harrison made a quick escape, he knows what Marley is like when he's in a rage. Valerie did not make an appearance. Huggy is the best of the lot, wish it was just Huggy and me, I have a lot to thank Huggy for.'* "

"What do you think of that?"

"That's when the counterfeit plates vanished then, Friday the thirteenth, unlucky for some," said Luther.

"Does it say Huggy knows who took them?" asked Dan.

"No, that is the only thing it says," replied Rhoda.

"Anything in your ledger of any interest?" Dan asked Luther.

"No, just the normal in and out stuff. Nothing that stands out."

"What about you Jacob?" Dan asked.

"No, nothing of interest in mine either, like Luther, normal in and out stuff."

"Anything of interest in the diary Cliff?" Dan wanted to know.

"More interesting than I wanted to know about. Damn it," Cliff told them.

They all sat looking at him, his head buried in the diary.

"This diary contains personal payments to people used by InGuesty, or Marley Burton whichever you want to call him, for favours rendered. One name that I have come across is no surprise, I was expecting that. The other, I was hoping against hope, his name would not come up, but it has. This confirms the rumours that have reached our ears. Too much to ask for, that the rumours weren't correct I guess," Cliff said.

"Who are they?" asked Rhoda.

Cliff looked up from his book and smiled at her, "Do you really want to know?"

"Yes, of course, I do. You can't come out with a statement like that and expect us not to want to know."

"The first name we all know about is Gary Harrison. The second name some of you might not recognise. Inspector Reg Longreen," Cliff looked pointedly at Dan.

"Christ," remarked Dan.

"Precisely," agreed Cliff.

"Who is Inspector Reg Longreen?" asked Rhoda.

"My inspector at Glaston Police Station," replied Dan.

Cliff continued, "We'd had suspicions regarding Inspector Longreen's honesty for a few months, but nothing concrete. So, when you and Jacob arrived at my desk and you told me you had been suspended for something you hadn't done, it came as no surprise to me.

"Coming back to Glaston with you both gave me a good excuse to try and do a bit of digging into things at Glaston without Longreen being suspicious. That's one of the reasons I showed interest in this case, but I was also looking forward to doing a bit of detective work as well. This chief constable job's all right but it's paperwork, paperwork, paperwork. And of course, there was an added bonus of working with Luther and Jacob again."

"What are we going to do now Sir," asked Dan.

"We are going to bed for the night lad, that's what we are going to do. Then in the morning, you are going back to work as if nothing was wrong, and I am going back to Barrow Police Station with all this lot. Let the professional moneymen take a look at it. And I think I need to have a meeting with the powers that be over Longreen. That's if we can beg a bed for the night," Cliff looked across at Luther and Jacob.

"You know there will always be a bed to lay your head on here Cliff, no need to beg," Luther told him.

"In that case, I will be off to bed now, I think I am getting too old for all this, maybe the desk job was a good move after all," Cliff stood up and Sally told him he knew where his bedroom was.

"Before you go Chief Inspector, may I ask you a question?" asked Rhoda.

Cliff stopped in his tracks and looked at her, "Of course."

"It's just that I have had a thought," confessed Rhoda.

"I will always be interested in your thoughts my dear," Cliff smiled at her.

"It was the other day really, I was wondering, well I know this is going to sound stupid but the thought just popped into my head," she told them.

"And that thought was?" asked Cliff.

"You know when all this first started and my father mentioned in his letters about a camera, has the camera ever been found?"

"It has not," Cliff told her.

"What does it look like?" Rhoda wanted to know.

"We don't know, nobody has seen it," Cliff replied.

"When I was going through my father's things before the house clearance man came, I found a shoebox in one of the cupboards. It had a little black thing inside, along with some papers. I took the shoebox home and put it at the bottom of my cubbyhole under the stairs. I have never examined the contents of the shoebox. I did intend to have a look, to see what all that paperwork was about. But I forgot. I only remembered it the other day," explained Rhoda.

Silence reigned in the room, then Luther stood up and held his hand out to her, "Come on, thought of the day, let's get you back to Chubb Lane and retrieve your little black thing, so Cliff can take it back to his tech men when he leaves tomorrow."

"It's not a big thing, and it doesn't even look like a camera, not that I took it out to examine it, it might be nothing," said Rhoda.

"It's the camera. We need to go now because Cliff is leaving first thing in the morning. We will leave the shoebox on the kitchen table for you Cliff, in case you are up and away before we get up. I will make sure Rhoda gets back to the bungalow before I retire, make sure she's properly tucked in for the night," Luther said.

"In that case, if you are taking Rhoda back to the bungalow, I think it would be more prudent if Jasmin and Bennie stayed here for the night." Jacob looked at Jasmin.

"I can find no fault with that plan," said Jasmin casting down her eyes in mock embarrassment.

"That leaves just you and me Sally. I had better walk you back to your little bungalow and make sure you are safely tucked in for the night," Dan remarked.

"I can find no fault with that plan," grinned Sally.

"In that case, after you." Dan stood up and held out his hand and Sally took it.

The next morning when Dan made his way back to the house and into the kitchen, Luther and Jacob were just finishing off their coffee. "Good morning, lazy bones," Sally remarked.

"Good morning to all of you too. That was the best night's sleep I've had for ages," said Dan.

"I wonder why," commented Luther.

Dan chose to ignore him and asked, "Where's Cliff?"

"Left at first light, said he had a lot to do," said Jacob.

"I'm glad I'm not in his shoes," Dan told them.

"I think that can be said for all of us," agreed Luther.

"Did you find the camera last night?" Dan wanted to know.

"We did. It's one of those high-tech jobs, must have cost a fortune. It was also a video recorder. I'd say it was what was used to record the information on the DVD. If the shoebox is not on the kitchen table, Cliff has taken it with him," Luther informed him.

"Where's Jasmin?" Dan asked.

"Went back to the bungalow, took the long way round along the path to give Bennie his morning run. Rhoda is going to make them breakfast. She's been taking cooking lessons from Sally so she's practising on Jasmin. Suits me, by the time we are married she'll be as good a cook as our Sal. I was leaving to come back here for my breakfast when Jasmin arrived back at the bungalow," Luther informed him.

"We have to be going too, Luther," said Jacob. "We have been neglecting the business these past few weeks. We will leave you in the capable hands of Sally. See you around."

Luther went over and kissed Sally on the cheek, then followed Jacob out to their cars.

"What was in the diary you were reading last night, Sal?" Dan asked.

"Don't know, I couldn't understand it, but I got the impression it was about a single person. No names mentioned, but whoever it is that the diary is about, he was a trained killer.

"It had something to do with being in the jungle, it didn't name which jungle and the brushes he'd had with the drug dealers. He'd had to learn how to kill with his bare hands because of the people he was dealing with. Drug traffickers, that sort of thing. No noise that way. Not a very nice read, believe me. He'd learnt some complicated kung fu moves whilst in China. Apparently, it was a fight for survival."

"It's Peter Squires writing about himself. Squires will have gone to China to do dealings with the drug traffickers. He told everybody that he worked away on the oil rigs as a cover story. I'll check it out when I get back to the station," said Dan.

"How are you going to check it out at the station?" Sally wanted to know.

"Ask Peter himself, and if he won't tell me, I'll ask Marley. Marley tells us anything we want to know," was Dan's answer.

"The diary said that this person had travelled the world and seen things he hadn't wished to see. He'd done things at first, that he didn't want to do, but he became an expert at survival. Getting rid of people who threatened him, was one of the things he had become an expert at. It had become a way of life and it held no meaning now, kill or be killed," Sally told Dan.

"You make the best breakfasts in the world Sal, that was delicious, I shall have to find a way of thanking you next time I see you, but I really must be off to work now. Will I see you tonight?"

"Here or your place?"

"I think my place would be nice for a change, just the two of us and no work. I finish work at five, I will be home for half past and it will be nice if dinner was on the table," Dan told her and he fished in his pocket and pulled out his house key.

He went over to her, took her in his arms and kissed her, "Here is my house key, you know my address,

256

please feel free to call any time you want, get used to the place for when you are living there permanently. See you tonight my darling, got to go."

Sally looked down at the key in her hand, closed her fingers over it and held her hand to her chest. Sally didn't think she would ever meet a man she would be able to trust again, and here she was madly in love and putting her trust in a man she had only known for a few days.

She slipped the key into her pocket and attacked the remains of the breakfast.

Back at the station, Dan decided to have Squires in the interview room, but because he knew Peter was a dangerous man, he went to see if Frank was working that day and discovered him working at the front desk.

"Hi Frank, is there anyone that can take over the front desk for about an hour while you come with me and sit in on an interview with the man you arrested at Beech Avenue, last night?"

"Eddy's next door, I'll ask him to take over."

When Dan had made sure everything was ready in the interview room, Peter Squires was brought in.

"Take a seat please Mr Squires," Dan told him.

The recording machine was switched on and all those who were present gave their names.

Peter looked at Dan and asked, "Are you the copper that brought me down at Glenda's?"

"One of them," confirmed Dan.

"Oh, there was more than one of you was there. That makes me feel better, you know if it took more than one copper to take me down. How did you know where I was?" Peter asked.

"Does it matter?" asked Dan.

"Hell yes, it matters. I have been to some pretty remote places and dealt with some pretty mean characters. It goes against the grain to be caught with my pants down. It matters."

"Well, I am not going to tell you and give you the satisfaction of knowing. What I will tell you is, you left the front door of Glenda's house unlocked. Now that was very shabby for such a professional survivor."

"I know I did. Very shabby indeed. But in my defence, I had to break the lock on the front door because I didn't have the key to gain entry. I had to get in as quickly as I could and hope nobody saw me. I had been into Glenda's shed prior to this, looking for a camera Huggy had told Marley he had hidden in there. In one of the drawers, I had seen some old bolts and sockets and a couple of old latches.

"I intended to wait until it was dark and go and get a couple of bolts to fasten onto the inside of the front door before I went to bed. I didn't want the neighbours seeing me going into the shed, better to do it in the dark. I didn't expect a visit from the police a couple of hours after I had gone to ground in Beech Avenue, or anyone else come to that. It was a crime scene and empty. But that is no excuse for leaving the front door unlocked, I knew better. I should have secured it somehow until I had managed to get the bolts."

"I have not brought you to the interview room to discuss your lapse on a survival strategy, let's move on, shall we? Why did you find it necessary to go into hiding?"

"I think you already know the answer to that."

"I would like to hear you say it, for the purpose of the tape recording."

"I received a phone call from your Inspector Longreen. He told me that the game was up, you had the gun that I had planted on Huggy and you knew it was I who had planted it. He also told me that you had the counterfeit plates in your possession and that Glenda Stanton had nothing to do with them.

"That in all likelihood, she had no idea where they were. He said I'd had no reason to kill her. Of course, I had. She and Huggy were an item. He owned Beech Avenue where she lived, rent-free and she provided Huggy with all the home comforts he needed.

"I also know that she used to innocently ask Harrison questions when he called to see her. If she got any dirt on anybody, she would pass it on to Huggy. She tried it on with me once, but it didn't work. I left her with the understanding that she had better not try asking me questions that she has no right in knowing the answers to. She never did ask after that, because she knew what would happen to her if she did," smirked Peter.

"Reg Longreen also told me that the counterfeit plates were found in Huggy's safety deposit box at the bank. That daughter of his had a key and she took the police with her when she went to the bank to open the box. She gave them the plates, bloody idiot, they were worth a fortune.

"I bet that's how Huggy knew about the plates. Glenda will have whittled it out of Harrison and passed the information onto Huggy."

"You don't seem to have any conscience with regard to providing information against other members of the syndicate as well as one of my fellow officers," said Dan.

"You will have found the ledgers and diaries that I took with me to Beech Avenue, it's all in there. No need to try to cover anything up. I know I am going down for a long time so what's the point in fighting it? Anyway, I have no liking for Reg Longreen, he thought he could get away with anything because of his position. I've made sure he will be investigated because there is lots of proof in one of the diaries of how much he's been paid and which bank it has been paid into.

"Before I left the country, I was going to post the holdall onto you. I had no need of it now the syndicate had been broken up. Longreen was not going to get away with the part he played in this."

"Why were the payments made?"

"A phone call was all it took. He knew when there was going to be a raid by the police because they had information that there was a party on. All we had to do was change the venue. Longreen provided information, I paid him a premium. He thought he was God that one, I've proved he wasn't. With the information in that diary, I've brought down more people than Reg Longreen.

"I'm happy with my lot. Marley's also banged up. When I first met Trevor Crast, I was a happy teenager, good parents, although at the time I fought against their restrictions. Trevor Crast found me late one night drunk out of my skull and he took me to Tree House. I could do what I wanted, when I wanted and he also provided me with money, I worshipped him.

"But as in life, nothing is free and I soon started to realise that Trevor was a bad man. I was introduced to drug dealing and because my parents had made sure I got a good education, Trevor put me in charge of his accounts. I came to hate him; I had gone from worshipping him to hating him with a passion. Then Marley came on the scene and my worshipping was transferred from Trevor to Marley, especially when Trevor vanished. I had no proof but I knew Marley had done Trevor in, did I care? Hell no.

"I soon became aware that Marley was even worse than Trevor. He had me travelling to other countries setting up drug deals with some of the hardest men you don't want to meet. I had to fight for my survival. He still kept me on as the accountant as well as making me travel the world. I was privy to some privileged information and unknowing to Marley, I made diaries with information in them that he had no knowledge about.

"It's all in the diaries, hidden money, covert payments, all listed. Clive Huggard was the most decent of the lot of them if you could ever class Huggy as decent. He did a lot of smuggling, not drugs, but Brandy, whisky and cigarettes. He refused to deal in drugs, how he got away with that is something we will never know now.

"If Marley said you deal in drugs, you deal in drugs. But Huggy's side of smuggling made Huggy and Marley, a lot of money. I think Huggy's circumstances were like mine; he came across Trevor Crast one night when he was drunk, and he was doomed before his life had begun.

"I know Marley has bandied my name around to you lot, Longreen told me. He'll have his day at my hands I can promise you that. If anyone is a God it's me. A measly accountant, bringing them all down. No point in trying to hide any of it, is there? And there is no point in this interview either, you have all you need to take us all down in the ledgers and diaries.

"The names in the ledgers you will not know, and you will never find out the identities of the people listed in the ledgers. False names are used in all transactions. But one of the diaries is for my own personal use. I listed names and account numbers that the money was paid into, in that diary. It was insurance in case a day like this arrived and I knew it would, so I named names. Marley does not know it exists."

"How did you become acquainted with Glenda?"

"Not much I can tell you about her. She was an idle cow, but Huggy liked her. He kept her for his own personal pleasures and when any of us wanted a favour, sex-wise, Huggy put us onto Glenda. Glenda provided the sex, we provided Glenda with money. Huggy didn't mind sharing her, we didn't mind using her," Peter confessed.

"In that case, you'll be escorted back to your cell. Interview ended ten forty-five," Dan said looking at his watch.

Back behind the front desk, Dan said to Frank, "I had to end that interview Frank or I would have knocked his head off his shoulders. I just couldn't sit and listen to what he had to say any longer. I need a partner Frank, if I can swing it would you be interested?"

"Would I be interested? I'd snatch your hand off. Going out and doing a bit of detecting work was really interesting and satisfying. I've been on desk duty for six months now, I'd love to get out on the streets with you," Frank replied.

"I'll have to have a word with Chief Constable Broadman about it. After what we've heard and what I have read in one of the diaries, I can't go to Inspector Longreen. I have no need to tell you not to talk about what you heard in the interview room with anybody else of course. The powers that be will have to deal with Longreen, thank God for that," Dan informed him.

Jasmin and Rhoda, after finishing off their breakfast took Bennie out for his walk. The summer was turning into autumn and the days were getting shorter and colder but it was a beautiful sunny morning, not too hot, just nice for a stroll in the sunshine.

"Jasmin, I'm bored. I'm not used to having nothing to do and the novelty has worn off."

"I know exactly what you mean, I'm bored too. I need a job. I know I keep harping on about it, but it's on my mind. This is not a life Rhoda; I need to be doing something. As you say, we need something to do to occupy our minds. If I do as Jacob says and have a credit card from him, I would feel like a kept woman."

"I've got plenty of money now, you can have a couple of bundles out of the safety deposit box. Less for the tax man to find out about."

Jasmin laughed, "That's very kind of you Rhoda, and it's not that I don't appreciate the offer, it is very generous of you. But being given money by you is no different to me being given money by Jacob. I need a job; I have a little money in the bank for my monthly mortgage to come out of, but that's not going to last forever."

"Luther said the same to me, about him having enough money for the both of us. I too didn't like the thought of being a kept woman so I know how you feel.

I did ask Luther what I should do with all this money from my father once it is transferred into my name. He told me I could do whatever I like with it."

Jasmin asked, "What did you tell him you wanted to do with it?"

"I told Luther that I would like to start up a dog rescue centre. I didn't know I liked dogs until I met Bennie and he has given me so much love and pleasure, and he has never demanded anything back in return. He was a rescue dog, and you rescued him. I don't like to think about what would have happened to him if you hadn't."

"That is a brilliant idea, Rhoda."

"Yes, I know it is. But when I think of what's involved to even start a centre up let alone run it, puts me off."

"It would certainly take some organising, I'll give you that," agreed Jasmin

"Well, they do say it's the thought that counts, so maybe I won't bother," admitted Rhoda.

"When do you think we can go home? If Peter Squires has been arrested, I don't see why we should have to stay here. Do you?" asked Jasmin.

"No, let's ask Jacob and Luther tonight if we can go home again. Give us a bit of space from each other and see if we all like each other then, as much as we do now," agreed Rhoda.

"I agree. At least something nice has come out of all this, our friendship," replied Jasmin.

"And Bennie. I shall be over to take Bennie for a walk whether you like it or not."

"I will like that very much."

"We haven't had our daily run yet," Rhoda said.

"Shall we turn around while Bennie is busy up front and start our run, when he sees us running, he'll give chase."

Rhoda looked at Jasmin with a sparkle in her eye, "I'm game."

Sally finished putting the breakfast things away and put on her coat. She was going to go to Dan's house and see what awaited her there. She couldn't wait to see it, to see what was to become her own home. A house on a public lane, with people walking past and the postman calling. Next door neighbours, she'd keep her fingers crossed they were better neighbours than Jasmin got when she had moved house.

Before she left, she went in search of Jasmin and Rhoda and as she walked along the path that led from Low Valley House to the bungalow, she saw them running for their lives and Bennie chasing them. They were both laughing and it made Sally feel so happy to see life on the grounds of Low Valley House, it had been a depressing place to live only she hadn't realised it until now.

Sally waited and watched as the two ladies headed towards her, a smile on her face. Bennie had nearly caught the ladies up and they were giggling with delight.

Bennie went charging past Jasmin and Rhoda when he saw Sally and she was greeted by enthusiastic barks and was nearly sent to the ground when he jumped up at her.

Sally in return, once Bennie had all four feet back on the ground, expressed her delight at seeing him by bending down and covering him with pats and hugs.

"Hello Sally, if we had known you were calling, we would have waited for you, and you could have come for a walk with us," Jasmin told her.

"That's very kind of you Jasmin but I had things to do. Dan has given me the key to his house and I am going to have a nose around, I can't wait. I am going to have a meal ready for him when he returns from work this evening," Sally told them.

"You're going to live at Dan's?" asked Rhoda.

"No, just visiting. But Dan said I had to go and see if living there with him will suit me before we both get hurt. He thinks I'll miss this place and all the luxury that goes with it."

"Will you miss this place?" Jasmin asked.

"No. I want a place of my own. I know I haven't known Dan very long but I'm not going to let this opportunity pass me by. To hell with the gossip, it's my happiness that's at stake, not theirs. If I have made a mistake then I will have to live with it, make the best of it, and let the gossipers say, 'I told you so'."

"Good for you, it's like Jasmin and me, we keep saying it's all been too fast for us all, but I am not as brave as you are Sally. I have had too many disappointments in my life to dare to grab what Luther has given me as permanent. I wish you all the luck in the world. I wish I dare do it," Rhoda told her.

"It will last with you and Luther, Rhoda. I have never seen Luther like this before. You have certainly made a huge impression on him," Sally told her.

"Do you think so? Oh, I do hope you are right."

"I must be going now, I came to see you to ask if you will have a meal ready for Jacob and Luther tonight. I am hoping to stay the night at Dan's, although he doesn't know it yet," grinned Sally.

"Of course, we will. It will be nice to have something to do for a change. Rhoda and I were just discussing going home. Now Peter Squires has been arrested there is nobody else for Rhoda and me to be frightened of," said Jasmin.

"If we are going to be in charge of the kitchen this afternoon, we will walk you back to Low Valley House. I am assuming your car is still down there."

"It is, and the door to the house is open, no need to lock it, nobody's going to get in."

Jasmin and Rhoda watched as Sally drove down the driveway and out of the side gates and waited until they had closed behind her.

"We have the house to ourselves Rhoda for a few hours, shall we go on an investigation? There must be rooms in a place as big as this that are empty. It will make a change from sitting in the bungalow and walking Bennie."

"No reason why we shouldn't," Rhoda said turning for the wide spiral staircase.

The house was vast indeed. Some of the rooms they had already been in, but some they had not. Some of the rooms were bare, some were sparsely furnished and some were beautiful and very tastefully decorated.

"What do you think about this house?" Jasmin asked.

"It's rather large," commented Rhoda. "I'm glad I'm not the one that has to clean it, I hate cleaning. Never mind having to pay the gas and electricity bills."

Jasmin laughed, "I think if you were the mistress of this house, you would be able to pay a cleaner."

"Did Sally do all this upkeep?" Rhoda wanted to know.

"I would say yes, it would have given her something to do."

"No wonder she grabbed Dan's hand off to go and live with him," said Rhoda.

"I don't think housework is the reason why Sally has gone to spend the night with Dan."

"What then?"

"They might like talking about nipples and crisps."

Rhoda and Jasmin looked at each other and burst out laughing. "Can't think of anything better to talk about," Rhoda said.

"Do you know what I think about this place?" Jasmin asked.

"No, do tell."

"I think it would make an excellent golf club. All these exquisite rooms with en-suite, and the grounds would make a perfect golf course, ups, downs, twists and flats. Perfect for a golf course.

"All the rich people would pay a bomb to be a member of a golf club here. Especially if glamorous girls were to be caddies instead of men. Also, why not have glamorous girls as golf coaches too? Men would flock to the place."

"You've got to be kidding me," Rhoda told her.

"No, I'm not. When I've been out with Bennie walking the grounds, the idea just popped into my head. Then walking around inside the house, it all seemed to click together. The perfect setting for a golf club."

"You know what you've done now don't you?" Rhoda asked.

"No, what have I done?"

"You've put the idea into my head, you've brainwashed me. Now when I'm out with Bennie I'm going to see golf balls flying through the air, and sand bunkers and flags stuck in holes."

"At the rate you are losing weight Rhoda, you could be one of the glamorous caddie girls. Not that I think Luther would allow it, but it's a nice thought."

"Like hell it is. Me a glamorous caddie girl? Get a life woman," Rhoda scoffed.

Jasmin and Rhoda shared the vegetable peeling, table laying and setting out of the cutlery and had an enjoyable afternoon pottering about in the kitchen and when Jacob and Luther entered the house, they were greeted by the smell of home cooking.

"Something smells good," remarked Luther as they entered the dining room.

"Hello you two, where's our Sal?" asked Luther.

"She went to make dinner for Dan. She told us to tell you she's stopping there tonight," Rhoda told him.

"Is she now, I only hope she knows what she's doing," said Luther.

"She knows what she's doing better than Jasmin and me, we have no idea what we are doing from one day to the next," Rhoda informed him.

"Don't you like living here?" asked Luther.

"Not at first, I didn't. Now I'm getting used to it. I enjoy the freedom and love all this company. I never dreamt I would have friends like you."

"Only friends?" Luther wanted to know.

"All right then, or a lover," admitted Rhoda. "Is that what you wanted to hear?"

"Oh, yes," said a satisfied Luther.

"Is Sally coming back?" asked Jacob.

"I think so. She said she was only staying the night," replied Jasmin.

"I was thinking, if Sally is leaving to go and live with Dan, we will be looking for someone to replace her," Jacob told them.

"You'd better mind your backs if Jasmin's thinking of taking over from Sally. She gets inside your head," Rhoda warned.

"What do you mean by that?" asked Luther.

"She got into my head this afternoon," Rhoda told him. "And the thought is still there."

"What thought has she put into your head? You have enough thoughts of your own without Jasmin adding to them," Jacob wanted to know.

"We had a proper look around the house this afternoon and Jasmin asked me what I thought about the house, I wish she hadn't now," complained Rhoda.

"Didn't she approve of it?" Jacob asked.

"Too much, she liked it too much. It got her imagination going and now I can't get the image out of my head," she replied.

"Are we allowed to share your image?" Jacob asked.

"I don't see why not. It's your house."

"And the image is?" asked Luther.

"Jasmin has turned this place into a golf club and she wants me to be a glamorous caddie girl for all the rich golfing nutters."

"Interesting," commented Jacob.

"Bloody fantastic image if you ask me," remarked Luther.

"You want to turn your house into a golf club?" asked an astounded Rhoda.

"Haven't got round to thinking about a golf club. Can't get you out of my head dressed up as a sexy caddie girl," he replied.

"Well, it's not going to happen. I am not dressing up as a caddie girl, so you can forget it," she informed him.

"We'll talk about it later," Luther said.

"You know, that's not such a bad idea," said Jacob.

"Not you as well. It's not going to happen, I am not going to get dressed up as a caddie girl and go parading around the grounds, not for you or for anyone else," said an indignant Rhoda.

Jacob laughed, "I didn't mean you getting dressed up as a caddie girl Rhoda. I meant about turning this place into a golfing club. You're right you know; it would make a splendid private golf club.

"In fact, Luther and I have been trying to think of another line of work. We have made a fortune in the computer business but we have had enough of it now. We could sell off the IT business and start up a golf club. What do you think Luther?"

"Sounds like a plan to me. Then I can stay at home and keep an eye on this sexy caddie girl."

Rhoda stood up and Luther asked, "Where are you going now?"

"I'm going into the pantry to see if Sally has left any crisps in any of the cupboards. I need comfort food." She left the table.

"Talk amongst yourselves," Luther said as he followed in Rhoda's footsteps.

Jacob looked across at Jasmin and smiled, "It's been nice coming home to find you in my house, Jasmin, it's a very comforting feeling. If Sally does leave and go to live with Dan, will you stay?"

"This house is a lot bigger than I am used to, it's taking some getting used to. But I must admit I enjoyed it in the kitchen cooking a meal for when you came home. I think like Rhoda, I am being brainwashed."

"Excellent," said Jacob.

"To be honest Jacob, I know it was my idea, but if I were to live here, I don't like the thought of people roaming around my house."

"I think I have to agree with you on that. We'll have to think of something else," agreed Jacob. "Will you stay until Sally makes up her mind one way or another, instead of going back home? I know you asked us earlier on if you could go home and it was agreed that we could see no reason now for you to be kept safe. As far as we know all danger has gone."

"We will stay until we see Sally again and see what has been agreed between her and Dan. Then we or rather I, will decide what I want to do. Rhoda will have to make her own mind up. But I think Luther has already decided what Rhoda is going to do. Don't you?"

Jacob smiled, "Oh yes. Rhoda's fate is signed and sealed. So is yours only you don't realise it yet. But I can wait at least another couple of weeks, but I warn you, that's all you're getting two weeks."

Jasmin looked across the table at the handsome young man with piercing blue eyes and said, "I like it when you're bossy."

"In that case, I shall have a sexy caddie girl outfit made especially for you so I can boss you around if that's what you are into. Luther is not going to get the better of me on this one."

"You haven't asked me what I think about that idea."

"You have no say in the matter. What's your favourite colour?"

"Yellow."

"Yellow caddie girl outfit it is then. Can't wait. I think it's a good idea if you and Rhoda stay here for the night," Jacob told her.

"Oh, and why would that be?"

"More convenient."

"In what way?"

"Easier for you to make my breakfast in the morning."

"What makes you think I am going to make your breakfast in the morning?"

"Because Sally's not here and someone has to make it."

"Are you offering me a job Mr Firth, or is it to be unpaid labour?"

"Can't think of anyone better to replace Sal, Miss Ward. You don't have to worry about payment, you will be paid, one way or another."

"I think I'll take you up on the offer of a bed for the night, but I will have to give the job offer some thought."

"Deal, my darling Jasmin. I'll have my secretary make up the contract."

Jasmin laughed, "You are impossible Jacob Firth."

"You will have to tame me, Jasmin Ward."

"I look forward to trying Sir."

"Good, let's go to bed."

"Can't do that, I have these dirty pots to see to, then I have to take Bennie for a walk."

"I shall help you take these pots to the dishwasher and accompany you and Bennie on your walk, then all three of us will be ready for bed."

"I wonder where Rhoda and Luther are?" commented Jasmin as the pots were stacked in the dishwasher.

"Knowing Luther, Rhoda will already be tucked up in bed."

A smile spread across Jasmin's face and Jacob said, "You and Rhoda have been the best thing that has happened to us in a long time. I have not seen Luther so happy since I met him."

"I think the same can be said about you and Luther for Rhoda and me. I think this has been the best time of her life. She didn't have a very happy childhood."

"What about you? Did you have a happy childhood?"

"My mother was a very good mother, but she was left to look after me when my father died. I missed him terribly. Since having to fend for myself, I realised what an exceptional job my mother had done. She must have gone without a lot to give me what she gave me and provide a roof over our heads. I have no complaints."

"Right Bennie, ready for a walk, boy?" asked Jacob.

Bennie on hearing the word 'walk' let Jacob know in no uncertain terms, he was ready for his walk.

When they were all seated at breakfast the next morning Jasmin said, "I have been thinking about what I said about turning this place into a golf club. Whilst lying in bed last night, I had a better idea. In fact, it was Rhoda that put the idea into my head, a few days ago. You said Jacob, that Luther and you have had enough of the IT business and it was decided that you would sell up and start up another project. The only thing with that was, you haven't hit on another project that takes your fancy yet."

"I haven't told you what to turn this place into," denied Rhoda.

"Oh, yes you did. I just haven't discussed it with anyone yet."

The overhead security screen pinged and Jacob glanced up. He saw the gate open and Sally's car enter.

"If I, were you, I wouldn't discuss it with Luther whatever it is. He'll turn everything round and you would end up turning this place into a brothel," Rhoda told them.

"Now that, Rhoda, is a suggestion to conjure with," Luther told her.

"If you make this place into a brothel, I'm out of here," Rhoda replied.

Sally entered the house to the sound of laughter and made her way towards it.

"Good morning, everyone. I think this is the first time the walls of this house have heard the sound of laughter," said Sally.

"Rhoda says she wants to turn this place into a brothel," her brother told her.

"I did no such thing," denied Rhoda.

"You little fibber, I may only have one eye but I have two ears and they can both hear extremely well and they heard you mention a brothel," countered Luther.

Sally looked over at Jasmin and Jasmin's eyes were brimming with laughter. A warm feeling of contentment engulfed Sally as she watched her brother gently teasing Rhoda. This lonely depressing house had suddenly turned into a happy place with laughter and dogs and love spilling out of the occupants' eyes.

Sally decided that she could now have a life of her own and she would feel no guilt in leaving her brother and Jacob to their own devices. They too had found that elusive word happiness.

"In that case, if this place is being turned into a brothel, I'm going to live with Dan. He asked me to go and live with him last night. I told him I couldn't leave my brother and Jacob to look after themselves. Now I know what you intend to turn this house into, all guilt has gone. I'm off. See you lot around, maybe." With that, she was off to pack her bags.

"She doesn't think you'll turn your home into a brothel, does she?" asked a shocked Rhoda.

"No, you goose, she knew I was only teasing you. Do you honestly think I'd let you live in a brothel? You had better not let me catch another man looking at you never mind thinking you belong in a brothel," Luther told her.

"Well, what is it that I said to you Jasmin, that gave you something to think about?" Rhoda wanted to know.

"You told me that you would like to start a dog rescue centre. It got my imagination going. Instead of just a dog rescue centre, what about an animal rescue centre?" Jasmin replied.

"You mean really set up a rescue centre? When we talked about it, I thought we agreed it entailed too much work," confessed Rhoda.

"Did you know," asked Jacob. "That Luther has hidden talents? He loves to sculpt. He has carved one or two beautiful figures that he hides away in a workshop just inside the wood at the back of Sally's bungalow. We could scatter these statues around the grounds and build some different size pens and a couple of aviaries to keep the animals and birds in, it would give us all something to do.

"We could invite the public in to see the animals and Luther's sculptures and make a minimal charge for entry to help pay for the animal food etcetera. I think that idea is much better than a golf club."

"It's certainly worth considering Jacob, I'll give you that," nodded Luther.

Rhoda looked at Luther, "Can I have a look at your sculptures?"

Luther replied, "My darling Rhoda, you may have a look at anything I've got, anytime the fancy takes you."

"Back to the brothel thing," commented Rhoda.

"I have also thought of something else for you to do. You can be a live model for me and I'll carve you in wood," Luther told her.

Rhoda was speechless.

Laughter was once again heard echoing around the walls of Low Valley House.

Chapter Sixteen

Reg Longreen, read the report on his desk. Not only was Marley Burton in his jail, but so was Peter Squires. A feeling of dread engulfed him. What was he to do? He decided to call back at the station that night when there was only a minimum of staff on duty and go and see Marley and Peter himself. He needed to know what had been said.

So far, he had received no files on either of the arrests, just the incident logs that have to be submitted at the end of each shift. Something was wrong. He needed to know what was going on. Reg dare not risk asking any of his men for the files of the two arrests. He didn't want to be seen taking undue interest in these two particular cases.

He finally allowed the two questions that had been pushed to the back of his mind to emerge. The first question involved Cliff Broadman and his continued presence at his police station. Cliff never discussed what he was doing there, he just turned up, did a bit of office work then went out. You do not question the chief of police.

The second question was, Dan Coltley. How did Dan Coltley come to be under the protection of the chief constable when he had suspended him from duty? There had been no discussion between Cliff and himself concerning the lifting of the suspension. Things weren't looking good for Reg, and he knew it.

It was eight o'clock that evening when Reg returned to the police station and only the skeleton staff remained. He went to the front desk and asked the officer in charge for the keys to the cells.

The officer handed them over to his superior without question, and Reg went in the direction of the cells. He had decided, that because Peter was the accountant, he was more likely to have information on him than Marley had. Reg unlocked the door of cell two, and in he walked.

"Well, who do we have here?" remarked Peter from his sitting position on the single hard wooden bed. "I was wondering when you would show up."

"Not so loud you idiot, keep your voice down," Reg told him.

"Who's going to hear us? Where's Marley?" Peter asked.

"In the next cell."

"I need to see him."

"Can't let you do that Peter."

"You don't have a choice."

"I can walk out of this cell and leave you to your fate."

"And I can tell your fellow officers where the account books are," bluffed Peter knowing full well that the police would have read the books by now.

"You'd do that?"

"Why not, what have I to lose? If you take me to see Marley, even if it's only for five minutes I might see my way to letting you know where the account books can be located. It might save you from joining Marley and me in the cells."

Reg thought about it and relented, "Five minutes, no more. Come with me."

Reg pushed Peter's cell door open and led him next door. When he had unlocked Marley's cell door, Reg ushered Peter in and pulled the door closed behind him, the cell door could not be locked from the inside.

"Visitors at this late hour, I am honoured," Marley said getting out of bed.

"Shut your mouth and listen," Peter told him.

"Not much point in threatening me, you are not going anywhere," smirked Marley.

"What I want to know is, have you told the police about me?"

"Of course. There was no point in trying to lie to them, they had all the information they needed to close the syndicate down. Huggy is the one you need to be mad at, he is the one that has been collecting information about the syndicate and hiding it all over the place. DVDs, photos and I think, it was Huggy that stole the counterfcit plates."

"You told the police about me; you shouldn't have done that Marley."

Without warning, Peter's right hand shot out and he placed a well-aimed karate chop to Marley's throat before Marley could do anything about it, Peter placed one hand at the back of Marley's head and the other under his chin and gave it a swift twist to the right and Marley went limp and slumped to the floor.

Reg was so shocked he couldn't move. Peter's right hand came up and the same karate chop hit Reg's throat and one of Peter's hands went to the back of Reg's head and the other under his chin and Reg joined Marley on the floor.

After checking to make sure neither of them had survived the attack, Peter calmly took the cell keys out of Reg's pocket, went outside into the corridor and locked the cell door behind him.

He pulled the spyhole back and looked inside the cell. He was filled with satisfaction. Marley down and Longreen down, a perfect ending. He didn't care what happened next, he wasn't going anywhere. He calmly flicked the cell keys back into the cell through the spyhole. He then went into his cell and pulled the door closed behind him.

He had done what he wanted to do; he had paid Marley back for all the hard times he had suffered just to make Marley a richer man. He had killed Reg Longreen because he didn't like the man. He too had personally gained out of his hard work and misfortune, and all the time being the perfect member of society. Neither of them would ever gain anything from his hard work again.

Peter felt good. He could have attempted an escape, but he didn't want to escape, he was tired, tired of running and hiding. He pulled the single rough woollen blanket off his bed, laid down, covered himself with it, and went to sleep.

By the time it got to midnight, the young officer at the front desk rang the inspector's phone line. No reply. He was not sure what to do for the best so, he rang Dan at home.

"Hello," came a sleepy voice from the other end of the phone.

"Dan, it's Ian from Glaston Police Station. I am so sorry to wake you, but something has happened and I don't know what to do about it."

"Why don't you ring the inspector, I thought he was senior officer on call-out duty tonight?"

"He is. It's just I don't really know how to put this without getting into trouble."

"Tell me, I won't tell anyone you rang me."

"Thanks, Dan. Inspector Longreen came back to work this evening and called at the front desk. He asked for the cell keys. I gave them to him; he didn't explain why he wanted them and that was at eight o'clock this evening. He hasn't returned with the keys yet. I have rung his office phone but there's no reply.

"Matt and Ray have had to go to a road traffic accident and Ken has gone to an assault. A man got drunk, went home and beat up his wife. That left only me at the station. I can't leave the front desk unattended and nip down to the cells to make sure everything is all right. What do you think I should do?"

Dan had by this time sat up in bed, "Ian, I don't want you to do anything. Do you understand? Don't say a word to anybody about this and I will deal with it. I'll be in touch shortly. Is that understood?"

"Yes, thank you, Dan."

"You are welcome. Goodbye."

Sally was woken by the sound of the telephone ringing and she turned to see Dan pulling on his underpants. "Trouble?" she asked.

"I would say so. Trouble is too fine a word for this complication. I am going to have to ring Chief Constable Broadman about this, see what he wants me to do." Dan turned and kissed her. "Wish me luck."

"Good luck," she said and when he had left the bedroom she turned over and went back to sleep.

"Hello, who the devil is this ringing me at this time of night," Chief Constable Broadman raged.

"Sorry Sir, it's Dan. I think we have a problem at Glaston. I have just had a phone call from the young officer on desk duty. Reg Longreen has taken the cell keys. He took them at eight o'clock this evening and he has not returned them to the front desk yet. What if he's freed Marley and Squires and done a bunk?"

"Devil take it, what was the young idiot doing giving the cell keys out? You'd better get back to the station and wait until I arrive. I'll put the blue lights on so expect me in a couple of hours or less. Have you got that?" He hung up.

Dan walked into the police station to find the young officer with a worried look on his face, "Dan, thank God you're here. Inspector Longreen has still not returned with the keys. What's going on?"

"Nothing for you to get yourself in a twist over Ian, can't say anything yet, but no doubt you and everyone else will find out sooner or later. Chief Constable Broadman is on his way and should be here in a couple of hours. I'll nip to the cells and see if I can see Inspector Longreen. Don't fret yourself, you will be all right," Dan told him.

Dan took the spare key to the metal security grill door that led to the corridor that housed the cells, from behind the front desk and headed in that direction. He pushed at the security door and it gave way. The door had been left unlocked. He made sure that the metal door was locked behind him before he went to have a look in the cells that held Marley and Squires secure.

He quietly pulled back the spyhole cover of Marley's cell. He was shocked to see Marley, with his head at an odd angle, laying on the floor of his cell. Inspector Longreen was laid next to him, his head was at an odd angle too.

Dan was about to take hold of the door handle and see if it was open, then he decided it would be better not to touch anything and wait until the chief constable arrived and let him deal with it.

Then Dan went to the cell next to Marley's and pulled the spyhole cover back. Peter was laying on his bed with his back to the door and the rough blanket covering his body. Was he alive or, like his fellow cellmate, lying dead in his cell? Dan could not tell. He left the cell corridor making sure that the metal door was securely locked before he went back to the front desk and sat next to Ian. They sat in silence and waited for the arrival of Chief Constable Broadman.

Dan and Ian were on their second cup of tea when Cliff walked into the police station. "Any tea left for me?" he asked.

"I'll make a brew and bring it into the office, you're going to need it," Dan told him.

Dan placed the cup of tea in front of Cliff and sat down opposite him. "Now then lad, what's all this about?"

"I don't know Sir. After phoning you I came over to the station and went to have a look in the cells. I got the shock of my life Sir, Inspector Longreen and Marley Burton are both lying on the floor and it looks to me like they have both had their necks broken." Dan went on to explain what else he had seen down in the cells.

"But there is only one of them that could have done it, nobody else has been near the cells. Unless Inspector

Longreen let someone in through the back door. I'm tipping its Squires. I didn't try his door for the same reason I didn't try the door to Marley's cell. Evidence. And anyway, I wasn't going to risk going into Squires cell on my own."

"You did the right thing lad. Longreen and Burton are both dead?"

"I would say so Sir, there's no way either of them could be alive with the position of their heads. But like I said, I didn't go into the cell. I hope to God they are dead; I would feel really bad if I could have saved either of them and I did nothing about it."

"This is bad business Dan."

"You don't have to tell me that Sir, that's why I rang you."

Cliff lifted the cup to his mouth and drained the contents, "How did you get into the corridor to the cells if you have no keys?"

"There's a spare key for the metal door to the corridor kept behind the front desk, for emergencies. I used that to gain entry and made sure the door was locked behind me after I'd seen the disasters in the cells."

"Better go and have a look then shall we."

After Dan collected the spare key from behind the front desk, Cliff followed Dan along the corridor until he stopped at Marley's cell. He pulled the spyhole back and stood aside for Cliff to have a look.

"Hell, fire and damn nation, it looks like you are right lad. Not much doubt their necks have been snapped. You haven't tried the door you say?"

"No, Sir, I thought it best not to."

"Quite right. But I think the cell door will be locked. I can see the keys on the floor. Not much we can do for those two. We'll have to get the crime scene people in before we do anything else. Which cell is Squires in?"

"Next cell on, Sir." Dan went and opened Peter's spyhole and Cliff looked in.

Peter was sitting up in bed and when he heard the spyhole open, he looked straight at it and put two fingers up to whoever it was that was spying on him.

Cliff closed the spyhole door and said, "That one's alive and kicking. Did you try his door?"

"No, Sir I did not."

"Good, then let's make a phone call to the crime scene people and let them do their stuff before we go charging in. Got to do this right lad, there is going to be a hell of a lot of unwanted publicity. Not good for the police, two of their own involved with a smuggling syndicate. The diary has confirmed that. Longreen and Harrison were on the take."

"What do you want me to do now Sir?" Dan asked.

"I want you to stay here and see to the crime scene people. Once they have arrived you should go home and get some rest. Nothing for you to do until the CSI has completed what they have to do, you will only get in the way.

"I am going straight back to the office, I need to inform people. I am not looking forward to this lad, but I'll tell you one thing, whoever did this deserves a medal, not an easy thing to do whilst being locked up in jail, murder two people, one an inspector of police at that. Got rid of a couple of hard cases to boot, and made the world a bit better place."

"What about Squires? It can only have been him that had access to the next cell. There is only him and Marley locked up at the moment. We can't just leave it like this. His cell door will be unlocked. It has to be, he can't lock himself in from the inside," Dan remarked.

"I think he's safe for now, if he had wanted to escape, he would have done so before we arrived. We made sure the security door to the cells was locked. If he does decide to leave his cell, he will only get as far as the metal security door," Cliff told him.

Before Cliff had returned to Barrow police station, he had rung his old mate, Sergeant Jack Webster, explained the situation at the station and told him that, temporarily, he was now in charge of the station. He told him to get down there as soon as he could and get abreast of things as best, he could. He told him that Dan Coltley was at the station and that he would explain things to him as he had to go back to Barrow.

The crime scene people arrived and the first thing they encountered was, Marley's cell door was locked, and they could not gain entry. Before Dan could go home, he had to go into the main office and sign the spare set of keys to the cells, out of the safe. He led the CSI team down the corridor, unlocked the security door and showed them to Marley's cell. He explained about the prisoner in the next cell and warned them to be careful. When Jack arrived to take over from him, Dan explained the situation, and then made his way home.

Sally was still in bed when Dan got home so he undressed and climbed in beside her. Sally turned into him and he enfolded her in his arms and said, "It is so nice to come home to a warm body in my bed. I love you, Sally, you do know that don't you?"

"Yes, I do, and I love you back Dan Coltley."

"I don't even know your surname," Dan told her.

"Deeman, my name is Sally Deeman. Deeman spelt D-e-e-m-a-n."

"Sally Deeman or Sally Coltley, I know which I prefer."

Sally smiled and settled more comfortably in bed.

Chapter Seventeen

Sally arrived at Low Valley House early the next morning and found all four of them in the kitchen. She told them that she was going to pack her bags.

After Jacob and Luther had left for work, Jasmin and Rhoda had helped Sally pack and then they found themselves once again alone. They set off into the woods to find Luther's workshop, with Bennie happily bouncing along beside them. Luther had told Rhoda that there was no key needed to access the workshop and they couldn't wait to see inside.

The workshop turned out to be more of a warehouse than a workshop, from the outside, only the front of the workshop could be seen but once inside, it was vast, "Some workshop, I was expecting a shed," commented Rhoda as she looked around.

"Oh my, look at these," Jasmin said as she pointed to the right-hand side of the workshop.

"Whooo, bring it on Luther," Rhoda replied.

"These are amazing, there must be at least fifteen," Jasmin said as she walked around the wooden statues.

"That's an understatement. Do you really think Luther has carved these?" Rhoda asked as she ran her hand over a huge piece of wood that had been carved in the shape of an owl.

"I don't see why not. Someone has to have done them and there are not many people inhabiting this place are there. Anyway, Jacob said Luther had done some carvings, so I don't see why we shouldn't believe him. Do you?"

"They are beautiful."

"They certainly are."

"I wonder why they aren't out on display?" Jasmin asked.

"I don't know, but they would look fantastic scattered around the grounds. Just imagine going for a walk amongst all these, you wouldn't know where to look," Rhoda replied.

Rhoda and Jasmin spent the rest of the morning looking around the inside of the workshop then went back to the house. Now that Sally was no longer there, they felt that they should take over where Sally had left off. But neither Jasmin nor Rhoda was very enthusiastic about housework, Jasmin decided to ask Jacob to get a housekeeper so they could go home.

"Do you want to go home?" asked Rhoda.

"Yes, I do. Even if it's only for a few weeks."

"Well, I don't. I have come to love living here with Luther, going back home to be on my own again is not a nice thought. I thought I did when I first came here but since the Peter Squires meeting, I prefer staying here. I feel safe here."

"Then that's the answer. You stay and look after Luther and Jacob and I will go home."

"You mean, leave me here on my own, like hell you will. If I stay, you stay," Rhoda told her. "Look at what you will be missing. I can't wait until Luther comes home tonight and tell him I think Jacob was right, the statues should be taken out of the workshop and scattered around the grounds. They would look stunning. How cool will that be?"

"The problem with living here Rhoda is I feel like a prisoner. We can't even go to the shop for a loaf of bread. Even if we go outside the gates, it's too far to walk to a shop, and if it's raining or snowing, we'd have to have a helicopter to drop us some food supplies."

"Now that's a bit of an exaggeration, I don't know how long Jacob and Luther have been living here, but I'm sure they have never had to have a helicopter deliver them food."

"Well, I might have exaggerated about that because Sally has been doing all the shopping as she can drive. Neither of us can drive. Don't you miss going out to the shops, even if it's only to look round and say hello to other human beings?"

"Yes, I have to confess I miss going into town and window shopping. My problem is, I am easily led. Ten minutes ago, I was content to stay here and feel safe. Now I want to go shopping."

"I'll tell you what, let's discuss it with Jacob and Luther tonight. But if we do decide to stay permanently, how do we get to the shops? There's not even a bus service anywhere near here for us to catch."

Rhoda could wait no longer, after seeing the wood carvings that Luther had done, so she took out her mobile phone and sent him a text, *'you are very talented'*, and she closed her phone and put it in her pocket. "I've just texted Luther, and told him he's very talented. I couldn't wait until he returns home tonight. I wanted him to know that we love his works of art."

"I think you have done the right thing, he needs to know that his sculptures are beautiful," agreed Jasmin.

Rhoda's mobile pinged in her pocket and she took it out and looked at the screen. Luther.

She read the message and she said, "Well, what do you think he's replied?"

"I've no idea," said Jasmin.

"He says, *'that's what they all say'*.

Jasmin and Rhoda looked at each other and burst out laughing.

"I really love that man," Rhoda said once she had stopped laughing.

"Yes, I know you do and I think you two have something special going on. I am so pleased for you Rhoda."

"Thank you. Are we going to do our running thing?" Rhoda wanted to know.

Jasmin looked over at Bennie, "Bennie's not watching us, let's see how far we can get before he catches up with us."

On hearing the sound of running feet, Bennie looked up and without hesitation, the chase was on.

The conversation later that evening was taken over by a discussion of the statues. Luther was, as always, modest and played it down when Rhoda said she thought he was very, very clever and she would give anything to be able to create something as beautiful as the carvings that he had done.

Luther pointed out that it was just a hobby, and because he enjoys doing it, he said he didn't feel he had any more talent than the next man.

The security screen pinged and Jacob glanced up at it as the gate opened and watched a car he did not recognise drive up to the front door. The car door opened and out stepped Chief Constable Broadman."

"It's Cliff," Jacob informed them.

"I'll go and let him in," and Luther jumped up and went to the front door.

"Good evening, everybody," Cliff said.

"Welcome, Cliff," said Jacob. "What brings you here at this late hour?"

Jasmin looked over at Jacob while he was talking and thought, *God, he's gorgeous,* and he felt her eyes on him. The look she gave him left him in no doubt about what she thought about him.

To cover her confusion Jasmin said to Cliff, "Dan's not here if you have come to see him."

"I came to see you all, not just Dan. Thought I had better come and let you all know what's been happening before it hits the newspapers and TV," said Cliff.

"Been movement on the case, has there?" asked Luther.

"Just a little bit. Inspector Longreen and Marley Burton are both dead," Cliff told them.

"Dead!" exclaimed Rhoda.

Cliff proceeded to relate to them the events of the previous evening and they all sat listening to what he had to tell them.

"Poor Dan, he got quite a shock when he went back to work and looked in the cells. We interviewed Squires and he told us everything. Weirdest case I have ever worked on. Never had so many confessions about a case in my long history as a copper. We were even told of a murder that we knew nothing about.

"When Squires had killed both Reg and Marley, he calmly took the cell keys out of Marley's pocket went out of the cell and locked Marley's cell door. He threw the keys back into the cell through the spyhole. Two murders, both silent, both professionally done and both inside the police station," Cliff concluded.

"Blimey," said Rhoda. "But I must say I am glad, at least that Marley bloke can't come round to my house any more and go through my drawers. But how can Squires have dropped the cell keys through a spy hole?"

"The spyhole in the door of a police cell is not like the spyhole you have in your door at home. It's a square, bit bigger than a man's fist with a little door that you slide to one side so the police officer can see all of the inside of the cell," Cliff explained.

"I don't think it was Marley going through your drawers Rhoda. He might have been the one to send someone to do it for him though," remarked Jasmin.

"Same difference. I bet it was Marley that sent Peter Squires to my house," Rhoda told her.

"The publicity department is to make an announcement on the nine o'clock news." Cliff glanced at his watch. Eight-thirty.

"We'd better go into the sitting room and have a glass of wine and turn on the TV and see what the publicity people have to say on the matter," Jacob told them.

"I'll stay and see to the dishes and join you shortly," Jasmin said.

"I'll stay and help, then we will be done in half the time," Rhoda told her.

Jasmin and Rhoda had only just entered the sitting room when the computer screen pinged, they watched as Sally's car drove through the double gates and drew to a halt at the side of Cliff's car. Out stepped Sally and Dan. No one stood up to let them in. The door was not locked and even if it were, Sally had a key. Jacob went to get two more wine glasses.

"Good evening, everyone," Sally smiled as she dropped into a seat next to Jasmin.

"Good evening to you too," replied Cliff.

"Hello Sir, we wondered whose car it was at the front door. Have you heard that there is to be a publicity announcement with regard to the killing of Inspector Longreen and Marley?" Dan asked the Chief Constable.

"I took the car out of the garage at Barrow, after all, I am working. It's costing me a fortune in petrol driving backwards and forwards between the two police stations. I have heard, yes. That's why I am here. I came to warn Jacob and Luther and Jasmin and Rhoda of course. Watch out, here is the news now."

Silence fell in the room and they all watched as the newsreader told them that a police officer was about to announce two deaths at Glaston Police Station.

Sitting at a long table were three policemen in uniform, facing the camera. The policeman in the middle began, "My name is Inspector Lee Deepcote and I am sorry to have to report that in the early hours of this morning, Inspector Reg Longreen was escorting a prisoner to the cells when the prisoner overpowered Inspector Longreen and unfortunately killed him.

"The prisoner then proceeded to take possession of the cell keys and unlocked the door to a cell that housed another prisoner. This second prisoner was also murdered by the prisoner that had killed the police officer. The two prisoners had a long and violent history going on between them. The murderer of these two men is a man called Peter Squires. The other prisoner who was brutally murdered was a gentleman that went by the name of Marley Burton, also known as George

InGuesty. The perpetrator of these two crimes is now detained at Glaston Police Station.

"That is all we know at the moment; further press releases will be forthcoming when more information is known. That is the end of the announcement and we will not be taking any questions at this moment in time. Thank you."

"Well, well," commented Cliff. "I think they got away with that for the time being. At least there is nobody to contradict the publicity announcement because nobody saw what happened. An internal enquiry will be set in place and Squires will be charged with murder, of course, no doubt about that. But Peter doesn't seem to care. He says living in a prison where all his meals are provided and laying on his back in a cell all day, beats drug running. He'd had enough. How he'll feel after he has done a couple of years in prison, is anybody's guess."

"Is that what really happened?" asked Rhoda.

All eyes focused on her, "Why is everyone looking at me?"

"Are you saying you don't believe what the policeman on the TV said?" asked Dan.

"I don't know. I was just curious. I don't care one way or another. They should all be dead then Jasmin and I can go back home and go shopping. Only it doesn't sound like the explanation that the chief constable gave us," she told them.

"Let us say that what the press officer said is what happened, because no one was there to say any different. I might have got it wrong," Cliff told her.

"OK," agreed Rhoda.

"Needless to say, I'm sleeping here for tonight, Jacob. I don't feel like driving all that way back to the office tonight," Cliff told them.

"You know where the bedroom is by now. Make yourself at home," Jacob replied.

And Cliff did. He said goodnight to everybody and made his way upstairs.

"I think Dan and I will stay at the cottage tonight if that's all right with you two?" Sally wanted to know.

"This is your home Sally, you will always have access to it and the cottage will be left empty for you to return to whenever you like, while Luther and I live here. I am hurt to think you need to ask," Jacob told her.

"Come on then Dan, I am ready for bed and you are up early in the morning for work." Sally stood up and held out her hand to Dan.

"See that, under the thumb already," Dan grinned as he allowed Sally to drag him out of the room.

"What was that comment you made earlier about going shopping Rhoda? Are you still wanting to leave here and go back home?" Luther asked.

"Jasmin and I were talking this afternoon; we feel that we need to be able to go out and have a look around the shops if we want to. This place is so isolated, there isn't even a bus route down the lane for us to catch a bus into town. That was all," Rhoda explained.

"I've been thinking about that," Jacob told them. "I was going to have a word with you both about putting you through your driving test.

"Once you have passed your test, we will provide you with a car each then you will be able to go shopping for food and whatever else you need."

"Are you mad?" exclaimed Rhoda.

"What's mad about that?" Jacob wanted to know.

"Me, driving a car. Do I look like someone who can drive a car?"

"All you have to do is take lessons and learn how to do it. It is the same for everybody, not just you," Jacob told her.

"I will get you a chauffeur, sweet pea," Luther said. "But it will have to be a lady chauffeur, I will not have you being cosseted inside a car with another man," Luther told her.

"Can I have a chauffeur?" asked Jasmin.

"No, you can learn to drive," came Jacob's reply.

"Why does Rhoda get the goody and me the baddy?" Jasmin asked.

"You have that the wrong way round, you get the goody and Rhoda gets the baddy," countered Jacob.

"How do you work that out?"

"Because I am making you independent and Luther is turning Rhoda into a milk pob."

"What's a milk pob?" Rhoda asked.

"Bread soaked in warm milk, all soft and gooey," supplied Jacob.

Rhoda thought about this for a moment and then said, "I'll learn to drive."

"Good. Is that settled then?" Jacob asked.

Jasmin and Rhoda looked at each other and nodded, "But," said Jasmin. "I need to go back home to see to my house. There will be a lot of rotting food that needs throwing away. We left in such a hurry last time we went back home and it was beginning to smell then. Rhoda rang me to say she had been burgled, there was no time to do anything at all. I also need my clothes and Bennie's bed."

"What do you say to me dropping you off at your house before I go to work in the morning, then come and pick you up after work and we'll go out somewhere for dinner? Hopefully, all danger has passed now, so we should be able to get back to normality. That will give you a day to sort some of the things out that you need to attend to. But on no account are you to let anybody into your house. Lock your doors and don't answer to anybody. Is that clear?"

"Yes, you made it quite clear. I am looking forward to going out for a meal. It seems a lifetime ago since I did that, thank you."

Rhoda looked at Jasmin and said, "Milk pob."

"Do you want dropping off at your house to do the same?" Luther asked Rhoda.

"No, I want dropping off at Jasmin's. Then when we have sorted out her house, we will go to my house and sort out mine. I will go back to Jasmin's with her, and you can pick me up at Jasmin's and take me out for dinner, just like Jacob is doing with Jasmin. I am never going back to my house on my own, ever," replied Rhoda.

"Milk pob," commented Jasmin.

"It's all right for you, you have Bennie, I don't have a Bennie to look after me," countered Rhoda.

The next morning, Jacob, true to his word dropped Jasmin, Rhoda and Bennie off at Jasmin's house and left them to it.

They watched his car until it disappeared and Jasmin said, "Before we go inside and get to work, shall we take Bennie along the canal? He needs his morning walk and I think he will enjoy the canal, don't you?"

"What a lovely idea, not only Bennie will enjoy it, so will I. I need to unstress."

"So, a walk along the canal to unstress has replaced a bag of crisps, has it?"

"I never thought I would hear myself admit to that, but yes, I think I would prefer a walk to a bag of crisps. Hell, how my life has changed over the past three months. You mentioned to Jacob you needed your clothes, so do I, but the clothes I have in my wardrobe will no longer fit me. They will drop down to my feet I've lost that much weight."

"You look better for it you know."

"I feel better about it. I have never in my whole life been so happy. I even like being called sexpot, sweet pea and a milk pob." Mischief was in Rhoda's eyes when they met Jasmin's. Life was good.

"I think we had better turn round and go back now, there is a lot to do. I don't know how long it's going to take us to get rid of that smell."

"I agree. Come on Bennie, we are going home," Rhoda shouted, and Bennie, hearing his name called, came galloping back.

When the door was unlocked and they entered the house, the smell of rotting food hit their nostrils and they stepped back outside.

"Leave the door open and let the smell out," Rhoda told her.

"You stay here with Bennie and I'll go inside and empty the pedal bin." Jasmin handed Rhoda Bennie's lead. "I'll leave the back door open to let the fresh air blow through."

Putting her hand over her mouth and nose Jasmin braved the stench and practically ran to the back door, unlocked it and then she went into the back garden and breathed in some fresh air.

When she had got her second breath she went back into the kitchen and opened the pedal bin, took out the black bin liner and ran to the dustbin with it. Then she took the pedal bin outside and taking up the garden hose she proceeded to douse it inside and out with cold, clean water. She stood the bin upside down to let the water drain off then she went back inside the kitchen.

Although the smell had not vanished altogether Jasmin went to the front door and taking Bennie off his lead he ran straight through the house and into the back garden. He was home.

"You do know that my place is going to smell just as bad, don't you?" Rhoda asked Jasmin.

"No doubt it will. I am going to lock the front door because Jacob said I had to, but with Bennie in the back garden, I am leaving the back door open. I will open all the upstairs windows too, that should help to get rid of this smell."

Rhoda used the hoover and Jasmin tackled the kitchen and by dinner time things were in much better condition than first thing that morning. The house smelled much fresher and looked a lot cleaner and because they had thrown all the food out of the fridge into the bin, they decided to have a walk into town and get something to eat, then go to Rhoda's and do the cleaning there.

All windows were shut and doors locked and Bennie was put on the lead and they went into town. They had fish and chips open and ate them while they walked along High Street in the direction of Rhoda's house.

The same procedure of cleaning was done at Chubb Lane and it soon smelled as sweet as Jasmin's. Sitting on Rhoda's sofa they drank Coke they had bought at the fish and chip shop.

"I've really enjoyed today, Rhoda. I was worried about us working together at Low Valley House but we got on all right, today, didn't we? I think I will enjoy working there better than in that little pod back at IT International. I will be my own boss and do what I want, when I want and not have to report back to anybody."

"And I am looking forward to setting out Luther's carvings, they will look spectacular don't you think? Luther says I can do whatever I like with them and put them where ever I like. I can't wait," Rhoda told her.

"That guy spoils you."

"I know," smiled Rhoda. "This is the first time in my life that I have been spoilt, and I like it."

"I think we had better get back to my house now, it won't be long before the men arrive to take us out. Have you got some clothes to change into when we get back? I don't know about you, after all that cleaning, I need a change of clothes."

Rhoda jumped up and said, "Blimey, yes, I had better go and see if I have anything that might fit me."

Ten minutes later Rhoda came into the room and said to Jasmin, "I've found some clothes that I outgrew years ago but they will do for tonight."

As they were approaching Jasmin's house Rhoda asked, "Is that car parked in your drive?"

They looked at each other and hesitated, "This is ridiculous, we can't spend the rest of our lives thinking that anybody who calls our house is going to murder us in our sleep," Jasmin told her.

"I know. But Jacob said you are not to let anybody in your house and you agreed. What do we do now?"

"Technically, he is not in my house and he is in full view of anyone passing. If he or she, for we can't tell from here whether it's a he or a she, was trying not to be seen, they are not doing a very good job are they?"

"Ring Jacob."

"He's at work?"

"Ring Jacob, it's his company, he can do what he wants, nobody is going to sack him. He can walk out without having to give anybody an explanation and no comeback. Ring Jacob."

Jasmin took out her mobile phone and rang Jacob.

"Hello Jasmin, is everything all right?"

"Yes, and no. Rhoda and I have come back to my house from hers, and there is a black car parked in my driveway. Have you sent him or her, I can't see who is inside?"

"No, I haven't sent anyone. Don't let whoever it is into your house. I'll be with you in fifteen minutes."

Jasmin looked at Rhoda, "Jacob's on his way. We haven't to let them inside the house."

"Good, we'll wait for Jacob."

"We won't, you know. I am not going to let them in, but I am going to see what they want."

"Not a good idea Jasmin, let's wait for Jacob."

"Rhoda, we can't go on like this, ringing Luther or Jacob every time we see a car and we do not know who it belongs to. I am only going to see what they want. Are you coming or not?"

"Of course, I'm coming, you don't think I'd let you go alone do you? What kind of friend do you take me for?"

Rhoda and Jasmin arrived at the bottom of the driveway and started to walk towards the car.

The driver must have seen them in his mirror for before they had reached the driver's door, it opened and out stepped a very elegantly dressed gentleman in his late fifty's, early sixties.

"Good afternoon, ladies. Is either of you ladies Jasmin Ward?"

"Yes, I am Jasmin Ward."

"I hope you don't mind me waiting in your driveway but I must have a word with you. It's very important."

"No, I don't mind you parking in my driveway if you have come to see me. But due to circumstances unknown to you, I have rung a friend of mine and he is on his way. He will be here shortly so would you mind waiting a few minutes until he arrives, then we can all go inside."

"What I have to talk about is private and confidential."

"I have no secrets from this lady or the gentleman that is about to arrive any minute, so anything you have to say to me can be said in front of them. May I ask who you are?"

"My name is Miles Standish, I am, or was, the solicitor for Marley Burton."

Both Jasmin and Rhoda were rendered speechless and could find nothing to say. At that moment Jacob's car pulled to a halt behind Mr Standish's car.

Jacob approached the people standing in Jasmin's drive and the solicitor said, holding out his hand to Jacob, "You must be the gentleman Miss Ward is expecting. Miles Standish, solicitor.

Mr Standish and Jacob shook hands. "Jacob Firth."

Jasmin went to the door and said over her shoulder, "Please, won't you all come in?"

Jasmin was relieved that the smell of earlier had gone and she showed them into the lounge and told them all to take a seat.

"Before I start, I have to ask you if you are sure you want to hear what I have to say in front of your friends, the information is quite personal?" Mr Standish said.

"Anything you have to say can be said in front of my friends," confirmed Jasmin.

"Very well. I am sure you will all have seen the news regarding Marley Burton's death." Mr Standish stopped and looked at Jasmin.

"We have," she confirmed.

"Good, then I have no need to go into an explanation regarding his death. Before he died, whilst he was in prison Mr Burton requested my attendance. I went to visit him and he told me he wanted me to make out his will.

"I attended Mr Burton in prison on quite a few occasions. Whilst making out his will, he insisted that I follow his instructions to the letter. He has made you, Miss Ward, the sole beneficiary and executor of his will. Now this bit might be a bit embarrassing for you Miss Ward, are you sure that you want me to continue?"

"Yes, I'm sure."

"Mr Burton instructed me, upon his death, to make sure you know why he had made this will out to you. He instructed me to tell you that if it had not been for your interference in his life, he would still have been a free man.

"You caused him a lot of unnecessary trouble by buying a dressing table. What he meant by that I have no idea but he said, you had caused him a lot of trouble and he was returning the compliment, by leaving you everything he owns, in his will. There will be a lot of official people looking into his estate and you are going to have to deal with it.

"Marley told me that his wife was dead and that there were no children involved, as they were childless. He hopes you find no pleasure in the financial gain that will eventually come your way. He also hopes you have a lot of trouble from the tax man and police until probate has been granted. This may take many years because of the type of business he was involved in.

"I am sorry to have to repeat all this, especially in front of your friends but that was one of the stipulations of Marley's will, and I have to comply with his wishes. There is not much more I can tell you except, if you wish me to deal with the probate for you, my services are there for you to take advantage of," concluded Mr Standish.

"Thank you for your offer to deal with the probate Mr Standish, but I have my own solicitors and they will deal with probate for Miss Ward," Jacob told Mr Standish.

"In that case, I will leave you with the paperwork that Mr Burton had his bank send over to me. It has all been very underhanded and very out of the ordinary, to say the least. The visits to the police station for one thing. I was allowed to visit Mr Burton at any time, and for as long as I needed, very unusual. No appointment needed.

"If I am to be honest with you, Mr Firth. I am grateful for you taking this off my hands. It is going to take a long time to bring this will to a conclusion, and it is going to be a very expensive case. I wish you luck. And you Miss Ward, I don't know what it is you did to Mr Burton but he wasn't very happy with you. I will leave you now, but if there is anything else you need from me, here is my card.

"Oh, and by the way, Miss Ward, one of the documents I have left with you, is a life insurance policy for Mr Burton. It states that if the manner of his death is murder, you get double jeopardy. That means if the policy is for ten thousand pounds because he was murdered, you will receive twenty thousand pounds.

"I have not checked to see or worked out how much the policy is worth. The above amount I quoted was just an example, but Mr Burton was a very shrewd man and I think the amount you will receive, will go a very long way to deal with the expense you will incur during probate.

"When Mr Burton was making out his will, I don't think he was expecting you to inherit the estate for quite a few years yet, his death had been most unexpected. He told me that he was making his will out now whilst he was in Glaston Police Station because he didn't expect to have as much freedom once he had been sentenced."

Mr Standish wished them all goodbye and was pleased to leave the problem of Marley Burton's will, on someone else's shoulders.

"Blimey," said Rhoda after the solicitor had gone. "And I think I've got problems."

"I'll ring Luther and tell him to call for a takeaway for us all for dinner instead of going out tonight. We'll go out for a meal another night when we are all less excited about this new turn of events. Are you both all right with that?"

"I am," said Jasmin. "In fact, I don't think I can eat anything after that revelation."

"Me too, but I think I might be able to tackle a takeaway," confirmed Rhoda.

Jacob smiled over at her and said, "It's back to Low Valley House then, is it?"

Neither lady declined the offer and the two of them and Bennie piled into Jacob's car and they were soon on their way back to Low Valley House.

Chapter Eighteen

Luther was told of this new twist in the proceedings whilst they ate their takeaway and said, "I think we ought to ring Cliff and see what he has to say on the matter."

"Why Cliff?" Rhoda wanted to know.

"It might help him with his enquires. I'm sure Jasmin would have no objection to giving Cliff a free hand with all Marley's affairs. It might also save her a fortune if the police can sort everything out for her. We have solicitors that will work with the police. Make things easier all way round."

"Ring Cliff," Jasmin told him.

"Chief Constable Broadman speaking."

"Good evening, Chief Constable Broadman, Luther speaking."

"What can I do for you, must be something work related at this hour of the day. I'm not on twenty-four-hour shifts, you know."

"It's what I can do for you mate, not the other way round. Got a bit of good news for you. Marley Burton made a will out."

"Did he now? And who is that will made out to?"

"Jasmin."

"Jasmin!"

"Yes, Jasmin. Now, are you awake?"

"Damn right I'm awake. This is a bit of good luck. She willing to let us have a free hand?"

"What do you think I'm ringing you for? Of course, she is."

"I'll get in touch with Dan tomorrow and ask him to call and see her. Got any documents related to the case?"

"I think the solicitor gave Jacob some but we haven't had a look at them yet. We are all still in shock over it."

"I'll bet. I might come over tomorrow if I can get away. I seem to be spending more time in Glaston than I am here at Barrow. It's a hell of a drive down there you know."

"Free bed and breakfast though Cliff."

"Yes, there is that about it, and the best company a fellow can have. Thanks for the information, Luther. Keep in touch."

Jasmin was busy throwing empty takeaway boxes in the pedal bin while Rhoda stacked the dishwasher.

"To keep you two up to date with what's happening with the IT Intelligence, Luther and I have put the company on the market," Jacob told them.

"Are you sure you want to do that?" asked Jasmin. "After all, you've had the company for a few years now and built it up from scratch and it has a good reputation."

"Both Luther and I have made enough money to retire on Jasmin. More than enough money to let it go and start a new project. We have a couple of private contracts we will keep dealing with, but we work on them from home. We won't be getting rid of the IT business altogether. We are looking forward to turning this place into something that we can all work on and do something worthwhile, as well as enjoy ourselves while we are doing it," replied Jacob.

"What about Jasmin and me?" asked Rhoda.

"What about Jasmin and you?" asked Luther.

"Jacob said you and he, there was no mention of Jasmin and me. Are you expecting us both to be housekeepers here for you?" Rhoda wanted to know.

Luther looked at Rhoda and was silent for a few seconds, "We haven't decided on a housekeeper yet, but now you mention it, thanks Rhoda, we accept."

"You can sod off," Rhoda told him.

"You mean you are leaving before you've started?" Luther asked.

"I mean, just because you and Jacob have money, you can't go around dictating to others what they have to do," said Rhoda.

"Well, to be honest, Rhoda, I can't remember asking you and Jasmin to be our housekeeper," complained Luther.

"No, but you implied it."

"Whose idea was it to place all my carvings around the grounds of Low Valley House?"

"Jacob's, but I agree with him."

"Whose idea was it to make this place into a golf club?"

"Jasmin's."

"We all agreed we didn't want people roaming around this house, didn't we?"

"Yes."

"Whose idea was it to make Low Valley House into an animal retreat?"

"Jacob's."

"Who put the idea into Jacob's head?"

"Me."

"So, Jacob and I are selling up the IT business, and are going to set up an animal rescue centre, scattering all my carvings around the grounds, and the person whose idea it was in the first place, I expect to be our housekeeper. Is that what you are saying?"

"Not when you put it like that. It was the money that Jacob talked about; it made me feel guilty."

"Rhoda, by the time you've got your father's estate dealt with, you are going to be rolling in it. So, I can't even say you married me for my money, now, can I?"

"Jasmin will have more money than me by the time all her legal stuff is sorted out," Rhoda said in her defence.

"Don't bring me into your argument, I have enough on my plate trying to come to terms with what Marley has done. He did it from spite you know. He wants me to have as much hassle as possible, and so far, he is getting his own way," Jasmin informed her.

"Talking about housekeepers, I had a word with my secretary Brenda, this morning. I explained the situation here and told her we had put IT International on the market. As she has an invalid mother to look after, I asked her if she would be prepared to come and live here. She could have Sally's bungalow and she could bring her mother with her.

"I asked her if she would like to be our housekeeper, then she would still be able to keep an eye on her mother whenever the need arose. No travelling to and from work during her dinner hour, and pleasant surroundings for her and her mother to sit in or have a wander round. They live in an upstairs flat at the moment. She jumped at the chance. She is going to find a replacement for her at IT International and once that is set in place, she is going to arrange her move here.

"I asked Brenda because we need someone we can trust and both Luther and I know we can rely on her. It will take two or three weeks to organise so would you two kindly step in and look after Luther and me until Brenda arrives?"

"I don't mind doing it for a couple of weeks if Jasmin will be here with me. What about Sally?" Rhoda asked.

"Sally can have one of the spare rooms here, there are one or two still empty. She can do what she wants with it and she and Dan can come over and sleep anytime they like."

"Sounds like a plan to me," commented Jasmin.

"Let's have a look at some of these papers that the solicitor gave me before the police take them away. Shall we?" Jacob asked.

"Good idea, it will be interesting to see what Marley owns for one thing," Luther replied.

The paperwork related to properties along the river bank, both up and downstream, along with the paperwork for the three houses in Glaston. If they had been bought by laundered money, Jacob didn't think the Inland Revenue people would be able to prove that. Marley had been a very shrewd man. There were five properties along the riverbank altogether, and each one was paid for. Tree House where he lived was by far, the largest of the properties and the deeds to all the houses were all there.

"Is this all there is?" asked Luther pointing to the paperwork they had seen. "Nothing about the syndicate?" Luther wanted to know.

"No, nothing about the syndicate. But I do have Marley's life insurance policy here and the solicitor was right. If he dies because of foul play, the policy is doubled. The policy is for twenty-five thousand pounds. That means you will receive fifty thousand pounds, Jasmin," confirmed Jacob.

"Good for you Jasmin," Luther told her.

"Bloody hell," said Rhoda.

"I'm speechless," said Jasmin.

"Plus, eight properties, all paid for, five along the riverside and three in Glaston, to say nothing about his financial affairs," added Jacob.

"This is a hell of a situation we find ourselves in again. When it is known that Jasmin inherits Marley's estate, I hope the syndicate doesn't come looking for her thinking she knows more than she does," commented Luther.

"You mean we have now got the syndicate after us," asked a frustrated Rhoda.

"I didn't say it would happen, I said it might happen," Luther replied.

"If my dad were still alive, I would murder him myself," Rhoda informed them.

Luther started laughing, "Let's not put the cart before the horse and wait until we see what Cliff has to say in the morning. He's going to try to get here, but he couldn't say for definite. He said he would send Dan over to have a word with us," Luther told her.

"Was Cliff pleased when you told him about Jasmin being the beneficiary of Marley's will?" asked Jacob.

"Over the moon, he even forgave me for ringing him when he was off duty," grinned Luther.

"I don't believe this is happening," Rhoda told them.

"You had better get used to it, it looks like we are in for a long wait before things get back to normal," Luther told her.

"I don't think I will ever get used to it," Jasmin said.

"Nor me," agreed Rhoda.

"Well, at least you will have something to take your mind off things. Whilst Jacob and I are at work, you and Jasmin can start deciding where you want everything to go for this animal rescue centre we are going to start up," Luther told her.

"You mean we really are still going to start one up?" Rhoda asked.

"Of course. What's to stop us?" Luther wanted to know.

"A damned syndicate, that's what," replied Rhoda.

"The syndicate won't give a damn about the rescue centre. Why would they?" asked Luther. "It's Jasmin they might be interested in if they think she is now the head of the syndicate. I will put the word out that she is not. Just to be on the safe side."

"How will you do that?" asked Rhoda.

"I have ways and means. Whilst going through some of Marley's emails on his computer, I picked up a few email addresses. I'll just drop them the word, let them know she wants nothing to do with the smuggling. They'll leave her alone."

"Do you think it would be a good idea if we placed all the kennels, aviaries etcetera on the bungalow side of the grounds and keep Low Valley House as private as we can?" asked Jasmin.

"I think it would be a good idea if we erected a fence between the bungalow and Low Valley House. To keep them separate and stop visitors nosing around here," suggested Luther.

"That is an excellent suggestion, Luther. I'll leave it up to you to arrange," Jacob told him.

"Which of the carvings did you like best Rhoda?" Jasmin asked.

"The owl, I love the owl," confirmed Rhoda.

"I liked the hare, sitting on its hind legs with a carrot in its front paws. Shall we put those two on either side of the driveway when you first enter the grounds?" Jasmin's enthusiasm was spilling over.

"I'm pleased to hear you have already chosen your favourite carving. My favourite hasn't been created yet," Luther looked Rhoda in the eye.

"It's not likely to be created either," Rhoda told him.

"It is you know. You needn't worry about anyone seeing you naked. There are no windows in the workshop and the door can be locked and bolted from the inside. We will be perfectly private," explained Luther.

"Naked!" shrieked Rhoda.

"I want to carve you in wood and preserve you forever. I want future generations to see what a gorgeous wife I had," smiled Luther.

"Oh my God, I give up," said Rhoda.

"I knew you would," grinned Luther.

"I'm going back to the bungalow," Rhoda told them.

"Me too," Luther said. "I'll walk you back."

Rhoda couldn't keep the smile off her face as Luther pulled her chair away from the table.

"Let's go and sit on the sofa and be comfortable, shall we Jasmin?" Jacob stood up.

Jacob poured them both a sherry and he went and sat beside her on the sofa, "I think Luther is making a mountain out of a molehill."

"About what?" she asked.

"About the syndicate."

"Why do you say that?"

"I think, once it is known that the police have Squires' accounts books, the syndicate will vanish. I don't think they will try this same system along the river again. The syndicate will relocate somewhere else."

"You really think so?"

"I do. Besides which, when names were written in the syndicate ledgers, false names were used. There will be no names listed in any of the ledgers that will lead to anybody's arrest. I think you are safe."

"But how can that be? I thought Reg Longreen's name was listed in Peter's accounts ledgers as well as stating George InGuesty, is really Marley Burton."

"I think they were listed in Peter's personal diary, not the accounts ledgers, he is a very vindictive man. I don't think he targeted any of the other people, just those two. Luther said he will email a few people and that will be the end of it."

"Will I be able to refuse to accept being the beneficiary if I wanted to?" asked Jasmin.

"I don't know about that. But I think that if there has been no will made out and there is no other member of the family to be able to claim it, the proceeds go to a member of the Royal family. Again, which one I don't know enough about to make a comment, it is not something that interests me.

"But looking at it like that, if you refuse the estate and there is no one else, which I don't think there is, I would say take the money and put it to good use, Jasmin.

"If you take the money, pile it into the animal rescue centre, give a few unwanted pets or even wild animals a bit of love and kindness before they are moved on. It is going to take a lot of money just on vet bills alone. I think you would put the money to better use than letting somebody who already has millions add it to their coffers.

"Besides which, it would irk Marley to know that you are putting the money to good use and enjoying it. That was not his intention, he wanted you to have an unpleasant time of it. Don't let him win."

"Do you want this animal rescue centre in your backyard Jacob? When Rhoda and I were discussing it, we were only daydreaming, we didn't expect it to become a reality."

"To be truthful Jasmin, I can't wait. From the age of fifteen, I have worked nonstop. When I say nonstop, I mean nonstop. Luther and I worked late into the night and most weekends when we set up IT International. There has been no pleasure in my life Jasmin.

"I know we haven't known each other for very long but all the pleasure that has come my way it has come from you. Then there's Bennie, I never dreamt I would ever sleep with a dog, but if he wasn't at the bottom of my bed now, I sure would miss him.

"As for sharing my bed with you, what can I say, my life is complete. To be able to build some cages, get out in the fresh air and do some physical work for a change instead of sitting at a desk staring at a screen all day, will make a refreshing change. Being able to help look after animals that need a bit of care and attention is going to be the most difficult task. For, I know nothing about caring for animals.

"But I can learn, and I am looking forward to it. It's going to be a completely new line of work for me. I can't wait to sell up and come and help you and Rhoda run the centre. Luther too has found what he has been seeking for many a year, he worships Rhoda.

"He can't believe his luck either. He is a very modest man, so when Rhoda sent a text message to him saying she likes his artwork, he was thrilled. He came into my office and showed me the text message on his phone, just in case I thought he was making it up. I have never seen him so hyped up before. That girl certainly knows how to push his buttons."

"The sculptures are beautiful," said Jasmin.

"I know, I have often told him to get them valued and start selling them but he wouldn't. He said, 'who would want to buy them?' I think spreading them around the grounds is a fantastic idea, I can't wait to see them in place, they will look stunning."

"Yes, they will."

"Shall we call it a day?"

"Can't."

"Why not?"

"Bennie needs his walk."

"You, Bennie, are a pain in the butt."

Bennie hearing his name spoken pricked up his ears and looked over at the two of them.

"Yes, I'm talking about you," Jacob said. "Want to go for a walk?"

That last word did it, Bennie was on his feet and charging over to Jacob, he was ready for a walk.

Early the next morning saw the arrival of Dan and Sally, and Jacob handed the paperwork over to Dan. Dan went off to work and Sally stayed behind.

"Luther rang me last night and told me that you are thinking of starting up an animal rescue centre and that you are going to put his carvings around the grounds. I think that's a brilliant idea. I was wondering if I could stay and help you. He also told me that Brenda is going to be moving here and is going to live in my bungalow. I am going to need some help in moving my things out and into a room in Low Valley House. Would you both be interested in giving me a hand with that?" Sally wanted to know.

"Of course, you can, this is your home more than ours. We would love to have your help, the more the merrier. And yes, we will help you move your things into the house. Things are begging to get more interesting and exciting every day," Jasmin said.

"Shall we go and make a start on it? Go down to the workshop and try to sort out the statues," Rhoda asked.

"Why not, it will give us something to do and make our day less boring," Jasmin smiled.

"Bennie, here boy, we are off on another adventure," Sally told him and Bennie was up for it.

The three ladies set off for the wood and Rhoda said, "Shall we do our daily run and make a dash for it while Bennie is otherwise engaged?"

Jasmin and Sally looked over at Bennie, his nose to the ground, his interest in them no longer existed. They all grinned, knowing what was about to happen, and Rhoda was the first to set off running. There was nothing wrong with Bennie's hearing and he looked up and saw the three fleeing figures. He too had never had so much fun in his life until he met Jasmin.

Bennie was happily bouncing beside them as they approached the wood. They slowed down to a walk as they entered the wood and made their way to the workshop.

Sally opened the door and Rhoda said, "Luther told me the workshop door is never locked."

"What do we need to lock it for? Nobody is going to get in," Sally told her.

"You can't positively say that. There is always the smart Alec that manages to break the code. Any code, nothing is impossible," countered Rhoda.

"Have a word with Luther. It's his workshop," Sally told her.

"But if someone breaks in, they might steal his carvings," Rhoda told her.

"To be honest, I don't think Luther would care if they did," Rhoda was informed.

"Well, I would. I love them, Sally. Don't you?" Rhoda wanted to know.

"They are OK, but my thing is not art," confessed Sally.

"What is your thing?" asked Jasmin.

"I like teaching," they were told.

"Teaching, but that's boring," exclaimed Rhoda.

"No, it's not. If I can help someone to learn something, anything, I get a feeling of self-satisfaction out of it. Like teaching you to cook, I really enjoy that," said Sally.

"And I really enjoy learning from you. Talking about learning, I can't get to sleep on a night for thinking about what Jacob said to us the other night," Rhoda told her.

"What did Jacob say to you?" she wanted to know.

"Jacob told Jasmin and me that he was going to put us through our driving test and get us a little car each. Scares me to death even thinking about it," Sally was informed.

"Don't you want to learn to drive?" Sally wanted to know.

"I do," chipped in Jasmin.

"Do I look like someone who would look good behind a wheel?" Rhoda asked.

"Why are you always putting yourself down, Rhoda? Since you have lost all that weight you should be feeling more confident. It's all in your mind," said Jasmin.

"When I look in the mirror, I don't look much different," confessed Rhoda.

"That's only your clothes talking. You need some new clothes, some that fit you. We could do with going shopping and fitting you out with a new wardrobe," Jasmin told her.

"We could go shopping right now if you want. There are a couple of spare cars in the garage. Dan took mine but that doesn't matter, I'll take one of the spare cars," Sally sounded excited.

"But we aren't allowed to go out of the grounds," stated Jasmin.

"You and Rhoda can get in the back of the car and crouch down. I'll throw a rug over you then no one will see you. Do you have some dark glasses? If not, I have some, along with a couple of wigs back at the cottage. You could put on a wig and dark glasses, crouch down in the back of the car and I'll drive over to Cintage, the next town on. Nobody will recognise you there. Will they?"

"I've never been to Cintage," admitted Rhoda.

"Nor me. But I don't have any money," confessed Jasmin.

"I've got a bag full," said Rhoda. "You can have some of mine."

"I can't do that, but thanks anyway," Jasmin smiled at her.

"You can consider it a loan if it makes you feel any better. Once you get Marley's will sorted out you can pay me back. Come on Jasmin, we need a bit of fun in our lives. We can't let the bad men dictate what we do or where we go. Let's get the wigs and dark glasses on and let Sally drive us to Cintage and all go and do some shopping. To hell with it," Rhoda begged.

"All right, thank you, I will consider it a loan. Let's go shopping," agreed Jasmin.

"Race you to my cottage," said Sally and she set off running.

Jasmin and Rhoda followed her and so did Bennie.

Jasmin took Bennie into Low Valley House and shut him in the bedroom. He showed his disgust at being left behind by jumping up onto the bed and turning his back on her as she closed the door and shut him in. Then Jasmin went back to Sally's bungalow.

Rhoda had a long black wig on that reached down to her shoulders and a fringe that covered her forehead. When she put on the dark glasses even Jasmin didn't recognise her.

Jasmin had a short blond wig with a side fringe nearly covering one eye and the dark glasses hid her bright-blue eyes. Sally opened the garage doors and drove slowly out. They all started giggling as Jasmin and Rhoda climbed into the back of the car and Sally threw a blanket over their crouched figures. Sally aimed her fob at the double gates. They opened and they were out on the road.

"Cintage, here we come," shouted Sally.

Once they were clear of Main Street in Glaston, Sally told them they could sit up.

When the three of them hit the shops in Cintage, all thoughts of being recognised or followed went out of their heads. They had an exciting and very lucrative shopping spree where money was no object and spend it, they did.

The time sped by and Rhoda said, "Gosh, I'm hungry."

"What time is it?" Jasmin wanted to know.

Sally looked at her watch, "Christ, it's half past two. We'd better be getting back. Let's call a bakery on our way to the car and get something to eat whilst we are driving back."

When they got back in the car, the boot stuffed to capacity, Sally said, "Don't forget to duck down and cover yourselves with the blanket when we near Glaston. Better to be safe than sorry."

Now back at Low Valley House, Sally told them, "You two be emptying the car while I start dinner for the boys. Keep them fed and watered and hope they don't throw a tantrum about us sneaking off to do some shopping."

"How are they going to find out?" Rhoda wanted to know.

"You must be joking," replied Jasmin. "With the security system that's about this place, we can't go to the loo without them knowing about it."

Rhoda was silent for a moment and after considering Jasmin's comment she said, "You mean when I go to the loo, Luther will be watching me?"

Jasmin and Sally both started laughing and Jasmin said, "No, of course, he can't. It's just a figure of speech."

"Maybe they won't know it's us with these wigs on," remarked Rhoda.

"I don't think Luther will have any problem recognising you, with or without a wig," Jasmin told her. "But I think he will be most impressed when he sees how smart you look in your new clothes."

Rhoda looked at her, took in what she had said then taking off the dark glasses and pulling off the wig, she looked up at the security camera and pulled out her tongue.

Sally gave a delighted laugh and said, "There's no wonder Luther idolises you, Rhoda, you are great fun."

"That's the first time anybody has called me great fun. My father didn't do anything for me while he was alive, but he's sure as hell made up for it since he died."

Jasmin looked at her and said, "You've changed your tune."

"That's because of the company I now find myself in. Friends, fun and shopping sprees with any amount of money to spend, never thought it would happen."

The security screen peeped and they all three looked up at it. The gates were opening and Sally recognised her car driving through. Dan had come to collect her. She ran to the door and opened it and stood waiting for him as he jumped out of the car.

Dan went over to her, grabbed her non-too gently and his lips found hers. Then, they both went indoors.

"Hello Dan, are you stopping for dinner?" asked Jasmin.

"No thank you. I have just called in to say hello and pick Sally up. And tell you that all the paperwork Jacob gave me has been passed on to the relevant people to sort out. We will just have to wait and see now, nothing else I can do. It's out of my hands," he told them.

"We've been shopping so there is no dinner ready for you," Sally told him.

"We can pick some fish and chips up on our way home," said Dan.

Turning to Jasmin and Rhoda, Sally said, "I've had such a good day today, if you don't mind, I'll get Dan to drop me off tomorrow as well. It's been fun."

"We will be glad to see you, Sally, I think we've all had a fun day," Jasmin told her.

"Where's Bennie," Dan asked.

"Oh my God, Bennie!" exclaimed Jasmin and she set off upstairs at a running pace and opened the bedroom door.

Bennie shot out of the bedroom, ran down the stairs and stood at the front door. Sally went to the door and opened it and Bennie made a quick exit.

"Poor Bennie, I had forgotten all about him," Jasmin said.

"There's nothing poor about Bennie. He has a better lifestyle than me. Being locked in for a few hours won't have done him any harm," Dan smiled.

Sally had left the door open and Bennie reappeared and made sure he had greeted each of them before he went in search of food and water.

When Sally and Dan had gone, Jasmin said, "We didn't have time to get anything ready for Jacob and Luther's dinner. What about making some homemade chips and egg for tea?"

"I'm up for that," agreed Rhoda.

Jacob and Luther were in their separate offices both engrossed in paperwork when their security screen peeped and lit up. The screen showed three women at the garage on the grounds of Low Valley House and Luther watched as Sally opened the garage doors.

Luther went out of his office and into Jacob's. Jacob was sitting at his desk watching the same scene that Luther had just seen. Luther perched on the edge of Jacob's desk and they both sat and watched as Sally drove out of the garage and came to a halt by the side of two other ladies, one a blonde and the other with long black hair. Both wore dark sunglasses.

The two ladies opened the back doors of the car and climbed in. Sally got out of the driving seat, went to the boot of the car and took out a blanket. She threw the blanket over the two ladies, got back in the car and drove off.

"What do you think that was all about?" asked Luther.

"I think they are going somewhere, shopping would be my guess," Jacob smiled.

"What's with the wigs and dark glasses?"

"A disguise, in case someone is watching them."

"There's no danger now is there?"

"I don't think so."

"Sal seems to be getting on well with Rhoda and Jasmin, don't you think?"

"Yes, I do, I am so pleased for Sally, Luther. She took it hard when you had to tell her about Henry selling our data programmes."

"She did, I used to hear her crying in bed sometimes before we moved here. It tore at my heart." Luther went back to his own office.

The day passed without mishap of any kind, but just before they left for home Jacob went into Luther's office and said, "Is Dan picking Sally up when he's finished work?"

"I've no idea, I didn't ask. Is there a problem?"

"No, I was just wondering if we would see him and I could ask him if he had heard anything about Marley's paperwork."

The security screen peeped and lit up; the ladies were back. Both Jacob and Luther watched as the boot of the car was emptied of boxes galore and they followed the ladies into the house. What the conversation was they did not know but they saw Rhoda take off her wig and glasses and look directly at the security camera and pull her tongue out.

"Hell, I love that woman. I like what she is wearing too. You were right Jacob, shopping expedition." Luther smiled.

"Time to go home then."

By the time they reached home, Sally and Dan had already left.

They were sitting in the living room when Luther asked, "Did you enjoy your shopping spree?"

Rhoda looked at him and asked, "How many times?"

"What do you mean, *'how many times'*?" Luther wanted to know.

"How many times have I been to the loo?" she replied.

Jasmin looked at Rhoda, Rhoda looked at Jasmin and they both burst out laughing.

Luther looked at Jacob with a question in his eye, "I shouldn't bother furthering it if I were you," Jacob told him.

The next morning Dan dropped Sally off and then turned the car round and set off to work. Sally went into the house to find only Bennie there to welcome her.

"Where is everybody, Bennie old boy?" asked Sally as she greeted Bennie.

Rhoda followed him into the room and said, "Hi Sally, Jasmin has gone into Glaston with Jacob this morning. He's taking her to a driving school. It's her first driving lesson today. My turn next, but I don't like the thought, it scares me stiff."

"I've got a suggestion to make."

"Which is?"

"We have a huge estate here, there are loads of lawns to be cut and we have a sit-on lawnmower. We have a gardener of course who attends to that, but how do you feel about me teaching you to drive the sit-on lawnmower? Off the road away from other vehicles. It will give you confidence to take a car out on the road and it's great fun.

"I know driving a sit-on lawnmower is different from driving a car, but you will see how easy it is and it will help you to learn how to steer. Nothing for you to be scared of, nothing for you to bump into."

"Can Bennie come?"

"Of course, wouldn't think of leaving him out," Sally said.

"OK, why not. Lead the way."

Sally, Rhoda and Bennie set off in the direction of Luther's workshop. Sally carried on into the wood and not far behind Luther's workshop, they came across a garden shed. Sally opened the door and standing in the middle of the shed, was a big red sit-on lawnmower.

"Blimey, it's bigger than I thought it would be," said Rhoda looking at it in trepidation.

"It doesn't look this big once you are sitting on top. I'll drive it out and you jump up onto the back axle and hold onto me or anything you can get your hands on. I'll drive very slowly so you won't fall off. Then when we get to the bottom field it's dead flat, you can practice down there," Sally told her.

The bottom field was reached and Rhoda's first driving lesson began.

At dinner that evening, they couldn't shut Rhoda up. She was so excited at being able to drive a sit-on lawnmower that she was constantly talking about it.

"For heaven's sake Rhoda, we get the message," Jasmin told her.

"Well, I am so excited. I never thought that I would ever drive, even if it's only a lawnmower. I am going to cut all the grass on the grounds before we put Luther's sculptures in place. How did your driving lesson go?" Rhoda wanted to know.

"Not very well. It turned out it wasn't a driving lesson but a computer-based questionnaire about the highway code. I got most of the questions wrong. Jacob said it's the best way to learn. Now I know what I am going to have to do, he says it will be easier next time. He's given me a highway code book to study. I have to go back in three weeks, to take it again," Jasmin told her.

"May I borrow your highway code book?" asked Rhoda. "But if you have to do a computer test then there is not much point in me learning to drive, I can't use a computer. I tried at school but couldn't get the hang of it. But we could get Sally to teach us to drive a car on the estate though. Then I would know how to control a car. She is a very good teacher, Sally."

"Of course, you may borrow the highway code book. And I think it's an excellent suggestion about getting Sally to teach us how to drive on the estate. I too would feel much more confident if I had a little knowledge of the controls of a car before I go out onto the road. I will teach you how to use a computer but even better, you have Luther. You can't have a better teacher than him," replied Jasmin.

"What a very good idea Jasmin. You already know about some of the highly confidential computer software we produce, if Rhoda is taught too, you can both help us out in the home office. A brilliant suggestion.

"Both Luther and I are struggling to keep up with the work we do here at Low Valley House, so if you come to work here in the home office and lend a hand, we will pay you. That kills two birds with one stone. We get help in the home office and you get money into the bank to pay for your mortgage," Jacob said with enthusiasm.

"I can't keep up with all this," complained Rhoda.

"Don't worry about it, sweet pea, we are all here for you," Luther told her.

"It will also give you both something to do. You won't have to stick to office hours you can do what you want any time of the day or night. Any help we can get will be most appreciated. Now we have that out of the way, I had a phone call from Cliff this afternoon," Jacob told them.

"Chief Constable Broadman?" asked Rhoda. "What did he want?"

"Yes, Chief Constable Broadman, he couldn't get away from work to come down in person. He tells me that it shouldn't take all that long to sort out the accounting books and he doesn't think we have anything to fear from the syndicate. So, there will be no need for you two to get dressed up as 1950s rockers again when you leave the estate.

"Cliff said your father's camera didn't reveal anything they didn't already know about. It looked like your father had transferred all the information from the camera onto the DVD and USB. The paperwork under the camera is all related to your father's bank accounts and personal stuff. He'll bring it with him next time he comes."

"You mean, we can go back to normal now?"

"Yes, you can go back to normal," confirmed Jacob.

"We will still be friends won't we, Jasmin?" Rhoda asked still not sure of herself.

"Of course, we will. After what we have been through, we are friends for life. Anyway, we have an animal rescue centre to set up, statues to scatter around the grounds, driving licences to pass, and our own houses to sort out. To say nothing about you learning to become a computer buff. Not much time to fall out I wouldn't think," Jasmin told her.

It was Sunday morning and Cliff looked at the speedometer on the dashboard, he didn't want to get a speeding ticket, he wasn't working. He hadn't realised how lonely his life had been until he had started the investigation into Reg Longreen's business, and how much he had enjoyed the company at Low Valley

House. He had decided that he was going to pay a visit that Sunday and have a relaxing day in the company of friends.

He was making his way up the long drive to Low Valley House when he nearly ran an elderly lady down, who was leaning heavily upon a Zimmer frame. He slammed on the brakes, switched off the engine and climbed out of the car. "Are you all right?" he asked.

"Yes, I'm all right, you didn't touch me. You did give me a scare though; I was told it was all right for me to have a walk anywhere I liked. I am sorry if I shouldn't be here. I'm lost you see," replied the old lady.

"How the hell did you get in here?" Cliff asked her.

"Jacob came and picked Brenda and me up this morning," he was told.

"Where is this Brenda then? Why isn't she looking after you?" Cliff wanted to know.

"She's at the bungalow cleaning it out for when we come to live here," the old lady informed him.

"Which bungalow?" he asked.

"The one behind the big house," she informed him.

"But that's Sally's bungalow."

"Not any more, she has moved her things into the big house and when everything is sorted out at IT International, Brenda and I are coming here to live. Brenda is going to keep house for the two men that live there."

"You are quite a way from the bungalow now. Would you like me to give you a lift back?" he asked her.

"My mother told me never to accept a lift from a strange man," her eyes sparkled back at him. "But when you get to my age, beggars can't be choosers. I would appreciate the lift, thank you."

Cliff helped the lady into his car, picked up the Zimmer frame and placed it in the boot of his car.

He pulled up to a halt in front of the bungalow and helped the old lady out. He followed her inside and found Brenda in one of the two bedrooms trying to put up a bed.

"Hello, you must be Brenda. I found this lady wandering around the grounds and she was lost," said Cliff.

Brenda stopped what she was doing and turned round. She was around the same age as Cliff, her hair was slightly streaked with a flash of grey here and there, but it was the eyes that got him. He couldn't look away, they held him captive.

"Thank you very much, I'm sure my mother appreciates it. I would have found her eventually. Keeping an eye on her here is going to be challenging to say the least," she smiled back at him.

"Can I give you a hand with that?" Cliff nodded at the bed.

"That would be very kind of you," came the reply.

Cliff took off his coat and rolled up his sleeves.

It was Luther that made his way to Sally's bungalow and came across Cliff's car, parked outside. He found, sitting in the sunshine an elderly lady reading a book, "Hello," said Luther. "You must be Brenda's mother." He held out his hand.

The old lady shook his hand and said, "Yes, and you must be Luther."

"I am. I have been instructed to come and see if you would like to join us for dinner."

"I would love to come and join you. I don't know about Brenda though, she's in the bungalow doing a bit of courting."

Luther liked this old lady and his one eye shone, "Do you think it's all right for me to go in then? I wouldn't want to interrupt anything. Who is she doing the courting with?"

"The guy that owns that car. Bit of a flirt if you ask me. Had no scruples about inviting me into his car, then as soon as his eye rested on my daughter, I became invisible."

"And the guy's name is?" asked Luther.

"No idea, he didn't say. I came out of the way, didn't want to be a wallflower."

"I think Brenda's Mum, that you and I are going to become great friends."

"Are you spoken for?"

"Yes, I am," smiled Luther.

"Pity," she replied.

Luther walked into the bungalow and found Cliff on his hands and knees with a screwdriver in his hand, "Well, well. Look at you, didn't know you had it in you."

Cliff turned and said, "Lady in distress, had to give a helping hand."

"Dinners at one o'clock, I'll tell Jasmin and Rhoda to add an extra plate." Luther grinned at Cliff and it was Cliff's turn to change colour. Luther loved it.

Over dinner, Rhoda said to Jasmin, "The other day when we were talking about everything we had to do, you didn't mention the syndicate stuff," Rhoda told her.

"I'm leaving all that for Jacob and his merry men to sort out. From now on, I am going to enjoy myself."

"In that case, seeing as I have left all my father's stuff for Luther and his merry men to sort out, I'll come and join you in your fun," confirmed Rhoda.

"Where do Jacob and I come into all this fun?" asked Luther.

"I would have thought that was obvious. You and Jacob are there to provide the *nipples and crisps.*

The old lady sat listening to the conversation, nipples and crisps, life had taken on an interesting new twist all of a sudden. She was going to like living there.